Anna Leland

Joys and Sorrows of Home

An autobiography

Anna Leland

Joys and Sorrows of Home
An autobiography

ISBN/EAN: 9783337013387

Printed in Europe, USA, Canada, Australia, Japan

Cover: Foto ©Raphael Reischuk / pixelio.de

More available books at **www.hansebooks.com**

JOYS

AND

SORROWS OF HOME.

An Autobiography

BY

ANNA LELAND.

"OH! THOU WEALTHY PAST,
THINE ARE OUR TREASURES."

NEW YORK:

D. W. EVANS & Co,

No. 677 BROADWAY.

1860.

PREFACE.

In these days of many books, multitudes of tales are told, whose only foundation is in the fancy and imagination of their writers.

How often after the perusal of these does the reader feel that Romance is, after all, less strange than Reality, and that from his own history or his own knowledge he might weave a tissue of facts which should be more interesting, and even more startling, than these airy structures.

To the indulgence of such a feeling may be ascribed the origin of this unpretending volume.

CONTENTS.

CONTENTS.

H O M E.

CHAPTER I.

MY MOTHER'S DEATH.

SILENCE and sadness were in the house of Sidney Leland !
A heavy sorrow was on every heart. The wife and mother
lay on her death-bed ; but for her the bitterness of death
was passed. Husband and children, her dearest earthly
treasures, had been given up—trustingly, lovingly resigned
to the keeping of one who she felt would never leave nor
forsake them, and with her mind staid on his promises of
love, she was kept in perfect peace, waiting only for the
summons—" the Master calleth for thee !"

Her husband had struggled long and fearfully to obtain
the mastery over his feelings, that, in her presence at least,
he might be calm. He had tried to say and to feel, " Thy
will be done ;" but his spirit rebelled at the agonizing
thought of a separation from the beloved companion of his
life.

Alone with his God, he had been pleading for strength to subdue his murmurings and to enable him to bear this heavy chastening from his Father's hand. Again and again within the last few hours, since he had been told there was no hope, he had stolen to the bedside, looked long and earnestly upon her pale face, radiant with calm and holy joy, as though he would have her image indelibly graven upon his very soul, and then hastened away again to pour out the bitterness of his heart's grief before Him who alone could give him aid.

Once more he stands bending over her, and gazing upon her loved countenance with an intensity of affection and subdued emotion in his manly face, that told more than words or tears could do, how deeply the heart of the strong man was stirred. Her eyes were closed. She had lain thus tranquil and silent through the day. Her thoughts were evidently not of earth. The communings of her spirit were with an unseen Friend, and her steady faith had rapturous glimpses of an unseen world. He tenderly pressed his lips upon her forehead. Slowly she unclosed her eyes, and gazed around for a moment in bewilderment, as if unconscious where she was, but as she met the agonized look of her husband, tears gathered in her eyes, and her arms were clasped about his neck, while she softly murmured,—

"The Lord bless thee and keep thee—the Lord make his face to shine upon thee, and be gracious unto thee—the Lord lift up his countenance upon thee and give thee peace"; then taking his hand in hers she sought to give him words of comfort, and added in a calmer tone, "Our Heavenly

Father has been very merciful to us, we have enjoyed much happiness together all these years, and shall we murmur now? Even now He is full of mercy and compassion. Never before have I felt the Saviour so near and precious to me. He is with me and I fear no evil, though I am passing into the dark valley. He will support and comfort you. He will be infinitely better to you and our dear little ones than any earthly friend. Do not grieve for me—rather rejoice because I am going so soon to be with Him. You will soon join me where we shall be for ever with the Lord.

"God will take care of our dear children; I have given them up to Him; He will help you to train them up for Him."

Her husband sobbed aloud; he sank on his knees, and clasped her thin hands in his own.

"Oh my own sweet wife! must I lose you, my best beloved? But I am wrong, Bessy," controlling his emotion with a masterly effort. "It is the Lord; let Him do what seemeth Him good. He does not willingly afflict, and oh! let me not murmur against His holy will."

CHAPTER II.

"EARTH TO EARTH AND DUST TO DUST."

"Oh! beyond that bourne :—
In the vast cycle of being which begins
At that broad threshold, with what fairer forms
Shall the great law of change and progress clothe
Its workings."

AH! well do I remember the mournful tones of the minister, the hushed silence, the solemn faces of the few kind neighbors gathered to attend my mother's funeral. I knew my darling mother was lying, cold and stiff, in the coffin, with my newly-found baby-brother on her breast.

They told me she was dead, but little indeed did I comprehend their words. Childish wonder, mysterious awe, with a dim consciousness of some mighty overwhelming evil, were confusedly mingled with the current of my feelings as I gazed by turns on all around me. All was strange as if in a troubled dream. My Father!—how fixed and dreary was his gaze as he strove to listen to the proffered words of consolation and sympathy from the holy man! while he struggled to gain submission and strength to bear up under his weight of woe. The light of his happy home, the mother of his babes, was gone for ever from his sight.

There was deep feeling in the faces of the little company as they looked upon the desolate man and the motherless group of seven, while the minister repeated in tremulous tones, the exquisitely touching and appropriate words: "She that hath borne seven languisheth; she hath given up the ghost; her sun hath gone down while it was yet day." As he spoke, his moistened eye and broken voice told how deeply his kind heart sympathized with the afflicted ones around him.

Ah! she had been well loved; she had been the pride of fond brothers and sisters, the joy of her husband's heart, and, alas! from her helpless band of little ones how ill could she be spared!

There was the youngest, the fair-haired Willy, of two summers, now hushed in Betsey's arms, herself the picture of despairing grief. Good and thoughtful Bessy! She, though only a child of twelve years, was ever wont to be the comforter, so quiet and so kind, while Mary, the eldest born, gave way to passionate sobbings, and hid her face in utter abandonment of sorrow.

But Alger, gentle and sensitive, the tender and peculiar care of his mother (for he had been dumb from his birth), how would he miss her soft hand and loving caress, her ready response to the mute appeal of his dark, speaking eye! And Grace, too, pale and fragile as the first spring flower, and as delicately beautiful, with quick mental susceptibilities, and feelings keen and varying like the breeze in April, how needful for her the gentle influence of a watchful mother. My youngest sister, the chubby-faced Hester, and myself, full of rosy health, were in our childishness too fond of sport and frolic to retain long our grief and half-frightened wonder. In after years we knew full well that that best of gifts—a kind, judicious mother—was not ours.

The precious remains of our loved mother were committed to their last resting-place, and sadly and silently the bereaved ones retraced their steps, and entered the dwelling from whence they had so lately borne her who had been its joy and blessing—gone now, never to return !

My father had before appeared calm, but as he now cast his eyes upon his motherless family of little ones, and thought what desolation Death had wrought in his happy home, his grief burst forth afresh. He sank into a chair, his head rested upon his hands, while his whole frame shook convulsively. We gathered around, weeping bitterly, and sought in our childish sympathy to comfort him by endearing words and caresses.

Little did we then understand his grief or our own great loss. He did not speak, but kissed and embraced each one, when a considerate friend gently drew us from the room and left him alone. Willing hands and kind hearts had they— our friends and neighbors ; our evening meal was prepared, and all needful care and attention ministered to us ere they retired to their own homes. Ah, that sad evening !

Little Willy had fallen asleep and had been laid on Bessy's bed. The rest gathered in silence round the table ; my poor father's voice trembled as he asked a blessing on our food. Mary refused to eat, burst into tears, and left the table. Bessy, dear, good Bessy, more thoughtful for our father, though she could not restrain her tears, quietly wiped them away, as she carefully poured out his tea and made every arrangement for his comfort. Thus was Bessy ever doing and caring for others and forgetting herself. My father scarcely tasted food ; he moved back his chair and sat long with his head bowed in silence. Mary and Bessy, with noiseless steps, carried away the tea-things, while we younger ones were grouped together still and sad, or spoke only in whispers. The very dog—old Hero, our companion and playfellow—seemed conscious that there was some unusual sorrow among us, for he walked from one to another, looking wistfully in our faces, resting his head in our laps a moment, and then lying down in his corner again. At length our father took down the large old Bible, from which he had read to us so many lessons of wisdom—the book our mother loved so well—I can almost see it now, that old Bible—and drawing his chair near to the light, he read a short portion to us in a low but steady voice ; then knelt and prayed ; at first in trembling tones, but as he went on, he gained strength and calmness. He brought us all before his Heavenly Father—he pleaded so earnestly, so trustingly, that, young as I was, I never forgot that prayer—I never can forget it. When he rose, my father looked calm and cheerful, and I well remember feeling that God—the God of my father and mother—had comforted him.

For several days one and another of our friends and neighbors would come in to cheer and aid us in our household duties ; but Mary and Bessy, though so young, had been well instructed, and with affectionate solicitude they strove to do their best, that they might, by that means, if possible, lighten the increased burden of care now resting on our father.

I was soon to be separated from the little flock. Not long after my mother's death, an aunt, my mother's youngest sister, who lived at some distance, came to see us. She kindly offered to assume for a time the care of one of the younger ones, and finally, after considerable deliberation and some alternations of choice from one to another, she selected me from the group to accompany her home. My aunt was a good-natured, easy sort of a woman, and withal a little selfish ; for, being the youngest of her family, handsome, and decidedly willful, she had been too much indulged in her youth, and now was little inclined to care for others so long as herself was at ease. Uncle Huntley, her husband, was somewhat imperious in manner, and occasionally peevish and fretful ; he was several years the senior of my aunt, for she was yet in the bloom of youth, and valued himself not a little upon his descent from a family of some distinction. Of him I was profoundly afraid, but in my simple little heart I thought aunt Hannah was so good-natured and kind, I should have a fine time with her and my two little cousins, both younger than myself ; so the tears I shed at parting with my brothers and sisters were quickly chased away by the bright anticipations of childhood.

CHAPTER III.

THE FIRST HOME AND THE SECOND

" Flowers there are that bloom apart,
With meekly consecrated charm,
Whose gifts of fragrance cheer the heart
Like healing balm."

My mother had been blessed with pious and tender parents, and had received, for those early times, a good education. Until the age of seventeen she had lived, with little change, in her sheltered happy home, in the town of Roxbury, just across Boston Neck. The house was but a few years ago yet standing. This neck of land, now widened on either hand by soil reclaimed from the sea, and covered with stately dwellings, was then a mere narrow road, almost washed by the tide, and formed the only means of land communication between Boston and the adjacent country. My grandfather, whose name was Lyle, had a numerous family of children, and being desirous of opening a new field of enterprise for his sons just entering upon active life, he was induced to purchase a tract of wild mountain-land in the remote township which we have called Wayland, the scene of the events recorded in the preceding pages.

Accordingly, he went to Wayland with his two elder

sons, and established them there among the pioneer settlers of those wild, wooded hills.   In the midst of prosecuting his plans, he returned from a journey to explore his new possessions, to find his beloved wife on the bed of death ; and in a few months he too was called to bid adieu to earthly things, to rest in the same peaceful grave till the morning of the resurrection.

The homestead was soon transferred to strangers, and the remnant of the orphan family, including my mother and some younger brothers and sisters, repaired to their inheritance among the hills of Wayland, finding a home with the older sons on their new-cultivated farms.   Bessy Lyle, my mother, is described as possessing much sweetness of nature, joined to a happy turn for humor and a winning sprightliness of manner, while no small share of personal beauty graced the bright bloom of her early youth.   My father was a neighboring farmer ; he saw and loved the young orphan girl, and ere long she learned with her full soul to do justice to his excellent qualities, his intelligent good sense, high integrity, and, above all, his deep-toned piety. She became his wife, joyfully sharing with him who had won her young heart's affection the toils and hardships, the hopes, too, and pleasures of a life in a wild region newly settled.

There, in that solitary farm-house on the hill-side, had she passed fifteen years, a happy wife and mother, though far from her early home, and isolated from society, save the few scattered rustic neighbors.   Her ready solace and cheerful smile were never wanting in the hour of difficulty and discouragement, and her kindly ways and loving spirit smoothed the rough places of life, making all around her better and happier by drawing out the best and sweetest sympathies of our common nature. Such was my lamented mother, whose children form the subject of this narrative—this simple, unvarnished story of home-life and home-scenes.

A few words respecting the town of Wayland. This was truly a picturesque and lovely spot, consisting chiefly of hills skirting the beautiful valley of the Connecticut. That valley is now the pride of New England, with its palace-like dwellings, its busy, teeming population, its restless hum of business, each hill and valley echoing to the sound of the untiring car, and everywhere the abode of wealth—its green meadows and upland slopes seeming one broad garden of luxuriance and beauty—but in that day it presented a far different aspect, for the narrative refers to a period immediately preceding our revolutionary struggle. Then a large portion of New England was an unknown land—its familiar inhabitants the wild fowl and savage beast, with here and there a straggling settlement in the valleys and along the borders of the streams. Many quiet, lovely nooks were hid among its hills, of which few now remain so sequestered from the busy world as not to resound with the shrill neighing of the iron-horse. Memory presents to my mind the vision of my early home, the scenes of my happiest days, glowing with young imagination's warm coloring, as a place of rare beauty. The principal elevation towered far above the surrounding hills, and was called Pine Mountain, from the lofty groves of that majestic tree crowning its summit. On three sides

it declined in long, gentle slopes, abounding with the chestnut and oak, furnishing fine pasturage, and well rewarding,
too, the labors of the farmers whose brown huts, scattered
on the knolls and ridges, sometimes peeped from among the
thick trees, sometimes were distinguished only by the curl-
ing smoke. Quite different, however, was the appearance
of Pine Mountain on its eastern side ; there it made a preci-
pitate descent to a deep ravine or chasm, called the "Gap ;"
through which was the principal road. This narrow "Gap"
gradually widened and opened into a valley, until the little
brook, at first rushing with wild music over its rocky bed,
overhung with thick trees and rocky precipices, at length
found its peaceful course among green meadows and fair
fields, already occupied by thrifty settlers. Their farms
extended up the slopes of the wooded hills on either side,
while their cottages, nestled in gardens by the road-side,
dotted the long, straight valley, till it became an undulating
plain, crossed and bounded by ranges of hills, whose dark
blue summits rested against the sky.

That valley at the foot of Pine Mountain !—Valley Brook
as it was called ! How the thought of its quiet loveliness
lingers in my heart, though long, sad years have passed,
and the sportive joys of childhood, the deep, full happiness
of youthful prime and of a wedded home, all alike have
drifted down the stream of time, untill their memory seems
like the far-off murmurings of that placid brook.

I remember the weather-beaten school-house on the brink
of the shallow brook, where we laved our feet in many a
pool, skipping from stone to stone, and under the rustic

bridge—a wonderful work of art to our childish eyes—the high bank, with the old broad-armed pine on its summit ; the sandy road, too. through the solemn old woods, on our way to school, so still, so dark—where we trod softly, and the beatings of our little hearts sounded louder than the pattering of our tiny feet. Oh ! Valley Brook ! To my partial memory thy green fields and gently rising hills ever rest in sunlight !

CHAPTER IV.

ATHERTON.

> " Childhood is the vernal season,
> Trim and train the tender shoot ;
> Love is to the coming reason
> As the blossom to the fruit."

THE journey to my new residence in the distant town of Atherton was a great event to me in my childhood. Everything to my inexperienced eyes was delightful. The broad beaten road, the long sombre woods, the hills, the winding river, all were new and wonderful to me.

The village of Atherton was older, larger, and altogether more imposing than the simple neighborhood of my father's house ; the long straight street, with its double row of smart white dwellings, seemed to me quite magnificent. My uncle's house was much larger and grander than my humble cottage-home ; it had been the old parsonage, for the father of Uncle Huntley was the former clergyman of the town.

The house stood with its gable-end to the street, shaded by two venerable elms in front ; in the rear was a garden and an orchard, with trees so thick that in summer scarce a ray of sunshine could glimmer through the branches on the soft green carpet below

The remembrance of two years which I spent in this place with my aunt, is mostly dim and confused, shaping itself to nothing marked or clear, excepting an intense desire, towards the last of the time, to return to my own home. My fear of my uncle I could never overcome.

He was somewhat querulous in manner, and his tone of voice was sharp and startling. I was always shy of speaking before him, or indeed of being in his presence at all ; timid and shrinking, I generally contrived to escape the notice of visitors, for I was keenly alive to the idea of fitness and good looks, and was frequently oppressed with a feeling of shame, as I thought of the appearance I made. An indistinct impression yet remains of having been neglected, of being unwashed, uncombed, sometimes even in tattered garments.

Not that my aunt was unkind to me—far from it ; with the best of feelings and intentions, she had taken me to her home. The addition of another to the number of her own little ones must have been a sensible increase both of labor and expense, and they were far from being rich. Her husband, though in many respects a worthy man, was sometimes exacting and hard to please ; her own children were troublesome, and so no doubt was I—a child of only six years, lively, impetuous, and full of robust health, feeling in every limb the bounding pulse of the dawn of life.

Love and gratitude have ever been deeply cherished in my heart for my kind, careless, easy-tempered, mirth-loving aunt. If in aught she failed in duty to me, her sister's child, that failure was solely the result of the thoughtless, good-natured negligence inherent in her disposition, which rendered her equally averse to the unwelcome task of correcting the faults of my character, and to the daily care of supplying all my childish wants. How I loved her children !

They were both younger than myself. Harvey was a gleesome noisy boy, my partner in many a merry play, as well as my opponent in many a little bickering. He was a very tyrant in exacting compliance with his wishes, well knowing that the trouble of curbing his turbulent temper would prove too great a task to be often undertaken. Little Mary, delicate in health, and somewhat peevish, was my especial charge, and, in my view, the " wee dearie" was entitled to the full gratification of every whim.

Another was added to the family during my stay, the darling baby Clara, whom it was my delight to fondle in my lap, gaze into her deep blue eyes, and press my lips to her sweet, rosy mouth, the dimpled home of kisses.

I was the little errand-girl of the household, too, to wait, and tend, and run, at each one's call.

When not employed, I roamed as fancy led me over the house, garden, or orchard, or played with the children, seldom heeded or questioned. My favorite resort was to a corner of the garden where a clump of rosebushes grew neglected. Deep in their shade, I made my little playhouse, and collected my store of precious things, the knowledge of which I carefully guarded from all. There, for many an hour in the long summer days, I revelled in my childish fancies, finding ever new delight in making dolls of poppies and roses, with their gay silken petals for dresses.

Even now I recall the pleased feeling with which I reflected that my dolls were more richly dressed than King Solomon, for, to my infant comprehension, they had quite as real an existence as had the Hebrew King of the Bible.

One day, near the end of the second year of my stay in Atherton, my father came to visit us, bringing with him my Uncle Huptley's widowed sister, Aunt Rhoda, as the children called her. She was very lively, and talked to me in a funny strain, quite delighting my little heart by the notice she took of me. My father was grave, but he seemed happy. He could not take me home with him then, he said, but he should try to send for me soon.

Just before he went away, he took me into the garden alone, and spoke most kindly to me for sometime about my duty to my Heavenly Father, to my remaining parent and friends. His words made a deep impression on me for the time, and led me to make many resolutions to be a very good girl. I am not sure that such impressions upon the mind of a child are ever entirely erased, though the effect may not be seen or known for many years. It is only by "precept upon precept," and "line upon line," that the heart can be duly reached

CHAPTER V.

THE NEW MOTHER.

Not long after the visit of my father, mentioned in the preceding chapter, my aunt came one night to the side of my little cot, saying that she had something to tell me.

I listened with wonder, as she informed me that a new mother had gone to take her place in my father's house, and that my father would soon send for me to go home. She told me I must love her as I had done my own dear mother, and that when I went back to Wayland, I must try to be a very good child. Her tone of unwonted seriousness left somewhat of fear and dread upon my mind in regard to this new relative, and I fell asleep full of dreamy apprehensions of some undefined evil.

My new mother was the sister of my Uncle Huntley, the same widow lady who had accompanied my father in his recent visit to Atherton.

She had been the only daughter of indulgent parents. She grew up with a strong, ungoverned will, little imbued with the spirit of self-sacrifice, so important an element in a true woman's character. Early in her girlhood she formed an attachment for a low-lived, worthless foreigner, employed in her father's family. Her father, naturally enough, having higher wishes for this, his only daughter, forbade her to see or think of him ; but his commands being disregarded, she was at length forbidden to leave her room. The strength of her will and her ungovernable temper, now spent their fury upon her physical system, and threw her into a slow fever. Her parents becoming alarmed, ceased their opposition, and, recovering her health again, she shortly after became the wife of her unworthy admirer.

His subsequent conduct realized the worst fears of her friends, for after some years of poverty and wretchedness, he abandcned her, and died in a distant town. His wife and three sons were left to the care of her relatives, who subsequently brought about the union with my father. By this marriage, she became the mother of seven children, five of them girls, between the ages of five and fifteen ; a situation demanding much prudence, gentle firmness, and disinterested love, expressed in acts of untiring kindness. This rare combination of qualities was certainly not possessed by my step-mother, whose unchastened spirit was but stung to impatience by her trials, or benumbed into sullen and callous indifference. "There are hearts whose sorrows all spring up into joys for others "—which become softened and purified by affliction—but these are natures of finer mould.

The shallow, brawling brook may glisten in the sun, and show many a shining pebble, but can by no possibility flow with the peaceful, yet resistless current of the deep river, whose placid surface, from its clear, calm depths, reflects the sky in ever-varying beauty.

Let me, then, in portraying character, do no injustice ; my step-mother had but ordinary endowments by nature ;

hers was a different type of womanhood from that which invests the hallowed memory of my own mother.' The one was like the shallow, babbling brook, the other like the deep, peaceful river. To my sainted mother belonged the wealth of affection of "the grand, full soul," self-forgetting, devoted, an ever-flowing fountain of tenderness and sympathy. A serene, deep-felt excellence like this my step-mother could not even comprehend.

Let me revert, in my next chapter, to the time just previous to my return home.

CHAPTER VI.

TEARS AND SMILES.

ONE afternoon my cousin Harvey came running in, with a bound and a jump, saying, " I want some water, mother. Anna, get me a drink." I obeyed ; accustomed to do what would best ensure quiet, for the wayward boy well knew that his mother's aversion to any trouble or disturbance gave him much power. "Hurrah !" said he, "father is coming home to night : he will bring me a present ;" and swinging his hat around, it brushed my hair, dislodged the comb that confined it, and swept my long clustering locks all over my face, leaving my new comb —no trifling matter to me, then—in fragments on the floor. Angry and vexed, I caught the offending hat and threw it out of the open window. He sprang towards me with a menacing air and clenched fist, and appealed loudly to his mother. I know not what scene might have ensued, but my aunt, who was just trying to hush the baby to sleep, vexed with the noise, gave us each a slap on the ear, saying angrily, as she shook my arm, " Why need you always be meddling with him ? There is no peace in the house when you are together." I stole away, feeling condemned for my share in the uproar, yet with a sense of injustice done me ; I was stung to the quick by my aunt's reproaches, and ran to my haunt under

3

the rose bushes, threw myself on the ground, and, in the first
tumult of my childish passion, I tried to stop my breathing,
so that I might die ; but this violent mood was soon over.
Presently the tears ran ; first of anger, then of grief, as I
thought of my brothers and sisters, the playmates of my
infancy ; of my father, too, and with him came the ever-re-
curring conjectures concerning my new mother ; whether
she would love me and be kind to me, with a vague, undefined misgiving on this point ; yet my heart bounded at the
thought of home, and I wished, oh, how much, for wings to
fly like a bird straight to my father's house, whither I had
been for weeks expecting, with the eagerness of childhood,
an opportunity to return.

But I was a light-hearted child, seldom retaining long in
my heart sad or angry feelings, and when evening came, I
had quite forgotten the whole affair, heartily joined in the
lively talk and curious conjectures as to what present each
one would have, for my uncle had been on a journey to Boston—no slight event in those days of slow and difficult travelling—and now his return was eagerly watched for by the
children.

A fire had been lighted in the kitchen, for it was a cool
October evening, and we were around it, listening at intervals for the sound of his wheels.

"But he won't bring you any present," said Harvey,
whose good-nature towards me was not yet restored, " it is
not *your* father, but only your uncle. "

I had been doubtfully revolving the same idea myself, and
was therefore the more easily vexed by his unkind sugges-
tion.

"I think he ought to bring me one as well as you, I am older than you," was my reply.

"But I know he won't," said he ; "will he, mother ?"

"Hush, children," said my aunt, "don't be troublesome."

"He promised me, he did not promise you any present, Anna," persisted Harvey.

"Be quiet, can't you, till he comes, and then you will all see what he brings," said she.

"I wish I could go home, then my father would bring me something," I exclaimed pettishly, "I hate to stay here."

"You are trouble enough here, I am sure," said my aunt; "you and Harvey are always quarrelling."

"I wish you would go away to-morrow," said Harvey.

Tears would come into my eyes, in spite of my most stubborn efforts, and I sobbed bitterly.

"What a foolish child," said my aunt ; then added, soothingly, "Don't mind what a little boy says."

Just then the wagon was heard outside ; the children ran to the door, and in the confusion of the arrival I escaped into a little dark bed-room, and hid my face in the pillow ; nor did I come from my place of concealment till after a time, peeping out, I perceived my uncle seated at the supper table ; a strange boy with him excited my curiosity, and I crept softly round to the corner behind the cradle, where, unnoticed, I could scan the face of the new-comer. He was a tall lad, of forward bearing, looked about boldly, and spoke in a loud voice that altogether impressed me disagreeably, and made me hope he would not spy me. I soon found out that this was Rupert Gill, the eldest son of my

new mother. He had come from Dorchester with his uncle
—for Uncle Huntly was his mother's brother—his residence
being in that place with two old maiden aunts.

He was now going to visit his mother, as I learned from
the conversation, and as it would afford an opportunity for
my return to Wayland, it was proposed that I should
accompany him, an idea that I did not at all like at first,
much as I longed to go to my own home ; for the appearance of this boy did not prepossess me in his favor.

Meantime he kept on talking in a brisk tone, quite at his
ease.

"What is your name, little fellow ?" said he, flippantly,
to Harvey ; " why, you are nothing but a musquito ; you
don't remember cousin Rupert, hey ?"

But without stopping for an answer, " How long is it
since I was here before, Uncle John ?" said he, turning to
my uncle.

I looked up at him, wondering at the bold, confident
manner in which he addressed my Uncle Huntley, who had
always inspired me with so much fear.

Aunt Hannah called me to her presently, and said to
him, " This is Anna Leland, Rupert ; your mother is hers
now."

I shall never forget the leer in his eye and the bold stare
with which he regarded me, while he said in a mocking
tone,

" You're a sly puss, I'll warrant."

This summary disposal of my character did not increase
my liking towards the new-comer.

"I should think, Rupert," said my aunt, "you would be very glad to visit your mother in her new home."

"Oh, yes," answered he, carelessly. "She is far enough into the bushes, I should think. Is it all woods there?"

"It is a very good place," said Uncle Huntley, rather tartly, which put a stop to the conversation.

Meantime the children had been hovering round their father's chair, and, after some solicitation, the presents were produced.

Harvey was made perfectly happy by the possession of a miniature gun, and Mary not less so, by a sugar man with a pipe in his mouth. We were all in the best possible humor; I quite forgot myself in my delight in the new toys. Harvey played with his gun, which went off with a snap, pretending over and over again to shoot Mary and me, each time with new bursts of merriment.

I saw no present for myself that night, but my mind was too much engrossed with the thought of going home, to dwell upon the omission.

The next morning, however, I was delighted to receive a little reticule, the prettiest I had ever seen, which had been sent me from Boston, by my Aunt Hastings, the aunt for whom I was named. Nothing since has looked more beautiful to my eyes, than did that gay, silken bag, and my joy was complete when I found within it a tiny thimble and a shining pair of scissors.

"How do you like it?" asked Aunt Hannah.

"It is beautiful!" I exclaimed—then added gravely, "If

I had been a little girl, I might have liked something else better, but now nothing could please me so well."

"Oh! indeed, you are quite a young lady, to be sure," said Rupert, who was standing by, with a laugh and a tone that sent the blood into my cheeks with sudden mortification, and I hastened from the room, wondering what I had said to excite ridicule, for my aunt too smiled at this assumption of womanly airs.

The next day, the bluff, jovial, self-important, but not ill-natured boy, went with me to my father's house—his mother's new home. That mother I longed, yet dreaded, to meet, questioning with myself whether she would be to me more like a mother or an aunt, whether she would love me and be kind to me, and doubtful if she could be as really my father's wife as was my own mother.

CHAPTER VII.

HOME AGAIN—RUPERT.

> " He was one
> Who could not help it, for 'twas his nature
> To flourish into glee, as 'tis a tree's
> To leaf itself in April."

" Are those hearths as bright as of yore, without the shadow of our figure ?"

I left my Uncle Huntley's with little or no regret, for, though I loved my cousins, I loved my dear brothers and sisters still more, and my little heart bounded at the thought of being once more among them in my own home.

It was a bright, cool morning, and as we rode off the rising sun shone out, clear and sparkling, upon the white-frost crystals which glistened upon every tiny spear of grass and every leafy shrub. I did not enjoy the journey much, for the arrogant airs of my new acquaintance, and his continual bantering, made me a little afraid of him, and quite uncomfortable.

Late in the day we reached the bank of a small stream. The little shattered bridge had been washed away by a sudden rise of water, occasioned by heavy rains.

"Whew !" said Rupert, looking about with pretended anxiety ; "We are to have a ducking now, I guess. What do you think of that, Nanny, eh ?"

"What shall we do?" I ventured to inquire.

"Do? Why, do as other folks do, to be sure. If there isn't any bridge to go on, we must make a bridge of the water. Don't you know how that is done? I'll take care of the horse and wagon, and you are so light, you can skip right over on your feet, if you run quick."

"No, I can't," said I, trying to laugh, yet slightly alarmed by his serious tone and manner.

"Well, I think it is queer if a great heavy man can keep up, and swim on the water, and a little thing like you can't do it. That don't suit you, hey? I'll get on the horse and ride over, then, and you may sit in the wagon and roll right along after me."

I was tired, and having been worried all day by his teaz ing, began to feel really alarmed. I could contain myself no longer, and burst out into violent sobbing and crying.

"There, there," said he, half laughing, but now really in earnest, "I didn't mean anything. I'll get you over, safe and sound. The water isn't deep; can't you see the stones at the bottom? We can ride through it easily. Come, cheer up, that's my lady. You are my sister, you know, and I am going to take grand good care of you." Then, taking up a little pebble, he sent it skipping and whizzing across the water.

"There, don't you wish you could skip over like that? I'm sure I do. I should like to ride over at that rate. Will you throw it if I'll jump on?"

I began to laugh in spite of myself. As we rode down into the water, he sank his voice into a confidential whisper, and said, "I can see some fishes in the water ; ain't you afraid we shall ride over them and kill them ? You won't tell anybody if we do, will you, for you know we can't help it."

This was such a funny idea to me, that I laughed heartily, and quite reassured, began to feel less afraid of my strange companion, and even to relish his comical jokes.

At length our journey was ended, and ah ! that meeting, in which joy, sorrow, and fear, were strangely blended !

I cried heartily, amid kisses and embraces. My beloved father ! how tenderly he took me in his arms and welcomed me home ; saying, in his quiet, solemn way, "God grant, my dear little daughter may live to be a blessing to her father." He greeted Rupert kindly, who seemed awed by his mild dignity, looking really a little abashed. Presently his mother appeared, and advancing to her son, she loudly exclaimed, "Why, Rupert, you are almost a man ! I declare I am quite afraid of you !" evidently admiring his dashing, bold, and forward air.

"And here's my little lady come home, too. Why, you're not sorry, are you ? Come here ; we are old acquaintances, you know."

But I shrank away, ran out the door, and cried more heartily than before. Bessy, following, encircled me lovingly in her arms, and gently led me round the corner of the house, talking cheerfully, and called Hester and Willie from their play.

"You have not grown so fast as Hester ; see, she is as tall as you." Then placing us side by side, she pressed our cheeks together, then our lips and noses, saying, " You are two little Chinese girls now. Do you know they always touch noses when they meet ?"

Little Willie would say nothing to me, but held by Bessy's apron. It soon began to grow dark, and we all went into the house again.

And now, how distinctly the picture comes up before me ! A bright fire was blazing on the hearth, for the chill autumnal winds were giving notice of the coming winter My new mother was bustling about, preparing the evening meal. The family were all together once more. Bessy led me to my father's side, who was in his accustomed seat, a settee—or settle, as it was then called—in one corner of the ample fire-place.

Huge shadows flickered on the low walls of the large, old-fashioned kitchen, dimly lighted by the uncertain blaze from the wood fire.

Mary, now sixteen, well-grown and really handsome, was seated by Rupert, who, with his very best air, was parrying with his jokes her lively sallies, both in high glee.

Grace and Alger sat opposite to them, in one chair, making, by signs, mute comments on the new-comer, glancing at him from time to time. I slid from my father's arm and joined them ; Hester took my hand, and we were soon in lively conversation, mostly carried on in pantomime. Bessy was helping our mother. She was taller than Mary, but stooped a little, as if called to exert her growing strength too much, and her countenance wore an anxious look.

After supper, my father took the family Bible, and all

was hushed in silence, while he read from its sacred pages, and then, in his own deep, earnest tones, commended his little flock to the care and guidance of the God of their Fathers.

Again I felt that I was at home—as if the past two years had been obliterated.

CHAPTER VIII.

"High hill and valley deep,
Where nature's beauties sleep,
Unknown, unnoticed by the crowd of men."

MY father's dwelling, in truth, was not situated in Valley Brook, nor yet upon the grove-dappled terrace which overlooked its smiling verdure and calm beauty.

A road from the valley, leading up its side to the steep, rocky brow of the hill, wound circuitously round, joining the main turnpike at a little distance; while a lane, branching off, gained the summit by a gentle acclivity, and brought to view the little brown cottage, situated a few rods down the green slope, and half hidden by a clump of cherry trees. Only one other house was visible, and over its roof the wooded top of Pine Mountain appeared, rearing its graceful crest. The outer declivity of the hilly ridge, unlike the steep side toward the valley, formed a long sweep of woodland and pasture, with here and there a cultivated field. The soil was deep and strong, and well repaid the labor of tillage, though the whole region seemed based upon a vast ledge of granite; sometimes the moss-covered surface of the rock just peeped above the ground; again it stood piled up in bold precipices, with overhanging trees and shrubs, wild flowers and creeping plants, springing from each fissure and crevice.

The sweetest berries grew around those rocks, and the cows that fed upon the patches of soil hid and interspersed among the crags and ledges, furnished the richest milk and produced the best of butter. The growth of fruit, too, was remarkably fine and abundant. There was an orchard on either side of the house, where more than one tree drooped its boughs, heavy with golden fruit, over a broad ledge or a steep rock.

We were a busy and frugal family, for it required the united exertions of all to bar want from the door ; to procure the comforts, or even the necessaries of life.

My father was careful, industrious, exact, and methodical in the management of his affairs, so as to secure always a uniform, comfortable provision for his large family. Another little brother, and ere long a sister, were added to our number, which, with my stepmother's youngest son, consisted of ten children, to be fed, clothed, and educated.

The state of the country for some years after peace was declared, was unsettled, and far from prosperous. Taxes were enormous, and bore heavily on the pioneer settlers, for the country was new, and quite inaccessible to the sources of wealth found in the older cities and villages along the sea-shore.

A frock of calico was the greatest luxury of dress that could be afforded by females in that retired district. The wedding dress of our mother was a wonder of beauty to our childish eyes ; it was of green calico, nearly covered with large gay figures of yellow, red, and blue ; its cost per yard was one dollar and twenty cents ; and for many years it was the dress she wore at every wedding, quilting, or social party.

Young girls ordinarily wore a short slip of calico or cambric, over a skirt of home-made materials ; and busy must be their hands, when not only must they perform all the every-day labors of the household, found so arduous by the young ladies of the present generation, but they must also both spin and weave. Through their patient industry, wool and flax must be converted from the raw material, into winter and summer garments, table-linen, and the complete habiliments of the bed, from the coarse tow covering of the straw mattress, to the fine linen sheets, " whiter than snow, laid up carefully with fragrant herbs, the thrifty housewife's stores."

With the early spring began the task to be performed by persevering toil. The preparation of the flax was the work of men and boys, the breaking and hatcheling, by which the finer threads were separated from the coarser and shorter portions of tow. Then, winding the silky fibres around the distaff, the females began the work of spinning, which is but the first step in the busy process of household manufactures. Even after the web is woven, the cloth made, the whitening, or bleaching it upon the grass, is still the work of many days. Many a pail of water must be carried out, the cloth folded together, then thoroughly wetted, and again spread out in the warm sun, that the rapid evaporation of moisture may aid in its bleaching.

Nor was school forgotten or neglected, in the midst of all these labors. In winter, the only season of comparative leisure, we wended our way, a light-hearted, merry troop, down the steep, rocky road, then through the dark, still, pine woods, and across the rude bridge, to the old school-house, even now standing as in those long-past days, on the brink of the brook ; the "*brick* school-house," as it was called, par eminence ; a quaint, old-fashioned structure, evidencing in the solidity of its walls, and the expense laid out in its erection, the value set upon the means of education by those worthy pioneers, and their belief in the necessity of permanence in such institutions. It was more than a mile from our own house, but we thought it no hardship, though not clad in furs, to bound through the deep snows, in face of the fierce blasts of a New England winter, till we reached our destination; stopping, however, at each house— they were but two—to warm. Well do I remember the matron of one of these cottages, good Mrs. Govey, who would watch for our coming, and meet us at her door, with her warmed woolen apron to wrap our aching hands ; then she would seat us on stools before the fire, pleasantly talking with us all the while. Noble woman ! Though acquainted with constant, severe trial, and many privations, yet she had a heart full to overflowing of kindness ; a spirit which could patiently and tranquilly endure the churlishness of her strange, austere, rough, and unpliant husband. Mr Govey, or "Old Govey," as he was usually termed, was a singular mixture of shrewdness, oddity, and ugliness. His eyes were so much turned, or crossed, that he could not see what was directly before him ; turning, squinting, and contracting his eye-brows and forehead, as if the organ of vision was in his ears.   He was totally indifferent to the claims of propriety in dress, seeming to be best suited with the most uncouth habiliments.   His spirit of contradiction was remarkable, always trying to confound and silence one by a rough retort, especially in matters of religion by a sudden or strange, and seemingly malicious, perversion of some part of the Bible.   He was well-informed, reading—or rather having his children read to him, for he could not see—every thing that came in his way.

Strictly honest, and very industrious, " Old Govey " had amassed a comfortable property, yet so churlish was he, and so niggardly, even to his own family, that it was with difficulty his wife could obtain the needful supplies of household comforts.

Many tales were told among his neighbors of his unkind and sharp replies to common questions and remarks, and he was never known to grant a favor without the accompaniment of surly, ungracious words.

Being sent one day by my father to borrow of him a carpenter's tool, I timidly made known my errand, remaining partly behind him ; turning sharply round, and twisting his stern, contracted features into a grim frown, he answered, in a loud, quick tone, " Yes ; and bring it back the minute he has done with it, or I'll cut your head off."   Though frightened, and glad to get away as soon as possible, the rough reply was no matter of surprise to me.   Uncle Harry, living near, once sent a boy to him for some trifling aid in his work, and was tartly repulsed with a direct refusal, causing my uncle some inconvenience. The same day, Aunt Kathy, his wife, chanced to receive a present of some nice honey. Knowing her surly neighbor to be remarkably fond of this luxury, she took a portion of it and carried it herself to his cottage, pleasantly asking him, in her own graceful manner, to share with her. Touched with shame at this kind return for his moroseness, he struck both his hands on his head, loudly exclaiming, " Oh ! you burn me, you burn me ; you heap coals of fire on my head !"

To all his harshness and ill-nature, his excellent wife was never known to reply but in mild and pleasant tones, and one of our neighbors quaintly remarked, " Old Govy has one redeeming quality, and that is his wife."

But to return to our description. At a casual glance Valley Brook would seem to comprise almost the whole of Wayland. The rich meadows and well-tilled uplands evinced prosperity and thrift ; already the buzz and noise of the busy wheels of machinery were heard, while the whirr of mills and the rush of waterfalls, made by intersecting dams, announced that the quiet stream was made to subserve the purposes of wealth to the inhabitants.

The passing traveller might well look back and linger as he left this charming valley and turned his steps towards the narrow and craggy road, through the gap, and pursued his solitary way. Above him, on one side, was the steep, overhanging mountain ; on the other, the wild tangled ravine, with its deep gurgling brook. Slowly ascending, he emerges at length on an uneven, rocky bluff, and there

4

stands the small, plain, weather-beaten church of Wayland, a few mean houses gathered near it, but all looking dreary and forlorn.

As he journeys on the aspect becomes still less inviting, till he exclaims, "What a barren, desolate region!" Yet hidden behind the hills, in the shade of chestnut groves, or among the dark pines, was many a snug old-fashioned farm-house, a sheltering nest for sturdy sons and fair daughters.

On Sundays that lone church was well filled, the congregation gathering in cheerful groups from every by-road and lane. The parents on horseback, the universal mode of riding, the wife on a pillion behind her husband, while a walk of two or three miles to church was deemed by the young, no hardship.

Ah, how vividly does memory paint the picture of my childhood's home! Much do I recollect, too, of the sunny hours of careless play in the open air. Each familiar haunt is before me, even now! The broad flat rock at the top of the hill above our house, where, after every shower, the water stood in tiny pools—where were innumerable little crevices, corners, and cunning nooks, charming as the haunts of fairy-land to our merry young hearts—this was our favorite resort at the close of the long, bright summer-day, when the sunset beams cast the long slant shadows in fantastic forms, and the gathering dews of evening brought refreshing coolness.

The large, wild pasture, too, where we skipped among the rocks, or followed the winding, shady paths looking with awe at the towering crags, and the dim depths of the dark old woods. The Indian kettles, too, as we called them, were objects of much curiosity, then supposed to be relics of the children of the forest, exciting, in later years, still greater interest with geologists as marking the action of water, and consequently an evidence that the whole region must at no distant period have been submerged. They were round, smooth cavities, of varying size, some several feet deep, others capable of holding a quart or two, some still smaller. We supposed them the work of Indians, made to pound their corn in perhaps, and much we wondered and fancied about their wild haunts and habitations.

The berries and the nuts, too, that we picked ! larger and sweeter they seemed than any now do. Those chestnuts ! We knew the place of each particular tree. In the brisk air of a November morning, how cheerily we tripped forth, with bags and baskets. The elder boys climbed the tree, or beat the branches with long poles, while our bright eyes searched among the crisp grass for the shining brown nuts, and nimble fingers gathered our winter store.

Oh, joyous playmates of my merry childhood ! loved and loving companions of my hopeful, happy youth ! How does my heart warm, and how do my eyes grow dim, as these fairy visions start up before my mind. Alas ! of all your blooming circle there now remain to me only Bessy and Hester ; and where is the free, glad step of the one, where the careless gaiety of the other ? Ah ! instead, the lines of sorrow and the burden of years are deeply traced in the pale, withered cheek, the stooping, tottering gait. But Time can only touch the outward form, the heart and the affection are still unchanged.

CHAPTER IX.

MY GRANDPARENTS.

"The good die not."

DOWN the green slope behind the house, over some broken ground, in a sort of dell or hollow, stood the nearest cottage, by the side of a little brook, shaded with large old trees. In that rude, yet romantic spot, my grandfather Leland had, many years before, made himself a home. Here, almost alone, amid the savage wildness of untamed nature, he had labored to win from the flinty soil its hard-earned products for the support of his large family. Here had been my father's early home, and it was now occupied by his youngest brother, Uncle Harry Leland, between whom and my father subsisted a most tender brotherly affection. Not a day passed in which they did not meet, always with kindest greetings. My father had a cheerful, yet serene temper, and seemed to live constantly under the influence of the religion he professed. Uncle Harry was gentle in his ways, but had a merry, frolicksome humor, ever with a smile on his lips, and a word of fun for the children, who all loved him dearly. Aunt Kathy, his wife, was of a pale, delicate mien, with a soft voice, seeming the impersonation of goodness and love, and her beautiful baby-boy was, in my eyes, the most lovely of children. After a few years, however

Uncle Harry removed to a distant town. This was, at the time, a sore grief to us, for we all loved most dearly our jovial uncle and his gentle wife ; and especially the darling little one was the great object of our childish admiration, and to be permitted to go to "the other house," as it was familiarly termed, was a special delight and favor to any of us. The old house—a mere hut—fell into decay, and scarce a vestige now remains to mark the place where it stood.

But a single recollection is left me of my grandfather Leland—his animated, earnest prayers, when so old and infirm as to be unable to rise from his chair.

My dear and venerated grandmother I well remember, then quite aged, with her meek, placid face, as she sat in the easy-chair in the corner, the little round table by her side, on which lay alternately, her knitting-work and her Bible, her constant companions. Earthly things were fading, as a feverish dream, and she was tranquilly awaiting her summons to a brighter world. She passed quietly away, was laid in her peaceful grave, and the busy world moved on.

She was well-known and well-beloved in that region. After the death of my own mother, she used frequently to come walking up across the field, supported by her cane, and sit all day mending garments for us. It was a great treat for any of us to walk back with her. At the half-way stone she would sit down to rest, talking kindly of our little affairs, or giving us advice how to take care of our clothes, and many useful hints in house-keeping.

I have been told by those who knew her in her younger

days, that she was very energetic and skillful, as well as truly benevolent. When the town was new and the inhabitants few in number, her superior intelligence and skill enabled her to act as a physician. In extreme cases of sickness, she was frequently known to put on boots and walk through woods in a dark night ; and in more than one instance she rode for miles, when travelling was dangerous, on horseback, behind the messenger who went in haste after her.

Nor were such the only instances in which were shown her courage and strength of character.

At one time, being alone in her little cottage, far from neighbors, she vanquished a bear, with the aid of the broom-handle. The animal had seized upon her best pig, which he had already dragged several rods from the pen, and was tugging with might and main to pull over a huge log that lay in his way. The cries of the poor pig attracted the notice of my grandmother, who ran out, and dealt such sturdy blows upon Bruin's head and face with her weapon, that, though quite intent on his spoils, he relinquished his prey, and made good his retreat.

Hers was true heroism, for such we may justly call that courage that conquers perils, overcomes difficulties and hardships, by patient endurance and active exertion.

In her faithful performance of the duties of her more humble and limited sphere, we recognize the same qualities that distinguished the noble women whose names are honored by fame, cherished and embalmed in our hearts with the memories of great deeds.

Her great-grandchildren are now acting their several parts in the crowded arena of life, scattered over the land, from the borders of Maine to the banks of the Mississippi—on the broad slopes and sun-lit glades of Ohio—among the fair, fertile fields of New York, and on the vast prairies of the West. Some are merchants in our polished Atlantic cities; some are farmers on the quiet hills of New England: and not a few preachers of the gospel. Could her dust be re-animated, and she now stand in the midst of her descendants—no small company—she would see many of them, thanks to her covenant God, her children indeed, in faith and piety.

Who can say how much of present blessing we receive in answer to the prayers of our pious and self-denying fore-fathers?

We do indeed venerate the memory and virtues of our hardy ancestors. Thanks to the influence of their noble example descending as the mantle of the prophet on us their children, we can see the moral beauty of high aims, devoted courage, patient endurance, and earnest faith and truth.

Yet to some, perchance, the simple record of these unpre-tending virtues may seem but the common-place of every-day life, and fail to awaken in their bosoms one spark of generous feeling or noble admiration for the good and the true, the really heroic in life and character. Fashionable idlers there are among us, delicate, soft, nervous beings, who weep, it may be, over the vapid pages of some modern novel, but are shocked into interesting helplessness at the sight of real distress; who cannot find time for the active duties of life, amid their numerous engagements. A life of useful exertion for a worthy end, has neither place in their thoughts nor savor of beauty in their eyes. It is their ambition, rather, to be admired by some perfumed lover, the round of whose duties consists chiefly in the care of his superb moustache, his delicate fingers, and gold-headed cane—whose existence is alike barren and aimless as their own. Much is said of the advancement of the present age, especially as respects the education of our daughters, and no doubt justly; they are intelligent and cultivated, the graceful ornaments of the drawing-room, the charm of the social circle; but is it not to be feared that, with all the culture, delicacy, and refinement of young ladies of the present day, they fall, in some important respects, far below the standard of those noble women now, alas! nearly all gathered, as ripe sheaves, by the reaper, Death?

The elements of a character, strong, high, enduring—one that stamps itself upon succeeding generations—what are they!

Are they created by the forced, hot-bed development of brain, by which the pale school-girl of sixteen, urged on by the stimulus of vanity and rivalship, to which that age is so susceptible, has traversed, with her overwrought, immature mind, the circle of the sciences, and can glibly repeat, as familiar words, the results of the life-long researches of a Newton or a Herschel!

The "well educated" young lady has, indeed, glanced over the broad field of knowledge; but neither basis, nor strength, has been given to her unformed character; neither discipline nor steadfastness to her inexperienced mind. The

matrons of a former age, making no pretensious to high-
sounding acquirements, yet knew how to think and reason
justly ; how to act promptly and nobly ; their powers of
intellect, heart, and conscience, were so trained as to enable them to take enlarged views, and form right conclusions,
in all the difficult circumstances of that period—teeming
with great consequences—in which their lot was cast.

CHAPTER X.

BROTHERS, SISTERS, AND COUSINS.

> "They grew in beauty side by side,
> They filled one home with glee,
> Their graves are severed far and wide,
> By mount, and stream, and sea."

I HAVE before mentioned that my grandfather Lyle owned a considerable tract of land, upon which his eldest sons early settled, in Wayland.

Uncle Francis Lyle died soon after his father, and his brother, my Uncle James, lived on the farm, which was large and productive, some two or three miles from us. This uncle was regarded by us with scarcely less reverence and affection than our own father. He was of noble and commanding appearance, and his knowledge and long residence gave him much sway and influence with his townsmen. He had twelve children, eight of them daughters ; two married before my remembrance, some of nearly my own age, some much older.

Their father took much pride in his large, promising family ; and justly might such a group be a parent's delight. The girls were handsome, lively, and reckoned sufficiently accomplished in the requisites of female education in tha day.

I may say, that personal beauty was an attribute of my mother's family ; finely rounded forms, clear, sparkling eyes, and delicate fairness of complexion ; such were my cousins, such were our own Grace and Alger. Mary's beauty was of a different style—hers was the full, dark hazel eye, the vivid bloom of the Lelands.

Uncle James' daughters, though our frequent companions and most intimate associates, yet being richer, better dressed, and in many respects possessing higher advantages than we, were naturally enough not insensible to their claims of superiority.

We were restricted by the straightened circumstances of our father's large and increasing family, and above all by the unwillingness manifested by our mother to grant any gratification or advantage to my father's elder children, seeming to consider all such expenditures as so much taken from her own.

My three elder sisters only attended school during the winter, yet they were not a whit inferior in their acquirements to their more favored cousins ; nay, I may not be mistaken in saying that they were better educated than most of their associates. That my sisters were well informed on the various topics of the day, read with keen relish the best English authors, and that the letters they wrote did them no discredit, either in style or execution, may be deemed faint praise in comparison with the present broad surface of female culture, yet even those acquirements they owed not so much to the facilities of learning afforded them, as to the care and instructions of our father ; who thus repaid to his children what he had received from his own excellent mother.

Bessy was, from a child, prudent, thoughtful, and discreet. Wholly devoted to the interest and welfare of the family, she early became the main trust and stay of brothers and sisters, and even of our father. She was timid, taller than Mary, and a little awkward, from the little confidence she had in her own power to please—shrinking from strangers, shy even with relatives, she loved to stay at home, where she was best known and most valued.

She had, withal, a fund of quiet but jocose humor, ever peeping out in an arch look or seemingly grave remark. Her intuitive sense of the fitness of things gave her an exquisite tact in detecting the ridiculous, or the smallest deviation from propriety in those around her. We all knew, and stood somewhat in awe of her sly look, and meaning smile. Her care and watch of Alger and little Willie were unremitting. When Alger came in, wearied with out-door labor—for all had a share as soon as old enough—Bessy was on the watch to perform in his place the many little services demanded of him by our inconsiderate mother.

Our dear Alger was regarded with much tenderness by us all, on account of his peculiar infirmity, which was commonly attributed to a fright received by our mother shortly before his birth. She was one day alone in the house, expecting a visit from one of her sisters; while anxiously awaiting her coming, the door of her room suddenly burst open, and a woman in tattered garments, wild and haggard in appearance, stood before her, menacing her with violent words and

gestures. My mother fled from the house, in extreme ter·
ror, almost as much bereft of reason as her insane visitor,
gained the house of the nearest neighbor, but was for some
time unable to speak. Alger, her unfortunate son, never
spoke. His temper and disposition were very lovely, but
his temperament was keenly susceptible, and during childhood he was at times almost insane, wildly running from
room to room in a state of high excitement ; at all other
times he was gentle and affectionate, and most closely resembled Grace in his delicacy of form and feature.

His early childhood had been sheltered from every sorrow
that a mother's love could prevent, but now his open brow
and sweet face often wore a downcast and clouded expression. We all shared in the solicitude lest he should be neglected or unkindly treated. My father's watchful eye, and
judicious management, could only avail for the short portion
of time when he was free from the demands of out-door
labor.

Our step-mother, probably, thought the tenderness we all
felt and manifested for our unfortunate brother, overween-
ing, and unnecessary ; or, perhaps, she hardly considered
the matter at all, for her errors seemed to arise chiefly from
thoughtlessness, and a total disregard of every thing not
connected with her own personal comfort, and from a too
partial love of her own children, a love, indeed, arising from
this very selfishness, for she *valued* them because they were
her own, instead of seeking their best good with genuine
affection.

Our revered father was patient, placid, and forbearing, in

word and manner, though many and bitter were the trials he endured. Often assailed by peevish complaints, even by coarse and abusive language, he achieved a triumph by his meekness and calm endurance, when the exercise of his just authority as a husband in merited rebuke, would but have aggravated the evil.

I am certain that his two eldest daughters, almost from the first, saw and felt for him in these trials, especially Bessy, with whom, when a mere girl, he was accustomed to advise.

Mary was sprightly, somewhat volatile, extremely fond of pleasure and gaiety—it must be confessed, averse to home duties and cares, but she was always in good humor, warm-hearted, and loving, often blaming herself for leaving Bessy to do more than her share, but somehow having a chief part in all amusements, laughing, visiting, joking, and singing.

She had a fine voice, and knew songs enough to sing all day long. She was often called upon in company, till, to avoid further importunity, she would go gaily on, from song to song, till her list was completed.

Sweetly winning in her ways, far removed from pride or stiffness of manner, she was almost lowly in her graceful affability to all.

It was Bessy who kept all aprons and stockings in such good repair—it was Mary who was the life of every company, and a general favorite in the gatherings of the young ; nor was it very uncommon for the lively girl to find herself in want of some important article just as she was starting away, and to come to Bessy's well-kept, though somewhat scanty stores, for relief in her difficulties.

To Hester and myself, the great object of ambition at this time was, to learn to spin. In the large chamber where our sisters plied each one a wheel, the merry buzz and the cheerful talk went on together, day after day. Sometimes we were allowed to be with them, assisting in some part of the work ; but we were chiefly employed with an allotted task of knitting or sewing, under the eye of our mother, until old enough to learn to spin, and to have, each, a wheel of her own.

One day, when about eleven or twelve years old, I had been allowed, to my great delight, to spend most of the fore-noon with my sisters. I had learned to manage the wheel, and was expecting one for myself as soon as it could be conveniently procured.

In the meantime, Hester and I were employed in making into sheets a long web newly bleached. Oh, how tired we were of the long seams ! but they must be done by us, for other and more difficult work was demanded of the older members of the household, so we worked away with weary fingers, while the summer breeze came in at the open door, and glimpses of the waving trees in the orchard, and the bright sky beyond, made our hearts spring like the bent bow as we longed to bound away on the green grass, and breathe the fresh, sweet air. I had, indeed, plied my needle diligently, thinking of the pleasure I should have in being constantly with the older girls, when I had my promised wheel, and with a womanly sense of being then no longer classed with the children, and having a daily task upon the never-ending seams. Thus busily thinking, my work had sped well, but poor Hester's was quite behind; her eye often wandered, she broke her thread, pricked her fingers, fidgeted in her seat, and, worst of all, surveyed despairingly the long piece, still uncompleted. Suddenly she exclaimed,

"There is Nabby coming across the field, with a tin pail in her hand! Oh, mother! mayn't I run and meet her?"

"No! sit still! She has come to racket and play, I warrant; but you shan't either of you leave your work till it is done."

"Mine is 'most done," said I. Hester began to look grave, for Nabby was her especial playmate, and meantime she entered.

"Heyday! here's little black-eyed Nab! I don't know what will happen, when she is grown up and the beaux come round!"

The little girl's eyes sparkled anew at this address from my mother, who well knew how to please children, though by no means always judicious in her remarks to them.

"I have come to stay an hour, and play with Hester. I've been tending the baby all day, and he's been so cross."

"No; Hester must finish her sewing. You may go and play, Anna, if you have done yours."

"Wait just a little while," pleaded Hester, now applying herself vigorously; "What is your pail for, Nabby?"

"Oh, mother sent to know if you would lend her some flour. Father promised to get some, but he didn't, and Un-

5

cle William came last night. Father will get some pretty soon, I guess."

My mother did not look very well pleased, but took the pail. In truth, it was not a strange thing for Nabby to come to borrow one article or another, and borrowing was frequently equivalent to begging. Our cousin Hannah, her mother, was poor, often much tried, sometimes poorly supplied with even the necessaries of life. Her husband was master of a lucrative trade, and might have provided well for his family, but spent too many evenings at the village tavern, and it became rather a matter of chance whether their pantry contained either bread or meat.

"May we go up stairs, mother, till Hester is done ?"

"No ; the girls hinder themselves enough by their own talk, without your going up to help them."

But Nabby was determined to go up stairs, and by dint of coaxing, she succeeded, highly delighted with the permission, and so, in truth, was I. She was bold and forward, asking questions about everything, ransacking the chamber, and peering into every corner.

"Here, little miss, you must not open that chest," said Mary, " I allow no one but myself to do that."

"Tell me what is in it," persisted Nabby ; " I want to see your things in there."

"Come here, Nabby," said Bessy, " I want to tell you something ; do you know how your eyes grow bigger and bigger all the time, while you look at other people's things ? I think they are about large enough now. I should not want them to grow faster than the rest of you, and they will, if you do so, and then people will say, 'there's Nabby Great-eyes !'"

"You don't know who has come," said the little girl, trying to turn the conversation.

'Come !" said Bessy, "I suppose a great many people have come somewhere."

"Oh, well ! somebody came to our house yesterday, from down below. It's Uncle William, and he said he was coming to see you to-night, Mary."

Mary's bright blush set me to thinking, for Nabby's Uncle William, when in town, had called over more than once, and made himself very agreeable.

"Now," said Bessy, laughing, "you are a wise child—do you expect us to believe you ?"

"Oh, fie ! Nabby," said Mary, "what a story you are telling. I shall make it a point in future to believe only half of what you say."

"Well—he asked mother if you were at home. I heard him"——

"Then just half of it is true," said Bessy

"Besides, I heard mother say something to him about coming here a great deal."

"So does Cousin David come here, almost every day," I interposed, "and he always walks home from meeting with Mary, every Sunday, too."

"Hush, Anna," said Mary, "you don't know what you are talking about." Just then I was called down stairs for something, and finding Hester crying over her unfinished work, I told her I would do it for her, if mother would let me take it up stairs, which, with some reluctance, she permitted. Hester ran gladly out to play with Nabby, while I was well satisfied to stay and listen to my sisters' conversation. Mary and Bessy began to talk of Cousin Hannah and her trials, Nabby's smartness and neglected training, and the bad influence of the examples by which she was surrounded. Mary's work, whilom apt to linger, did not now; her wheel buzzed merrily, amid some quiet fun on the part of Bessy, and much gleeful teazing by me, especially as I chanced to find out that Mary contrived to put a nice piece of new cheese slily into Nabby's pail when she left.

Before evening Mary's work was done, herself made tidy, and, sure enough, William Homer came, and I fancy it was rather a late hour in the evening when he took his leave. The next afternoon he came again, mounted upon a fine horse, and leading another, for a ride; and blushing Mary, looking bright and beautiful, rode up the quiet lane with him, just as the sun was setting over the top of Pine Mountain.

The warm glow of sunset was all around; the burnished tree tops, the deep shadows on the green fields, the melody of singing birds, all found echo and were reflected in their young hearts, as, gaily talking, they disappeared over the brow of the hill

CHAPTER XI.

DREAMS AND REALITIES.

"Rarest of all things on earth is the union in which both, by their contrasts, make harmonious their blending; each supplying the defects of the helpmate, and completing by fusion, one strong human soul."

WILLIAM HOMER's parents were old residents of Wayland. The eldest son, Nabby's father, has been already mentioned; the younger, William, was smart, intelligent, but rather gay, so that he was termed by some, "a wild young man;" he was very handsome, almost fascinating in his pleasing address and easy politeness, not lessened by his residence "down below," that is, in or near Boston, where he had obtained a situation in a dry goods store. Mary's sprightliness suited well with his gaiety and high spirits, and that he was pleasing to her, there could be no doubt. But my father's air of gravity and reserve in respect to him, notwithstanding the frequent, and often unseemly jests of our stepmother, caused Mary some anxious thoughts; and I used to hear her at night—for I occupied a bed in the same chamber—in earnest conversation with Bessy. This was but the commencement of her first anxiety, and to Bessy she instinctively turned for counsel. No sisters could be more closely united in feeling, more confidential and communicative to each other in their affairs.

This confidence was not extended in the smallest degree to our mother ; nor joys nor griefs were entrusted to her keeping, nor could they have been, with safety.

I do not think we ever failed in outward obedience and respect towards her, yet, that she possessed not the key to our deeper feelings, was early and thoroughly understood by us all.

She herself marked a division, so to speak, by her commonest words and actions, between herself and her own children on the one hand, and her husband and step-children on the other. It was not uncommon for her, in the morning, after the family breakfast of plain but wholesome food was dispatched, and the family had dispersed to their different tasks, to prepare some little delicacy for herself and her own little daughter. I recollect one incident, not unlike others of common occurrence. An altercation had arisen at the dinner table between Willie and our youngest brother, Royal. My father, probably from seeing the younger most in fault, reproved him. His mother instantly interposed, exclaiming, while she caressed her son, " You take care of your child, and I will of mine !"

" Why," said I, " isn't Royal father's child too ?"

But I was bid to be silent, for her husband never permitted the least improper or disrespectful treatment of her by his children. Besides this, her carriage and deportment were too often subversive alike of the dignity of matron and mother. She was perpetually lowering herself by querulous trifling, petty contests with the children, or bandying low jests with the hired workmen, enjoying with much seeming relish the coarse laugh and the rough retort ‹ We were often mortified by the negligence, even uncouthness of her dress ; for in this, as in other respects, she loved to stand upon the outer verge of decorum, and slight the thousand little decencies of life and manners.

One day, when in one of her worst plights, Deacon Peters and his wife, special friends of my father, and she a lady of much refinement, came unexpectedly to visit. When my mother first perceived them, she stood almost aghast at being surprised in such a predicament; but, as they approached the house on their horses, a sudden thought struck her; she caught out her skirts with either hand, like an opera girl, struck up a lively tune, danced a jig in the open door, and skipped out to meet them. Mirth and hilarity followed this ludicrous performance, which, however well it might have succeeded as a *ruse* to conceal her chagrin, seemed more in keeping with the character of a harlequin than with that of a dignified and courteous lady, welcoming valued guests. Her nature lacked the quality of earnest, reflective seriousness, no less than a nice perception of propriety. The contrast in habits of thought and feeling between her and my father was great. She could neither lighten nor share his burdens ; but upon his faithful daughter, his Bessy, he could and did rely for constant aid, and even counsel, in his many cares.

She has since told me, that he was accustomed to converse with her freely upon family matters, and that many a time, when riding to church on horseback behind him, she was affected to tears, with the thought that young, inexpe rienced, and unfit as she felt herself to be, her father should seek her advice and make her the repository of his paternal cares and anxieties. My much-loved, honored father.! how unwearied were his cares, his love, and his efforts for our good! How vividly his kind, grave face rises to my recol·lection, and with it come his words of tender counsel, of wise caution, or reproof, almost always in quotations from the scriptures. His acquaintance with the Bible was so intimate that some apposite proverb or word of exhortation would seem to rise spontaneously to his lips, suited to every occasion ; casually passing through the room, perhaps, some passage gently repeated would check our foolish jesting, idle talk, or noisy glee, with an effect which has proved great and lasting. The truth thus early implanted in the "seed time" of life, applied to daily circumstances in our childish feelings and actions, formed the very life of the moral nature of his children—nay, constituted the foundation, deep and strong, of the religious character of later years. Even in thoughtless girlhood, amid all its heedless waywardness, when tempted to indulge in envious or unkind feelings, how often have these words of wisdom flashed across my mind, with all the tender and solemn sanction not alone of an earthly father, but of an Heavenly !

Nor was this influence less salutary on others. Neighbor Fleming, significantly termed "shiftless," who occupied a miserable hut near by, and was literally taken care of by my father, came one day with a child in his arms, complain-ing bitterly of the behavior of his wife, for they often disa·greed ; presently she appeared with another child, alleging that her husband was alway finding fault, let her do what she would. My father gravely repeated, "Better is a dinner of herbs where love is, than a stalled ox and hatred therewith." "The beginning of strife is as when one letteth out water," and similar quotations—his only words. On another like occasion, his answer was, "Tug at the beam, neighbor Fleming, tug at the beam, and the mote will disappear."

CHAPTER XII.

IN due time my wheel was procured, and Hester, too, was initiated into the spinning department, for, as the season advanced, there was greater press than usual in the household work.

Bessy had, with some difficulty, obtained permission to make a web of fine table linen, being desirous of learning to weave this, the most difficult fabric of home manufacture.

Cousin Lucy, a niece of my father's, much valued by him, and beloved by us all, who was frequently at our house, came now, and spent a week to instruct Bessy in the nice and complicated process of weaving it, for she was well skilled in the art ; and with much satisfaction a long web of the firm texture, variously figured, was laid on the grass, and carefully tended, till it rivalled the snow in whiteness.

After this, came the work of preparing winter clothing ; the wool was to be picked, cleansed, carded, and spun, then dyed and woven, that we might be in readiness for the rigors of the severe cold ; labors much more arduous and disagreeable than those of preparing the flax.

This year brought some changes in the usually unvarying tenor of things in our quiet family. Our dear Grace came home on a visit of some weeks. I should have mentioned, that she had lived most of the time since the death of our mother, with our Aunt Hilliard, at Alstead, New Hampshire. Aunt Hilliard was a younger sister of our own mother, a noble, true-hearted woman, and well and tenderly had she cared for and instructed her sister's child. Uncle Hilliard was a physician, at first settling in Wayland, he had afterwards removed to the still newer region of Cheshire county, and there established himself.

Oh, how glad were we to see our own darling sister, so long separated from us! She was joyous as a bird in spring ; with a clear, dancing blue eye, lightsome step, and airy motion, she seemed to have a glow of happiness about her enlivening the whole house. None was more happy in her return than poor Alger, who said, in his expressive language of signs, "When Grace comes into the room, the sun shines." He was nearest to her in age, and from childhood they had been special companions.

Grace herself was almost wild with joy at being again with us, giving us lively accounts of her home in Alstead, often making us laugh by her witty descriptions of what she had seen. She had much skill and ingenuity with her needle, and was of essential service in that respect, though she was then only a child of fourteen.

But the principal event in the family this autumn, was Mary's first visit to Boston, to spend a few weeks with Aunt Hastings. Uncle Hastings was a hardware merchant, with a comfortable income. They lived in some style, in a large, square, wooden house, at the South End. The dwelling is still standing, though having undergone in modern times considerable renovation. Aunt Anna Hastings was admired, loved, reverenced by us as quite the standárd of perfection in almost all respects. She was one of the most winning and lovely women I ever saw, as well as the kindcst of aunts. Bessy, her only daughter, was a little younger than Mary ; her son was older, and remarkable for his personal beauty. To make a visit to this beloved aunt was quite the summit of our wishes, and it suited well with the gaiety of Mary's disposition to mingle iu the exciting scenes, and witness the life and animation of the city. The journey was an important event in our retired country life, and there was much grave consultation on the matter of preparation. No pains were spared to make her simple wardrobe presentable in the eyes of her cousins, yet she found she must content herself to rest in the comfortable conclusion to which Bessy's good sense conducted her.

"You are a farmer's daughter," said she, " as every one who sees you will know ; you will not be expected to appear in the fashion and finery of rich city girls."

" But," said Mary, "I should be sorry to have Cousin Bessy ashamed to introduce me to her associatcs."

"Oh, that is not likely at all," rejoined Bessy, "it is no dishonor to a country girl to appear iu a country garb, and if anything is really wanting to make your dress respectable, Aunt Hastings will tell you. After all, Mary, you must, no doubt, depend on something better than fine dress to give you favor with others."

This conversation was the evening before Mary was to leave. We were seated on a spot half-way between the house and the barn. It was a ledge just appearing above tne grass, and forming a short, abrupt descent, where we often sat, or reclined, on summer evenings, and waited for the cows to come home to be milked. While Mary and Bessy were talking, father came from the barn on his way to the house, and paused where we were. Pointing to the glowing sunset sky, and the distant trees resting on its bright bosom, he said :

"That glorious scene brings Heaven to my mind, with its peace, its blessedness ; how mean and trifling are the things of earth, in comparison with Heaven's glories ! Keep God, and the world to come, in your thoughts, my children, and the little annoyances and mortifications you will meet, will have small power to disturb you. Remember this, my daughter, in leaving your home ; new scenes will doubtless bring new trials and temptations. Learn all you can ; your aunt will aid and guide you in whatever is necessary for your respectable appearance among her friends. Esteem it of little consequence, comparatively, what is thought of your dress, but be careful that all have reason to approve your conduct."

Then taking out his well-worn purse, and putting some pieces of money into her hand, he said :

"Here is a trifle more I can spare you."

"Oh ! father," said Mary, " you have given me so much already ! I am afraid it is selfish for me to take any more."

Her father looked at her with a kind smile, as he said, " It will not seem like 'so much' when you see so many things you would like in Boston, and you need not think you are selfish, for I don't."

As we walked towards the house, I saw a big tear roll down Mary's cheek, but she quickly brushed it away, as she caught the anxious glance of Bessy, and all that evening she seemed determined to keep up our spirits, by her lively chat, and cheerful, hopeful prophecies of her brilliant *début* in Boston. The next morning she left us

CHAPTER XIII.

A LITTLE LOVE, AND A LITTLE TROUBLE.

"Every life must have its own romance."

MARY went away buoyant with hope and expectation; she had the happy faculty of extracting pleasure from every source within her reach; but her anticipated enjoyment was somewhat clouded by a circumstance of which I knew nothing till long afterwards, but which had an important bearing upon her destiny in after life.

A week had passed, and she had been the happiest of the happy, each day receiving new delight in visiting, chaperoned by her cousins, the various objects of interest. Everything had the charm of freshness and novelty to her eyes; the sumptuous dwellings, the brilliant shops, with their windows temptingly decked with the new, the costly, and the beautiful. Then, how delightful the evening promenade in the Mall, among crowds of people, well dressed, looking happy and elegant—all was like enchantment to her unpractised vision.

One day a ride to Roxbury was proposed, a family carry-all was engaged, and all were to be ready as soon as dinner was over. Light-hearted and happy, she was singing through the hall as she went up to dress for the ride, when a knock was heard at the door, and from the top of the stairs she heard a well-known voice inquire for " Miss Mary Leland."   Her heart beat loudly as she went down to meet her old admirer, William Homer, who, hearing she was in the city, had called to see her. A variety of contending emotions flushed her cheeks, and deprived her of all presence of mind ; maiden timidity and bashfulness, joiued to fear of her aunt, whose ideas of nicest propriety she knew, with an almost unacknowledged consciousness that the handsome young man whom she looked upon with so much favor, was, after all, not the character to meet the approbation of her friends as a visitor to herself.

Feeling at the moment, that she could not invite him in, to be recognized by her friends as her suitor, she treated him with coolness, almost with incivility.

He saw her embarrassment, but knew not its cause. So, after a word or two, coldly spoken, he took his leave, feeling his presence unwelcome, both grieved and indignant at his repulse. Poor Mary crept up stairs, overcome by a whirl of feelings. A sense of relief that he was gone unseen by any of the family, was soon succeeded by great uneasiness at the recollection of his look of chagrin and vexation. Reproaching herself bitterly for the cold and uncivil demeanor which so belied her heart, she burst into tears. Soon, however, consoling herself with the idea that she should make all right at some future meeting, she dried her eyes.

Though her thoughts wandered, and a shadow was upon her spirit at first, she became cheerful, and even animated, by her ride. Roxbury was at that time a succession of fine farms, with comfortable, and even elegant dwellings. The scenery was charming, and Mary's love of nature was all aroused. It was, too, the early home of her own mother, the place of dear associations, and of many valued friends. The next day, as she sat at work with cousin Bessy, a letter was brought to her by the penny-postman. The handwriting made her cheek change color, and her hand trembled so she dared not open it. Covering her confusion by a question about the messenger, she escaped to her room, and found it to be what she had anticipated—a letter from her indignant admirer. It was written in great agitation, and in all the bitterness of wounded affection. He declared that he needed no more proof of her indifference, than was given in her reception of him the preceding day ; that he would trouble her no more with his attentions or his presence, though all his cherished hopes were blasted ; that his life would henceforth be a burden too valueless to be worth the trouble of preserving ; and much more, in the strong, passionate language of resentment, injured feeling, and disappointment.

This was trouble, indeed, for poor Mary ; his fine appearance and winning manners had captivated her youthful fancy ; her heart was touched by his regard for herself, manifested even in their childhood. In many of the sunniest hours of her joyous young life he had been associated ; and did not his image find place, too, in her bright visions of the future ? That future, indeed, she had but vaguely pictured to herself, nor were her thoughts and feelings in regard to him very clearly defined in her own mind. She lived in the happy Present.

6

The period of girlhood is that of quick susceptibility, nay, of strong, o'er-mastering, passionate feeling ; but it is also the time when fancy and imagination bear sway—subtle Fancy weaving its airy web in the warm tints of imagiuation's bright coloring.

The true depth of earnest, serious affection, must have underlying it, the higher, purer, stronger powers of the soul, that the judgment may, in its sweep, bear along the passions and emotions in delightful harmony.

This was Mary's first love, and though it was the love of the girl, rather than of the woman, it was still deep and true.   Sometimes she half resolved to write to him, desiring him to come to her, and then to explain all, and seek reconciliation ; but her maidenly pride forbade. With all her love for him, and her regret for her unkind treatment, she could but feel that he had been hasty, and unjust ; that, as he had left her in a fret, she knew not how to stoop to win him back ; but neither did she know how to bear this estrangement for such a trifle.   She was sorely tried, and her evident unhappiness, swollen eyes, and air so different from her usual buoyancy, could not escape notice ; anxious looks and inquiries only added to her trouble, until at length her aunt, taking a favorable occasion, when Bessy was spending the day abroad, set herself seriously to probe the wound.   In a kind, considerate manner, partly by affectionate entreaty, partly by her right, as standing for the time in place of mother, she drew from Mary a reluctant confession of her feelings, and the cause of her present cloud of sorrow.

Aunt Hastings read the letter attentively, and after a few minutes' thoughtful silence, said kindly,

"I quite sympathize with you, my love, in regretting your incivility. There is no keener suffering to a generous mind than regret for a wrong done ; it was due to yourself, and due to him, as a gentleman and friend, to treat him with kindness and courtesy. But, my dear girl," she continued, "this letter betrays great lack of a candid, manly temper, and a want of high principles of action, making all due allowance for the strength of his feelings. The young man who would suffer himself to be hurried along by such a torrent of mad passion as his letter betrays, is unfit to be trusted with the happiness of another. He is not the one for you—think no more of him."

"But, aunt," sobbed Mary, "he is so unhappy !"

"Not so unhappy, perhaps, as you imagine, my dear," quietly rejoined her aunt ; "such extravagant misery is not apt to be lasting or deep ; if, as I judge, he sports the character of the light-minded, fancy-flitting beau, you can well dispense with any further attentions from him, and he will soon recover his spirits. What is your father's opinion of him ?" she continued.

Mary colored, then hesitatingly answered, "He never said much about him."

Aunt Hastings went on. "It is of the first consequence that you be able to look up with respect, and repose perfect trust in the man you call your husband ; this can only consist with steady, thoughtful self-restraint, subjecting the mind and character to the rule of firm principle. Love, not founded upon these qualities, is as evanescent as the dew on the summer flower. Can you thus respect and trust William Homer? Do you believe him to be under the control of strong principle? Think and judge calmly, my dear."

Mary was obliged to acknowledge, when her serious judgment was thus appealed to, that some points in his character did not please herself, and that she was by no means sure that his attentions were approved by her father.

"But I can't help wishing this had not happened," she said, sorrowfully.

"My dear Mary," said her aunt, kindly, "I am satisfied, quite satisfied that it is best as it is. Nay, I am disposed to regard this as one of those turns in Providence, in which, by a trivial act or circumstance, a new direction or different character is given to a long train of events, perhaps a whole life. All our ways are directed by our Father above," she exclaimed, reverently looking up, "nor can we advance a step, but at his bidding."

A glow of earnestness suffused her expressive countenance as she added, thoughtfully, "How different from the whirl and excitement of passing scenes and present emotions, is the cooler and more distant view that retrospection gives ! A few years hence, you may look back on this occurrence, now so painful to you, my dear girl, as one of the most fortunate circumstances of your life. It is only in scanning the backward path, that the cloud becomes luminous. We walk in darkness seeing but the footsteps we are treading, and that imperfectly ; all objects before us appear in gigantic and fanciful shape, like a landscape enveloped in fog and mist ; while behind us the long pathway, however winding or rugged, beams in light."

This conversation was not without its effect on Mary's mind. It revealed clearly to her, what she had before dimly seen—that William Homer was deficient in some of the elements essential to a noble, manly character ; and, though her heart still pleaded in his favor, her reason and conscience declared that her aunt was right in saying—" It is best as it is."

CHAPTER XIV.

"You live, sir, in these dales, a quiet life;
Your years make up one peaceful family."

MARY returned home from Boston somewhat sooner than she at first intended, Uncle James Lyle being unexpectedly at the city on business. He performed the journey on horseback, then the usual mode, leading by the bridle father's old grey mare, for Mary's use. Long as well as lonely was the way, two or three days being occupied in travelling the same route now passed by railroad in a few hours. At that time, neither wagons, nor carriages of any sort, were in common use in Wayland. The weekly mail was brought upon the back of a single horse, where now the daily car carries the news of these more noisy times in papers and letters, by the hundred weight. About this time we were delighted to receive a visit from our cousin, Lyman Gove, who lived upon one of the West India islands. His mother, Aunt Cass, was a dear sister of my father's. Her house was near the church, and there my father invariably spent the intermission between services on Sunday ; and it was a season of sweet enjoyment and Christian converse, for they were both one, in tender affection and devoted piety.

Aunt Cass had been twice married, and Cousin Lyman

was the son of her first husband. He had married a Creole lady, and had with him on this visit, his two little sons. Funny, little, dark-complexioned, frolicsome fellows we thought them. It chanced once, when they were staying at our house for a few days, that there fell, during the night, a little light snow, as sometimes premonitory signals of winter will come, in the latter part of autumn, while the weather is yet mild. In the morning Sidney, the eldest, having gone out early, came bounding into the house in wild excitement, screaming to his brother,

"Oh, Martin! Martin! come out here—the ground is all covered with white sugar!"

Their wonder and curiosity about the snow—for they had never before seen any—afforded us much amusement.

During this visit, Aunt Cass's daughter, Lucy Cass, was married; but of the wedding, or its festivities, I remember nothing. The event was chiefly memorable to us, because our sister Hester, Lucy's especial favorite, accompanied her to her new home in Rutland, Vermont. She stayed there more than a year, and always retained a vivid recollection of "Father Haynes," the well-known colored preacher of that place, and of her sport with his little girls. When she returned home she managed her horse without assistance, during the whole ride of sixty or seventy miles, riding fifty miles in one day, which made an impression on my mind, as being esteemed a remarkable feat for a girl so young, for she was not quite eleven years old.

The cold weather came on apace, and no period of my childhood or youth rises before me in brighter, warmer coloring than this. We were a merry group of sisters; Mary and Bessy, Grace and' myself, occupied one chamber, and at night, after retiring, was the special time of sisterly conferences on all topics. We all attended school together, and when the rays of the early morning sun sparkled all over the dazzling winter prospect, the expanse of field and hill, then would Grace and I bound over the snow, piled on either side of the path, often so hard frozen and firm that we could slide down the drifted hillocks, or run as we listed over the smooth, shining surface of the fields. Oh! I can see again the slight, flexible figure of Grace, as, swift as a fawn, with a wild ringing laugh, she would start on a race, and leave me far behind at the first; but I was fleet and nimble too, and besides, she would soonest loose breath, for her slender person could not oppose the rude Borean breeze so well as my shorter and firmer knit frame. Oh, how the keen, cold, cutting air made the young blood dance in our veins, raising our spirits to the most hilarious delight, as we careered along on our way, to gain betimes the old square-roofed brick school-house.

There the uproar of shouting boys, noisy talk and glee, rose and swelled ever louder and louder as the moment neared for the master's grave approach, with rod and ferule, to still the tumult into awe-stricken silence and order.

There was a singing-school, too, that winter, the first I ever attended. That was pleasure, indeed, and neither hunger nor cold were felt in our enjoyment of its hours. We lived quite too far away to go home and return again for the evening, so, if it chanced that a morsel of bread and cheese was left of our dinner, we were glad ; if not, we could dispense with our supper, without a thought, and enjoy, oh, how much ! the gathering with our mates around the large open fire-place, as the ruddy glow faded from the west. As the night shut in, the blazing fire of huge logs piled one above another, roared in the ample chimney, casting its red glare on the motley group assembled around it, talking, singing, or, perchance, whispering fearful tales to the credulous, suggested by the darkness without, or the strange, gigantic, flickering shadows moviu, and darkening on the walls within.

The capacious chimney was built in the wall, opposite the door, leaving a large recess on either side ; one was the receptacle of the formidable pile of logs for the evening's consumption ; in the other was the smaller pile of pitch-pine knots, contributed from various quarters, " of the best kind, carefully selected." This mode of lighting an apartment, so novel in our day, was then quite common, being both economical and convenient, and as the dry, resinous wood blazed fiercely up, every nook and corner became bright and cheerful as they were filled with the brilliant light.

For those who loved music as well as I did, where could be found such a whole evening full of enjoyment as was here afforded ? The strong, hearty voices of the young men and maidens rolled out the notes of Coronation, and Russia, and chased each other through the labyrinthian passages of Exhortation, Sardinia, and Delight.

Are the parties and formal visits, which now usurp its place, really any pleasanter, with their chit-chat and fashionable small-talk, than was the singing-school, where were commenced and cemented lasting friendships, aye, and *loves* too, for half the "courting" was done there in those primitive New England times.

CHAPTER XV.

SUITORS.

> " That heart, methinks,
> Were of strange mould, which kept no cherished print
> Of early, happy times, when life was fresh,
> And love and innocence made holiday."

MARY, strange to say, required solicitation to induce her to join in the singing, wont to be her delight. A change had come over her spirit, her character was becoming deeper in its tone, more earnest, she was intent upon her studies, improving each spare moment. Evening after evening was now spent in poring over problems with the teacher, both absorbed in study, or conversation on various knotty points.

The teacher's visits, indeed, became so frequent, as winter sped, as to excite some doubts as to their disinterested nature ; but, to Mary herself, they were at that time only the means of more rapid improvement in her favorite studies.

This teacher was the only son of Colonel Lyman, who occupied a farm in a remote part of Wayland. The father had served with honor in the Revolutionary war, was a high-toned gentleman, priding himself on his standing and character. He was, indeed, regarded with a respect bordering upon awe, by many of his neighbors. His farm was valuable, his house the best in Wayland, being built in antique English style ; large, square entrance hall, long kitchen.

and spacious, wainscoted rooms, an ample, well-furnished farm-house ; in later years the home of Mary.

Col. Lyman employed several workmen, and was accustomed to take his meals with them, though always preserving much commanding dignity in his demeanor. His wife, usually designated "Madam Lyman," was extremely penurious, careless of the opinion of others, with vast energy of character, chiefly displayed in her thrifty housekeeping and good management. I have heard my father relate an anecdote characteristic of her. At the evening meal, which was ordinarily of bread and milk, her husband's dish was distinguished by a silver spoon, while the workmen were served with pewter. On one occasion, one of the men adroitly slipped his own spoon into the colonel's dish, and exchanged the bowls.

No sooner had the colonel commenced his repast, than, stopping short, he pushed back his chair, then instantly conceiving the trick and its motive, he angrily exclaimed,

"Wife ! have you given us skimmed milk to eat ? New milk is none too good for me ; and my workmen shall fare as well as I do."

With some confusion, Madam Lyman took away the dishes, and re-filled them with richer and more palatable milk ; and it was long before she tried again that method of saving. She was fond of money, seldom missed an opportunity of making or saving a penny, nor was she over-scrupulous as to the means of doing it. They had four daughters. The eldest was the wife of a thrifty farmer living near us. I remember her for her high, whining tone of voice, sounding as if she were just ready to cry, and for her habit of interspersing "dear" in her conversation, very freely, to every one, and on every occasion. She was much like her mother ; in her eyes no amount of moral excellence could compensate for the want of worldly advantages. She, consequently, was not well pleased with her brother's intimacy in our family, when she became aware of his liking for Mary.

The next daughter, Xenia Lyman, was observable for her high pretensions, lofty air and carriage, o'erlooking and o'ertopping all her companions. She was aspiring, and really talented, and was subsequently principal of a celebrated female seminary in Boston, where she remained till her death. I well remember her tall commanding form at church, as, with head erect, she walked with slow and stately step the length of the aisle to her father's pew. Her two sisters usually followed, Mary, with the most meek, down-looking, unpretending air, and Abby, taller than Mary, though the younger, an awkward girl, with a heedless, wandering gait, her teeth protruding through her half-opened lips. Few then would have seen, in the uncouth girl, the germ of the noble, accomplished woman she afterwards became. With her is associated the memory of some of my happiest days, and she is still living, honored and useful in one of our most favored cities.

Our teacher, Samuel Lyman, an only son, was early imbued with ideas of family importance, but was a young man of noble, elevated character, with high regard to honor and upright principles of action. He was somewhat awkward, and not very prepossessing in appearance, yet he was well

educated and sensible, chiefly noticeable, however, for a certain pompous manner of expressing himself, rolling high-
sounding words out from the depths of his throat, seeming,
but for his perfect naturalness and simplicity, like inflated,
ridiculous bombast.

There where others, too, who were applicants for Mary's
favor, and who sought to renew her interest in her former
gaieties ; for, though cheerful and even gay at home, since
her return from Boston, and her chapter of heart experience there, she had become indifferent to company, and to
attentions from other admirers.   Our cousin, David Leland,
a familiar guest, had long manifested a preference for her,
and would have compassed sea and land to win her heart,
but he well knew his wishes were vain.   Charles Coke, too,
was a frequent visitor, though in quite a general way ; indeed, he seemed to take more notice of Grace and myself,
simple, mirth-loving little girls, as we were, than of Mary
or Bessy.   He was just about Mary's age, rather handsome,
and even then spoken of as a fine young man.   He spoke
slowly, in a mild, grave tone, and thought seemed to sit
waiting for utterance on his broad, serious brow.   His gentleness, sincerity, and sweet, cordial manner, won our hearts.

His father, Mr. Jacob Coke, was an early resident, and
occupied the finest situation in Valley Brook.   He owned
a large farm, several mills, and was reputed. the richest
man in Wayland.   His house had a noble site on the slope
of the valley, overlooking the green meadows and the
flowery banks of the clear running brook, and commanding
one of the boldest and most picturesque views of Pine

Mountain. On the other side, the level road stretched far down the opening valley, traced and dotted by farm-houses and cottages, half-veiled by tall poplars and rows of bowery maples. There was a large family of the Cokes, twelve in all ; several of them grown up, and distinguished rather by sound, practical sense and upright stability of character, joined to a warm-hearted genial nature, than by any high pretensions or shining qualities, either of person or mind. Of Charles, I shall have occasion to speak again, a little further on in my story.

Bessy, too, shy, awkward, silent Bessy, began to have her share of attention. Our neighbor, Jonas Crokey, school companion in years gone by, when I used to stand beside him in the class and look up to him, an over-grown, thick-headed boy, half in fear, half in mirth, as in sullen discomfiture he was wont to yield place after place to quicker-witted scholars of half his stature. Jonas got quite into the habit, about this time, of "coming in" of an evening in a friendly way ; not, indeed, that he made himself remarkably social, apparently he had few thoughts in his head, or small power to express them.

He would sit and gaze like the Laird of Dumbiedikes, not, indeed, at Bessy, but alternately at the walls and ceiling, most of all, fixing his eyes pertinaciously on the brightest spot in the blazing fire.

When he did venture a remark on the weather or the news, he invariably addressed Bessy, who had to bear a multitude of jokes on his account. She took all in good part, however, disclaiming any particular concern with his visits; yet I noticed more than once an air of vexation pass over her face, when he would come familiarly to the kitchen door, raise the latch, and announce himself with "Good evening, Miss Bessy, it's a pretty cold night;" then seat himself and gaze into the fire as usual.

It must be confessed, we were somewhat disposed to make fun of him, but my father would allow nothing of it in his presence, always treating him with marked courtesy. It was not until the beginning of summer that Jonas found courage, or perhaps a fitting occasion to make a formal declaration of his wishes to Bessy. At the close of their interview, the unsuccessful wooer took from his purse a silver piece, and offered it to her, remarking, "Money is scarce and hard to be got, or I would give you more."

Painful as it was to her to accept a bit of money from a discarded suitor, she would not wound his feelings by refusing it, while, on his part, it showed that he felt the genuine sympathy and exquisite kindness by which she softened her refusal.

This affair was still more painful to her, because his suit was favored by our father. Entering the chamber that night, I found Mary and Bessy busily talking; Bessy in tears. She had just had a conversation with our father, in which he had expressed much regret at her decision, asking her to reconsider the matter. He represented to her the eligible home it would secure her, near him—for Jonas had a good farm, and was steady and industrious, and if he knew little else, he was not ignorant of the state of his flocks. It might seem that our father was unduly influ enced by worldly considerations ; but he was poor, with a family of nine children, six of them girls, for whom he could hope to do but little.

Bessy could scarcely expect a better opportunity to settle in life, since, plain in person and shrinking from notice, her merits would be overlooked.

Invaluable, almost essential, as were her services in the family, yet his anxiety for her good made it a sore disappointment at the time, that his beloved daughter should decline so good a situation as being the mistress of the smart red house and broad fields of Jonas Crokey. Bessy, truly humble in self-estimation, fully believed no other prospect could be in store for her, and she desired no other than a life of patient, unnoticed, self-denying toil, forgetting herself, and finding her happiness in ministering to others.

6

CHAPTER XVI.

"Touch us gently, Time!"

As spring advanced, Grace began to droop; she became languid, her step feeble, and, her fragile form seemed to fade away before the warm breath of the renewing year. She had been too severely taxed the past winter, by exposure to the cold, and exertions in attending school, and more than all, by the long evening walks after singing school, which yet, she enjoyed too much to forego willingly. Now, the exhilarating cold and pleasant excitement were succeeded by the relaxing, sunny days which often herald the reign of summer. The reaction proved too much for her frame, a fever set in, and she was reduced to the feebleness of an infant, hovering between life and death.

But we were spared this great sorrow then. On the night of the fever's crisis, when she lay in her utter weakness, in a sort of stupor, wrestling with death, our afflicted father called us together around her bed. Then kneeling, he prayed to his heavenly Father, "with strong crying and tears," that He would not cut her down in her youth like an untimely flower, but bid her live, to serve and honor the God of his fathers. His low, earnest voice became broken and faltering, as at length he bowed his head humbly, submissively saying, "Thy will be done."

I slept little that night. I believed my father's prayer would be answered. I tried to pray, many thoughts crowded into my mind—thoughts of neglected duty—of forgetfulness of God; above all, the agonizing fear of death, that dark portal to an unknown land. The form of my sainted grandfather rose before my mind, as seated in his chair, too feeble to rise, he would pour forth his earnest pleading prayers. The many kind counsels and warnings of my grandmother too—alas! so long forgotten and neglected, now came fresh to my recollection.

Lovely and beloved, as was my sister, conscience too plainly whispered, that she too had been careless of prayer, —had been intent upon the pleasures of her joyous young life, and not upon the high duties and solemn destiny of her immortal soul.

I felt that she was unfit to die, and yet, she might even then be passing through the dark valley. The resolutions I made that night, were never afterwards quite forgotten. The next morning Grace was awake and conscious, colorless as the sheet on which she lay, her eye uncertain in its languid gaze, but the danger was past, the fluttering spark of life though feeble now brightened, and joy and thankfulness reigned in the house. Slowly and gradually recovering, she regained at length, her usual buoyant activity, and even increased vigor and firmer health, as if the ebbing springs of life pressed back to their source—had started afresh, purified and strengthened by the mighty struggle. We felt that she was once more ours.

Mary commenced this summer, her first experience in

teaching, and she continued for several successive seasons this excellent discipline for the mind and heart. Her first effort was in a small obscure town adjoining, and much is revealed of the state of things in those early times, by the fact, that she received in pay a written promise of "a good cow with a vantage heifer," as it was quaintly expressed in the obligation. This was deemed better than the "town order" usually given, and a mark of uncommonly high estimation of her services.

Cousin Bessy Hastings visited Wayland this season. She was a fair, delicate, gleeful girl, finding infinite amusement in our country ways and rustic habits, accustomed as she was to the bland, polished airs of the city, and to a mode of life remarkably quiet, unvaried and methodical. She was nice and exact in her ideas of propriety. Sometimes she was quite scandalized at the greater latitude of manners in rural life, on our free hills. The first day after her arrival being Sunday, she rode to church behind uncle James on horseback, which, though quite the post of honor according to our customs, was a great annoyance to her, and she complained piteously to us the next day, half in mirth, half in vexation.

"How I felt," said she, "perched up so high on the horse, with my feet dangling, and to be obliged to put my arm round a *man*, and hold on by the button-hole of his coat. I was so ashamed!"

She was quite ignorant of the modern fashionable practice of embracing one's partner in the waltz! My gentle cousin became in time, quite familiar with all like honors, and spite of a little over-fastidiousness, her visit gave us much delight, she was so genial in her mirth, so fertile in finding pleasure in everything. She acquired considerable skill in managing a horse, and liked it extremely. She attempted too, to learn to spin, but her merriment over the wheel prevented much proficiency. She carried home a much deeper color on her cheeks, and a far better acquaintance with nature, than was hers, when she took her first lonely journey through the long patches of woods, and viewed with astonishment the lofty trees pointing skyward, excluding all prospect save its blue canopy, and looked almost bewildered upon the wide extent of field and hill, the waving verdure, and the ever-changing beauty of a country landscape.

CHAPTER XVII.

HOME LIFE.

THREE years had passed. We were again seated on our favorite rock, watching the slowly setting sun, on one of those mild, hazy autumn days in which the waning year seems to pause, brooding over the tranquil earth. The woods were just tipped and sprinkled with pale yellow and crimson, amid their dark depth of verdure; all was in sweet harmony with the joy and content of our hearts.

Grace had that day returned to us, after another absence of more than a year. We had much to say. We were all five clustered together, in various attitudes, all talking by turns.

Alger, too, was there, seated a little lower down, on the edge of the rocky hillock, his back partly turned towards us, gazing at the western sky, often turning his eyes to drink in every word that was said; yet with the quiet, grave air which was his wont. Oh, how lovely looked our Grace, as with animated, happy face, she spoke from the fullness of her warm heart of the kind friend with whom she had been staying!

"Dear Mrs. Brintnall has been so good to me!" said she; "If I had been her own daughter, she could not have been more watchful to consult my happiness in every thing; loving and caring for me for the sake of our dear mother, whom she loved so well. And Bessy, I have borne your name almost all the time !"

" Why was that?" asked Bessy.

" Oh, at first, Mrs. Brintnall would constantly mistake, and call me by my mother's name, because she thought I looked so much as she used to ; and afterwards she said I must let her call me so while I stayed, for it brought back her childish days."

" Did she and our mother live together when they were little girls ?" asked Hester.

" Yes ; she says they lived side by side, and went to the same school; they shared the same tasks, and played together among the beautiful groves of Roxbury Common, and she told me much of their frolics on the shady banks of the pond on the plains, then so wild and lonely. Oh, she is a noble-hearted woman ! She has been like a mother to me. You know her husband left her but a small income, and she has her two boys to provide for; yet she would purchase things for me, and instead of letting me help her in her work, she has taken great pains to give me some of her own exquisite skill in different kinds of sewing. And so, young ladies," said she, smiling and courtseying, "I have the pleasure of introducing to you Miss Grace Leland, fashionable dress-maker ; and if you do not choose to. patronize me, I will volunteer my services to remodel my *father's* wardrobe."

" Oh, never fear," said Mary, "but we shall all be disposed to bring your numerous accomplishments to an immeliate test."

"I do not doubt you will find exercise for all your skill," said Bessy; "and nothing could be more kind and considerate for Mrs. Brintnall, as she knew the circumstances of the family, than to fit you to be useful at home, instead of filling your head with all sorts of fine notions."

"She used to say," said Grace, "that, among several daughters, one should have it her province to know how to do all kinds of sewing."

"Oh, Grace," said Mary, "do tell us about your visit to Boston; I want to hear all about Aunt Hastings and Cousin Bessy."

"I went there with Mrs. Brintnall last June. She and Aunt Hastings enjoyed so much together, talking of old times! Oh! Aunt Hastings is so beautiful, so queen-like! she could hardly speak to me at first; she looked steadily at me a moment, and then her eyes filled with tears."

"It was because you look so much like our mother,' said I.

"Yes, she said it recalled her sister to her mind, just as she was in their young days, when they were at home together."

"Did you go out to the Plains?" asked Mary.

"Oh! yes, a party of us went out there; and what a paradise it is! more beautiful than you told us, after your visit. The little groves of high trees close on the banks of that beautiful pond, and all around so level, and green, and smooth. Did you see Mr. Willard's house?"

"No," said Mary, "it was not built when I was there; all around the pond was covered with woods."

"It is an elegant mansion," said Grace, "overlooking the pond; winding paths lead from the gardens, through the shrubbery. It is wild and solitary, yet it is a lovely landscape. It often goes by the name of Jamaica."

"But do tell us about Cousin Bessy."

"Oh, she talked a great deal about her visit to Way land, and says she means to come again next summer. Her brother is very agreeable. He will soon be married. I never saw a finer looking man. But Alger says the dew is falling; see, his hand is quite wet where he has felt the grass; let us go in."

Half an hour after, Grace and I were walking back and forth on the turf before the house, in the soft moonlight, our heads enveloped in the same shawl, while we busily talked on various topics.

"Do tell me about this doctor, that comes to see Mary."

"It is young Dr. Emery," said I; "Clark Emery, you remember, son of Mr. Emery on Flower Hill. He has been away from town, some years, pursuing his studies. He is considered a good scholar, and quite skillful."

"Oh," said Grace, "I can just recollect him at school, but I had quite settled it that Mary would marry her old beau, Sam Lyman."

"So had I, and I sometimes think she does prefer him; I half believe she would have him, if it were not for his mother and sister, Mrs. Goldring, you know."

"Oh, nobody minds Mrs. Goldring," said Grace, "she is always whining out some complaint or other."

"Well, both she and her mother have said some ill-natured things that Mary will not easily brook, sweet-tempered and forgiving as she is, about his marrying a penniless girl, as they say."

"I hope she will not *condescend* to accept him," exclaimed Grace. "Her noble qualities and real loveliness are worth more than all the dowries in Wayland."

"I do not doubt Sam is quite of that opinion, and if he were entirely independent of his mother, it would matter little to him what *she* thought. But you recollect Colonel Lyman died suddenly, the property is somewhat embarrassed, and Madam Lyman and her son manage it together."

"How finely Mary looks," said Grace; "she is handsomer than ever, and her face has such a sweet, serious expression."

When, again, we were all together at night, there was much free and happy talk, and many sportive jests on Mary's dilemma, and the course she had best pursue. She, herself, as lively as any of us, asked each one in turn, half laughing, half serious, which of her suitors she should accept. Mary was, indeed, sorely puzzled to decide between the two rival claimants for her hand. Young Lyman had persevered long in his attentions, and probably would before this have won her consent, had she been sure of being cordially welcomed into his family. To Dr. Emery there was no objection; he was kind-hearted, manly and sincere; a tall, dark-haired, good-looking man, and a good physician. It was not long before her decision was made in his favor, and soon after he received a pressing invitation to visit the province of Maine, with a prospect of an advantageous settlement in his profession.

He determined upon going, to return in one year for Mary. He urged their immediate marriage, but that was overruled ; they were, however, "published," just before he - left, in compliance with his wish. Mary, too, being not unwilling that her relation to him should be generally understood.

Next came the great era in Bessy's life. At the distance of a mile or so from us, lived a family of the name of Cotting. Mr. Seth Cotting was one of the deacons of the church, a most exemplary man, remarkable for the sobriety of his habits, and the precision of his manners. He had, apparently, never deviated in the smallest minutia from the customs of his father Seth, which customs he again was transmitting inviolate to his son Seth. This young man had reached the age of twenty-seven or twenty-eight ; a sober, steady, truly excellent character, seldom mixing in any company, and though among young men of that period, habits of general gallantry prevailed, he was never known to offer any particular mark of civility to a female, scarcely. indeed, to raise his eyes, or speak to a young lady. He had never been at our house, unless it might be an accidental call on business, nor were we at all acquainted with him This shy and bashful, but really meritorious person, was seen one day slowly coming down the lane towards the house. Bessy espied him from the window, and afterwards declared that with an instant flash she divined his visit, and

that its motive respected herself, with a sudden conviction
on her mind that they would do for each other, and that it
would be altogether a suitable and proper match.

Of their quiet courtship there is little need to speak ;
nothing occurred to ruffle its tranquil course. One evening,
however, as they were sitting together in the common room,
the family having retired, Bessy chanced to fix her eyes on
a crack in the old wooden ceiling which separated this
room from our parents' sleeping apartment, and became
conscious that a large grey eye was peering through the
crevice ; it was our stepmother, who could not resist the
temptation to witness the interesting *tête-à-tête* of this
steady couple. Though Bessy was a trifle vexed at this
mode of gratifying her curiosity, it was so characteristic
that it furnished us all some amusement when she told it
next day, with a grave, comical air.

In the course of the following year Bessy's home was
transferred to the pretty red cottage prepared for her on
the brow of the hill overlooking Valley Brook, with its
moving panorama of life and beauty. There

> "Her virtues blossomed daily, and poured out
> A fragrance upon all who in her path
> Had a blest fellowship."

There, peacefully, her quiet, unobtrusive life has flowed on;
contented and happy in her retired, sheltered home, her
visions of happiness have been more than realized ; and if
moderate and tranquil have been her joys and pleasures,
light, too, have been her sorrows   More than fifty years

have passed away, no change has come to their dwelling, save such as are brought by the gentle touch of time, which, coming on unperceived with stealthy steps, has gradually transformed the youthful Bessy and her sober and bashful, but most kind and faithful partner, into an aged couple, with silvered hair and feeble step, tranquilly looking toward the grave as the entrance door to a new and glorious life.

The house echoes to the sound of little feet, and merry voices, and surrounded by their children's children, they still live on the well-stocked farm. That old red cottage, if dimmed in its brightness, looks most truly comfortable ; the tall pines still throw their broad sheltering shadows on the green hill above the house ; even the stone horse-block casts its quiet shade under the front windows, as of yore, and while the most rapid and startling changes, amid whirl and din, announce the unparalleled progress of modern times—while traffic, arts, society itself, move forward with railroad speed, all is calm and unvaried *there!*

CHAPTER XVIII.

ALGER—MARY.

THE next year commenced with scenes of affliction, our first great sorrow since the death of our beloved mother. Alger—our dear Alger, was suddenly stricken down by the fell destroyer!

I do not know why my memory recalls so little of this favorite brother. During all the period of which I have been speaking, it has ever been a matter of regret, deep but unavailing, that so few recollections remain to me of his short life, overshadowed as it must have been, by a growing consciousness of his peculiar calamity. How have I wondered since, that I could have been so selfishly absorbed in my own trifling pursuits and pleasures—the foolish, giddy thoughts and vain imaginations, that so often steal from youth its precious short-lived advantages! Oh! if I had but sought to win access to the inner cell of his gentle, sad spirit! Oh! to possess that balm—the memory of having soothed and sweetened his impoverished life, and made some atonement to a heart defrauded of half the sweet charities and kindly sympathies of nature!

As a child, Alger was cheerful and lively in his demonstrations of feeling, making known his thoughts and wishes by rapid signs and gestures, often unintelligible to all but Grace, who being much with him in early childhood, had quick interchange of ideas, and could interpret his different shades of meaning. But he had grown up quiet, grave, reserved, as if interrogating his own soul, dumb indeed, in outward speech, but all the more intense in its silent communings.

None knew—perhaps none sought to know, what surges of conflicting thoughts rose and swelled within the shut caverns of his soul, and swept over his straitened and isolated being.

He was tall and slender, just verging towards manhood, with all its aspirations, its hopes, and its high purposes. He felt the weight of his coming responsibilities and trusts, and was visibly oppressed by it. I distinctly remember his pale, high forehead, the sad expression of his face, and his long-drawn sighs, as he sat among us, mute with an absent, thoughtful air. Was his spirit burdened by the foreshadowing on his clear vision of the invisible, eternal world, which he was soon to enter? Who can tell of the world of thought? Is it not God's history written in imperishable characters, to be read in the day when the secrets of all hearts shall be made manifest?

I often noticed his aspect, but oh! with what strange, heedless unconcern! giving to the workings of his mind but a momentary thought.

He was taken ill in the evening, while assisting our father in some preparations for the early morning's work. The agonized expression of his face was noticed by us, for he did not complain. The remedies applied afforded him but a partial relief. He grew worse, and died after a few days' suffering. Peacefully he passed away, for death met him in a gentle sleep. Hester and I were sent for, from school, a few hours before he died ; but the sands of life were feebly running, he scarcely knew us. Two or three physicians attended him, but his disease baffled their skill. Oh ! how we mourned him ! As we had felt a peculiar tenderness for him while living, so our sorrow took a depth of gloom from the suddenness of his departure, still deeper that we knew so little the emotions of his sealed spirit. It was a cloud, without anything on which the smitten heart could rest for relief. The winter was a sad one. My father's prayers were deeply affecting and earnest, expressed much in the words of Scriptures, and I remember being much moved by this passage, " Show us, O ! God, wherefore thou contendest with us." It was a time of serious thought with us all, and an air of tenderness and solemnity pervaded the house.

Mary, in the ensuing spring, made a public profession of religion, and Bessya few months later. Mary had, indeed, become the thoughtful, earnest woman ; always obliging, and sweetly winning in her disposition, she now added the lovely grace of a self-denying spirit, regardful of the happiness of others ; instead of the gay, giddy, volatile girl, there was the cheerful, refined, loving woman. Her sprightly conversation, and the animated play of her features, betokened her vivacity, and had singular power to entertain and charm.

The time was drawing near, when she was to leave her father's home, to accompany the husband of her choice to the distant province of Maine, then newly and sparsely settled, regarded as an inhospitable clime, and an almost savage land.

It was, in fact, an unknown, untamed wilderness, except on the sea-coast, and along the borders of the rivers.

Dr. Emery's letters announced his satisfaction in the prospect opening before him—his wish to remain, and his speedy return to claim his promised bride.

Now was coming the first change in my hitherto monotonous life ; for, save the two years of my childhood spent in Atherton, my knowledge and experience, if not my thoughts, had been bounded by the neighborhood of my father's cottage. Mary wished me to accompany her to her far-off home, and the idea was most delightful to me. My father gave consent, and preparations for our departure in the early autumn, went on with great alacrity. It was arranged that I should go to Boston for a visit of several weeks, where Mary and her husband should join me, when ready to set sail. I was at this time just sixteen, and it would be difficult to find one of that age more unsophisticated in the ways of the world—more childlike in ignorance and simplicity,—more entirely uninitiated in all the numerous little arts and appliances that form the framework of society. I was excessively shy, blushing at the least thing, with a painful consciousness of my own deficiencies.

I had, too, a very humble opinion of my own personal attractions, often contrasting the beauty of Grace, her delicate bloom, sparkling eyes, and the light airy movements of her lithe figure, with my own less pleasing face and form, for my darker complexion and vivid color lacked delicacy,

8

and I was far too timid to be at ease in the presence of strangers. Bessy and Grace were taller than Mary and I ; and Grace, so round and straight, was elegantly formed. We were all, indeed, sufficiently straight, thanks to an early acquaintance with the spinning-wheel. The blooming girls of that period possessed the expanded chest, the well-developed bust, the firm springing step, which belong to this healthiest and most graceful of all indoor employments—an elasticy of motion which dancing-masters sigh in vain to reach.

The handsome forms, as well as firmer health, and longer lives of the women of that day, compared with the bent shoulders, and stooping gait of their more feeble daughters, are matters of general observation, nor need we seek far for the cause.

CHAPTER XIX.

THE JOURNEY AND VISIT TO BOSTON.

> " Oh, recall
> Those past delicious hours,
> Which made me happy as a bird
> In its sweet home of flowers."

I WENT to Boston in company with Major Huntley, of Atherton, brother to my stepmother, who was also of the party. We rode in Major Huntley's chaise, a new, and at that time quite a grand conveyance. Vain would be the attempt to picture the pleasure this visit afforded me; retired as my life had been, the most trivial things had power to charm; my senses were alive to all impressions, for every object wore the gloss and fascinating garb of novelty. This period was painted with the gay coloring of the dawn of existence, was invested with all the bright hues of a young, fresh imagination, just wakened into life by its own delighted exercise

It has ever been most vivid in my memory, as if graven with a diamond's point on the plastic metal, while whole long years of dull, weary existence, have vanished like the light tracing upon the sand, washed away by the next returning tide.

The journey itself was most delightful; it was in the loveliness of early summer; pleasure was written on the fair earth, and still fairer sky, and bright hopes and flattering anticipations of new scenes soon brushed away the lingering sadness of leaving home. Major Huntley was a most amusing companion, full of jokes and comical observations. Mother was in the gayest spirits, and returned joke for joke.

We stopped the first night at Marlborough, setting off again the next morning with the early dawn, to gain betimes a march upon the noonday sun. Beauty and fragrance were all around ; sparkling dews, and the sweet warbling of bird-voices filled the morning air.

As the day slowly waned, my two companions being chiefly engaged with each other, I sat forward, watching the ever-changing landscape, arrayed in summer verdure and luxuriance. Many lovely spots have my eyes looked on, since that glowing spring of my youth, but on none more charming than was that succession of green woods, smiling villages, and waving fields ; the shifting forms and hues of the silvery clouds, and the fast flitting shadows from hill to plain, from the glancing river to the deep, dark woods. A moving panorama of ever-changing beauties. We rode slowly that blissful afternoon, for the horse had travelled a a long and weary way.

About the time the sun was setting, we neared the place of our destination. This was in Dorchester, the home of two sisters of old Madam Huntley, and aunts of my step mother. They were elderly maiden ladies, quite rich, living in a great, old-fashioned farm-house near the beach.

I had heard much of these rich, eccentric, old Aunt Pettys ; they had occasionally sent to mother some articles of apparel, from their well-preserved and ample store ; a scarlet, hooded mantle, and a large-figured, bright-colored brocade cloak, of the oddest and most ancient style, were among the treasures laid up in mother's chests, presented by these precise maidens. The mantle, mother persisted in wearing to church, to our grief, for its oddity excited both observation and ridicule.

I had heard of drawers and chests full of gay-colored, grotesque attire, kept for years, and all made in the same antiquated fashion, for they would have nothing new or modern. The house and all its appurtenances were as quaint, odd, and old-fashioned as themselves, though not without an air of stiff and stately grandeur, in the square roof and carved wooden shutters.

We rode up to the door under the shade of an old elm tree, that threw its shade almost all over the venerable mansion. Presently a large, good-natured looking old lady came out to the gate, the bright red ribbons fluttering on her cap, as she screamed out a welcome ; while a little, prim, sharp, black-eyed person appeared in sight a moment, then vanished, and we heard her shrill voice calling " Rupert ! Rupert !" and he, too, of childhood memory, soon came forward, and after greeting his mother and uncle, led away the horse.

We were conducted to the family " keeping-room," and seating myself on the broad stool of an open window, I looked around me almost bewildered, and quite unheeded, while mutual inquiries and congratulations passed between the older persons.

The window in which I sat looked out upon a large yard, in the rear of the house, stocked with a variety of domestic animals; at the furthest corner, a cow stood peacefully chewing her cud under a tree. Rupert turned our weary horse, now freed from his harness, into the enclosure, where he testified his delight in the green grass, by rolling himself over and over on the dewy carpet.

Within all was strange; the great clock in the corner extended from the top to the bottom of the room, carved in a curious device; the fireplace was filled with fragrant branches, gay blossoms, and boughs of asparagus, with its brilliant red berries, and decorated above with some pictures of scripture scenes. On either side were two large painted fire-screens, which, no doubt, had faithfully served for many long years to protect the fair maiden faces of the sisters from the too ardent gaze of their winter's fire.

My observations were stopped by the entrance of Rupert, now a dashing young man of nineteen or twenty, looking bold and assured, like the same lad in former years. He came up to me, saying,

"Ah, ha! I wish you a very good evening! How are you? As demure as ever? Just from the upper regions, eh? How goes it up in the bush?"

I could have little to say in reply, and that coldly, for I was both abashed and displeased by his free manners and confident tone. Just then I was requested to assist the maid in taking our things up stairs, and my mother, with characteristic thoughtlessness, added—

"See that you don't meddle with anything, nor stop to look round, as if you never saw anything before."

This address, than which nothing could have been more uncalled for, made my cheeks burn with mortification. In fact, I had rather an uncomfortable time during my stay there, for I felt little claim on their hospitality, and Rupert's free, half mocking air, both embarrassed and vexed me ; but, fortunately, he was not present much of the time, and I was greatly amused with all I saw. The antiquated tea service at supper, with china of the oddest device, the high-backed, stuffed chairs, too, covered with black leather, and the round, carved table, so dark and polished ; and I could scarcely refrain from laughing outright at the queer, almost grotesque, attire of the mistresses of the domain. These sisters formed a perfect contrast to each other in looks and air, and even in dress, though both equally singular ; continually interrupting each other with, " La ! sister, why do you say *so* ?"

The darkened rooms seemed to make fearful, unwonted echoes, as we made the circuit of the house the next day, mother being curious to see it ; and, indeed, she looked with wistful eyes at the great, old chests of drawers, which she doubtless conjectured might contain much store of coveted household gear, about which, however, her curiosity was not gratified. The old trees about the house waved in the wind to a stately, formal measure, and a large flock of geese stalked majestically about, as if conscious to whom they belonged, while ducks, hens, and flitting doves, all seemed to smack of the olden time. These ladies lived

apart from society, seldom going abroad, except occasiou-
ally into Boston to church on the Sabbath.   They had one
friend, a sort of connection, a widow lady, living not far off.
Patty, the maid, was dispatched to invite her to come and
spend the day in honor of their visitors. Major Huntley was
a favored guest, everything he did or said, delighted them ;
he had a lively, witty vein in conversation, and kept the
good ladies in excellent spirits. The lady guest was arrayed
in stiff brocade, with three broad, white ruffles round the
neck, extending to the waist in front, while the cap looked
almost ponderous, with its weight of frills and ribbons.
Briskly the talk went on, between these ladies and my
mother, and when Major Huntley was present he kept them
laughing, shaking themselves in the best of humor, and saying—" La, me ! what a man !"

The next day was Sunday, and the family vehicle, a sort
of small open coach, was brought out, and furbished up, to
go into Boston to church.   As there was not room for me,
something was said about Rupert's taking Major Huntley's
chaise, but he did not seem particularly to desire it, and
nothing would have been less pleasing to me than a ride
into Boston, delightful as it might have been in itself, under
Rupert's protection.   No doubt, in his estimation, my dress
and appearance lacked the elegance and fashion of the city,
and would, he thought, do him little credit.   As it was, I
expressed a desire to stay behind, and the vehicle set off
without me, Rupert on horseback by its side.

I had just seated myself in the vacant room, for a little
quiet reading, when a slight figure came gently and swiftly

to me, just glancing over my shoulder at the book I was reading, then brushed past me and lightly dropped into a chair. I was startled, and gazed at my visitor with a mixture of curiosity and pity, though at no loss to divine who she was. I had been told her story, and it interested me greatly. She was a relative of Aunt Petty's, who had been insane from early youth, and had with kindly care been cherished by these good sisters since the death of her parents, a period of fifteen or twenty years. She was perfectly harmless, and generally very quiet, going all over the house and amusing herself as fancy dictated.

She had been the child of wealth and distinction, eminently beautiful and accomplished, and was still fair and child-like in appearance, her brow clear, and innocent-looking, though her long silken hair was slightly silvered. Her air was so sweet and gentle, that nothing betokened her mental malady, save a restless glitter in her light blue eye, and her extreme liveliness of manner, which never varied, except when she was in a sort of stupor, and kept her bed. This had been the case since our arrival ; so that I had not seen her till she appeared so suddenly before me. Apparently struck with my surprise, she began an apology, saying, in a soft, gentle voice, " I fear I have interrupted your reading ; pray go on; let me not disturb you ; may I inquire what book engages your attention ?"

I showed her that it was the Bible, and smilingly asked if I should read to her.

" Oh, thank you !" said she ; " nothing would be so delightful !" Then, without waiting for me to begin, quick as thought, she took from the table a volume of poems, and read herself, without raising her eyes, several pages, in a clear, melodious tone, giving the accent and expression admirably. "Is it not exquisite?" said she, looking up at me with a bright smile. I expressed my admiration, and commended her reading. She inclined her head with much grace, saying, "I am more happy to please you. Madam Sontelle taught me poetry; did you ever learn of Madam Sontelle? Did you attend her school?" repeated she. Without giving me time to reply, she turned to me with the most affectionate manner, and commenced speaking rapidly, her mind probably reverting to her school-girl days and to her instructress. "My dear young friend," she began, "nothing so infallibly distinguishes the accomplished young lady as true gentleness; but gentleness is not the air of soft languishment that some young ladies affect, nor the simpering prettiness worn like the best dress, an ornament in company; such are mere coverings to conceal pride, and ill temper. Gentleness, my dear girl, has her seat in the heart, and is ever attended by her sweet sister, Humility, the lowly and graceful handmaid of all the benign virtues." This she said with inimitable grace and dignity; but, abruptly stopping, she seemed to make an effort to recollect herself, and sat awhile gazing vacantly at me; then rising, she tripped along, seized my hand, and said, "Permit me to lead you to the music room."

I had before noticed a large old harpsichord in the adjoining room, and went with her, greatly interested and amused. She began, lightly sweeping the keys; but waking the slumbering echoes of the past, old scenes and associations, she became more and more excited, the expression of her face grew rapt and intense, her thin fingers flew faster and faster over the instrument, till, completely exhausted by her own emotion, she drooped her head, touched a few plaintive notes, and commenced softly and sadly, by singing that beautiful ballad of Goldsmith, "Turn gentle hermit of the dale," &c.; but her voice sunk in sobs, and she fell into a violent fit of weeping. I was distressed, and tried to comfort her, though I could myself scarcely refrain from tears. She permitted me to lead her away, and seek Patty, the kind maid. The good girl came up and put her arms round her, saying, "You dear lamb! don't you cry so! poor dear thing! she's worked herself up till she's ready to drop, she's so tired." So the affectionate girl coaxed and comforted her, as one would a weary child, till, unresisting, she was led to her room, and was soon in a peaceful sleep. I did not see her again, for we left the next day, and she was usually kept much from visitors, on account of her excitability, and consequent exhaustion. This incident affected me much. Poor Susy Loring! How sad the spectacle of that unhinged and crushed intellect! How mysterious the workings of that crazed but gentle spirit, groping round the walls of its tenement, searching the haunted cells of memory in the mockery of vain endeavor, yet ever true to the impulse of her affectionate heart. She was always sweet-tempered and patient, even in her greatest sorrow. The image of this poor demented being was deeply impressed on my memory, and her sweet, suffering face haunted me long afterwards. I thought of her happy and favored youth, her bright hopes, and of the rude blow that had bruised and blighted her affections, jarring upon her finely-tuned soul, till for long years it had been like a harp with broken springs. Many years are gone since she passed to her long resting-place, but the sad and tender recollection of her rises to my mind fresh as if of yesterday.

I have dwelt long on the scenes of these few days, for a vivid picture of them is painted on my memory, and I love to recall their events.

A word about Rupert. He had been taken by these kind, though somewhat penurious old aunts, when quite small; he was then a bright, witty little fellow, was petted and caressed by them, and would doubtless have succeeded to their well kept possessions, had not his own conduct turned aside their intentions.

It must be allowed that they were not free from blame, in their capricious management of him; being sometimes severe and rigorous, then facile, and indulgent to every whim.

Aunt Grizzel, good-natured, and averse to noise or exertion, was too easy, unless thoroughly aroused by some heinous offence, when she employed the greatest severity; while Aunt Lois, the younger, was quick-tempered, querulous, and irritable, but easily cajoled by his playfulness, and sure to take his part, when he fell under the anger of her sister.

Thus, by extreme indulgence in one, and alternate pettishness in the other, he had grown up from a pert, witty boy to a self-willed, overbearing youth, undutiful, and even insolent, to those kind women to whom he was so much indebted. He became, at length, the grief and torment of their lives, until at last they cast him off, with a small gratuity.

He afterwards married, but, by idleness, reduced his wife to poverty, and was finally compelled to learn a trade. After this he lived comfortably, though still poor, in an obscure house, near the worthy relatives whose kindness he had so abused, and whose favor he had lost.

CHAPTER XX.

BOSTON AS IT WAS.

" Come, let us paint a picture of the past, for the eye of the future."

It was towards the last of July, that I found myself, for the first time, in the New World of a gay metropolis, at the house of my Uncle Hastings. All here was in perfect contrast to the singular domicile of Aunt Petty's, yet equally new and strange to me. I could scarcely act myself at first, and was covered with confusion, when Uncle Hastings, with the most formal politeness, as was his wont, entered into grave conversation with me—a simple little country girl, with hardly courage to say a word. I believe my blushing, shame-faced timidity, must have appeared very foolish to him.

Aunt Hastings, as ever, was full of grace and loveliness, with much too in her air that was noble and commanding. Cousin Bessy, six years my senior, undertook in due form my guardianship, and kindly and faithfully did she perform her task.

In acquaintance with books, I was not at all inferior to my cousin, for reading had always been my delight, and, thanks to the press of that age and my father's care, it had been tolerably well selected. My father had much relish for books, and so good was his memory, that he would repeat long passages from his favorite authors. Many such from Milton and Pope are familiar to me now, forcibly recalling my dear parent to memory. My cousin—pretty and lively as she was, and engaging in her manners, lived within the polished but narrow circle, that too often bounds the city life of young ladies of genteel income ; a round of calls, visits, and promenades, in which a surprising variety of agreeable nothings are said ; embroidery, with its never-failing excitement of new patterns, and the daily news, well conned and commented upon, fill up the intervals.

Thus the shining small coin of conversation passes briskly from smiling lips, with many pretty airs ; while the golden eagles gained by reading and reflection are almost wholly wanting, being esteemed quite too weighty for the cheerful, vivacious minds of young persons engrossed with passing trifles.

Solid reading, while it furnishes the mind, and gives higher range to the thoughts, by no means helps one to the use of that "pretty little small talk" which has so large a share in the common intercourse of acquaintances. While I was surprised that no one cared to read, or apparently to extend a thought beyond the ordinary occurrences of the day, I was myself, quite heedless of the various minute observances of time and place, the thousand little decencies that make up the "*comme il faut*," in decorum and outward propriety, and doubtless committed many unconscious blunders ; my recollection assures me of several occasions in which a hint was given, making my cheeks mantle with blushes for my ignorance. I knew not whether my dress was fitting or otherwise; I thought little about it Cousin Bessy, indeed, took unwearied pains to aid my inexperience in my little purchases, and once, when we were going out shopping, as I waited a moment at the hall-door for my cousin, Aunt Hastings came along in her smiling, graceful way, and slipped a bank-note into my hand, with a word or two playfully spoken, and away again, almost before I was aware of what she had done.

Uncle Hastings' house was about a mile from "the Neck," which space was by no means thickly settled, while the Neck itself was simply a narrow road, or sandy beach, on either hand almost covered with salt water at every high tide. Towards the Common, too, there was a large open space, even before reaching the old burying ground, now forming part of its boundary. This spot had been anciently the enclosure of the church, long since passed with its worshippers into oblivion and forgetfulness. Here, old Governor Dudley, one of the crown-appointed rulers of the colony in primitive times, had been buried; and the spot where his bones reposed, was pointed out to me with much reverence by Cousin Bessy, for he was one of her paternal ancestors. An old monument on the other side of the Common interested me very much; it recorded the deeds of our fathers, and particularly of Washington; it has now decayed, or given place to other memorials.

The Mall was planted with trees, and was already a favorite resort on fine days; a walk then answered the purpose subserved in our day, by the genteel and formal "call." The young and gay went thither to while away the time in pleasant converse; the fashionable belles flaunted along with their lap-dogs, their trains gracefully sweeping the ground a yard or two behind, or negligently thrown over the arm, in rare instances confided to the custody of a little colored boy, who thus helped his aristocratic mistress bear the burden of her finery. Ladies of less pretentions had the more moderate length of their trains fastened up to the waist. Most amusing and delightful to me, was this promenade, the daily recreation of all young people who made any attempt at fashion and gentility. The well-trodden walks are still pressed by the feet of morning and evening visitors; grave men pace thoughtfully, sit meditating in the shade of those old, old trees, with the hum of a mighty city around them. Stately matrons enjoy the fresh breeze in the sultry days, and bounding children too, are there, while young men and maidens still walk arm in arm beneath the whispering leaves. But in that olden time all was free and joyous life and animation, when the flippant jest, the light laugh, and gay flirtation ruled the hour, while the trees were yet young, and amid their branches opened many a passage to the bright sunshine.

The big "old elm," indeed, was there, even then looking almost as venerable as now, but, instead of the little pond, with its sparkling fountain, was only a low, marshy spot, which, with the flow and ebb of the tide formed alternately a deep pool, and a muddy hollow. The whole common was a green pasture; while Beacon street, now so thickly studded with its elegant mansions, was then, for the most part, a rough, unsightly hill, disfigured by rocks and sandy knolls;

9

toward the Common, however, it was levelled, and the State House was already erected, and in process of completion.

We sauntered over the ground many times, and with ever fresh delight to me, lingering on the western slope, in the delicious summer afternoon, to gaze on the beautiful country across the calm water, or watch the sun go down into the sea, like a monarch descending to rest.

Rarely, indeed, could a finer prospect be found than was there seen, of the fair young city seated as a queen upon the water—environed by the fine open expanse, adorned with wood-embosomed dwellings and glittering spires.

The funeral of Samuel Adams took place soon after my arrival, but none of the family attended, Uncle Hastings being rigidly opposed to the federalist party. As it was to be quite an imposing spectacle, Aunt Hastings wished me to go ; so, giving me many careful directions, she sent her maid to attend me. Securing a station on the steps of the State House, I saw the march of the long procession of sable carriages, drawn by black horses. Slowly, and with steady tramp, they advanced to the old monument, then, making a circuit, the Dead March commenced, with muffled drums. This, heard for the first time, powerfully affected me ; tears ran fast, and long after they had all passed by, I stood, indulging the thrilling sensations awakened by the scene.

Soon after this, Aunt Hastings received a visit from a relative and old friend of my own mother, who lived at Jamaica Plains. The beautiful spot now recognized by this name, had at that time a far different appearance from what

It now presents, being occupied by newly cultivated farms, except on the border of the fine pond, which began already to be a favorite summer resort for pleasure parties.

This relative, usually called Aunt Brooks, was a large, good-looking lady, very easy-tempered, and extremely fond of reading ; for a new book or magazine she would neglect even pressing engagements and necessary duties. Bessy and I being seated at the window, saw her, through the blind, approaching the house, and Bessy telling her mother, Aunt Hastings hurriedly said, "Put away those papers, . then, quick ; for I want to enjoy her company a little, this time ;" which Bessy hastened to accomplish before she entered. She was carelessly attired, but her face ! how luminous it was with the expression not only of intelligence, but of a certain large-heartedness, which was indeed a part of her character.

She regarded me with much interest and kindness, for the sake of my lost mother, whom, she said, she had often held in her arms. On leaving, she urged me warmly to go and spend a week with her, saying her son came in to market every day, with produce from the farm, and would call for me in the morning. I gladly assented, and sure enough, the next forenoon a large, ruddy-faced man called at the door, with his market-wagon, and I was soon jolting along, feeling somewhat queer with my stranger companion. He, however, made himself quite sociable, informing me of the names of residents on the way, and occasionally telling an anecdote, or describing the character of some one of them

Sometime after noon we reached the plain old farm-house, very large, and unpainted, standing apparently in the middle of an apple orchard. Here, after a day or two, I felt myself quite at home. There was a large family, and the farm seemed as productive as a garden, being cultivated with a view to supplying the city market. One of the daughters, Milly, was about my own age ; a pleasant, good-natured girl. She made considerable pretensions, though I thought her rather coarse, as indeed all the family were, in comparison with the mother, with whom I was soon on intimate footing.

Though she was so much older and wiser, and I looked up to her with reverence, yet I found it wonderfully easy to converse with her, and my natural reserve and bashfulness all left me in her presence. I enjoyed my stay there extremely. The situation of the house and grounds was wild and picturesque, and quite charmed my youthful fancy. The house was on the side of a hill, and a ledge rose immediately behind it, so high as to hide from view all beyond Trees were growing on the top of the rock, and their thick branches almost came in at the open window of the chamber where I slept.

Every morning I was awakened by the sweet carol of a multitude of birds, in their leafy bowers close to my head, beginning with early dawn, and giving me exquisite delight, as I lay entranced, listening to the charming notes.

Accompanied by Milly, or alone, I wandered over the wooded knolls and rocks. A great part of the farm was solitary and wild. I gathered curious pebbles and shells, and stored them up, which by chance coming to sight, long years afterwards, brought back in all its freshness, to my mind, this delightful visit.

CHAPTER XXI.

AN ADVENTURE.

ONE afternoon while I was at Aunt Brooks', Milly obtained the management of old Grey Dobbin with the wagon, to take me a ride, as she said, to show me the country. We were full of mirth and enjoyment, finding amusement in everything, and rode long and far, but where, I have not the least idea, except that we stopped, tied our horse to the remnant of a fence, and roamed over Bunker Hill.

Milly told me she had often been here to pick barberries, and, indeed, the spot was covered with tall grass and bushes, the luxuriant growth of the soil watered by some of the bravest blood of the Revolution.

We endeavored to trace the few indistinct marks, the uncertain vestiges of the signal battle fought there before we were born. My companion, struck, as it were, with a sudden spark of patriotism, assumed a tragic air of mock heroism, and exclaimed, "Here the precious blood of the brave ran like rain! Here their valiant heads were laid low! Oh, how I should admire to stay here all night and write blank verse!" of which she had about as just an idea, probably, as of the odes of Anacreon in Greek; her words, and the air with which they were spoken, were irresistible, and I burst out into a hearty laugh, seeming to her, no doubt, altogether devoid of fine sentiment or poetic taste. She seemed inclined to verify her words, for we lingered until the sun was set, and even till the stars began to take their places in the clear blue sky, and the last plaintive notes of the birds died away in silence.

Much as I enjoyed the loveliness of the scene, fear and the sense of unprotected loneliness began to be stronger, and I entreated Milly to return. But she assured me there was nothing to fear; that she should "admire," to ride home in the evening, and that she meant to show Bill, her brother, that she was not afraid to drive old Dobbin anywhere, for he was always saying it was not safe to trust her. At length, however, we were on our homeward ride, as silent as we had before been lively and talkative.

Milly was continually employed in urging the slow-paced beast to greater speed, for I believe she began to have some misgivings at the lateness of the hour, and the distance still to be traversed. As for me, I was tortured by fears; the way was strange; I had heard stories of violence and robbery, and everything we met made my heart flutter. We were not destined to reach home without accident; as we were slowly ascending a long winding hill, there came suddenly upon us a man in a gig, driving down at the top of his speed. He was somewhat intoxicated, and not seeing us in the darkness, or too reckless to heed any obstacle, he dashed along and struck our vehicle at full tilt. It gave way with a crash, while he drove on, and was soon far behind us, leaving me on the ground and Milly in the wagon, holding fast to the reins. Our faithful steed stopped short, by which means Milly was saved from fall-ing. We were both uninjured, and found our way as best we could to the house, which luckily, was not more than half a mile distant. The family were somewhat anxiously watching our return, for it was now quite late in the evening. Poor Milly, somewhat crest-fallen, told her mis-hap, and bore as patiently as she was able, her brother's ireful reproaches.

"Strange, what silly critters girls are !" said he. "They never know how to act; for ever trying to do something they can't. I knew there'd be some difficulty, sure as they went on such a rigmarole errand !"

I stole away in the midst of the noise and talking, and as I was going up to my room, thoroughly tired and much troubled at the dolorous issue of our excursion, I heard Aunt Brooks, in her placid manner, trying to make all smooth.

"It's no great harm done, after all, since the girls are not hurt ; only to think of their meeting Tom Sikes, when he was so drunk. I don't see as they could have done anything, so say no more about it ; come cheer up Milly, it might have been a great deal worse."

So Bill went to take care of the horse and the broken wagon, and the good motherly woman mixed a cordial for us "to settle our heads and better our spirits," she said, charging us to think no more about it, but to go right to sleep. This was not easy for me to do after such excite-ment, though Milly was not disposed to talk much about our adventure

The next morning I had no sooner risen and gone down stairs, than a sudden faintness came over me, and I was glad to be assisted back to my room and betake myself to bed. I was soon restored by the gentle, kind nursing of Aunt Brooks, and declared myself as well as ever, but she insisted on my keeping quiet, saying it was best for me to be quite alone for a time, that ruffled spirits required the rest and relief of solitude, and would come out clear and bright from silence and calm; so she arranged everything for my comfort, and left me reclining on my couch opposite the open window. The pure morning air came in, breathing freshness; the birds caroled their matin songs, and the checkered light glimmered through the green branches, and danced with the stirring of the leaves. The light soft motion, hushing to rest every unquiet feeling, tranquilized the soul and disposed to reflection; at first, a delicious, dreamy sort of reverie came over me, deepening unconsciously into clear, serene and happy thought. It was one of those times common to the experience of most, when the imagination, sense, the whole conscious being, seems silently to retreat to the inmost chamber of the spirit. How much was sweetly revolved in my mind during those few hours! The agitating scenes of the preceding day seemed to recede far into the past, like some faded dream, and the past to stand out before me, a vivid picture hung in the memory.

I meditated long letters to my father and sisters; all that had happened since I left them passed in review—Aunt Petty's dwelling with their poor insane charge, having a full share; then making a sudden transition to the dim regions of the shadowy future, imaginings of all sorts filled up the broad but vague outline of my bounding anticipations and hopes.

It was a delightful day to me, standing out even now from its fellows in peculiar brightness. The afternoon was spent alone with my kind and revered Aunt Brooks, whose very presence had power to diffuse around calm and sweet tranquillity. She read to me from a new magazine, and conversed entertainingly upon it. The subject was Shakespeare, of whom I had before scarcely heard. From her remarks were derived my first correct impressions of his writings and wonderful genius. I expressed surprise, saying that I had considered plays as only written for amusement, and at best, a doubtful kind of reading. In her reply she said, as nearly as I can recollect, that no other writer had portrayed our sex with such nice appreciation— such intuitive sense of the inherent qualities of woman— such exquisite truth in his portraitures, to the noblest and loveliest of her attributes; and that the study of his best female characters could not fail to have a most refining and ennobling effect upon the mind; "at the same time," added she, "there is so much in these plays that cannot be approved in spirit and tendency, that they should be read but sparingly by the young, and perhaps not at all, except under the eye of some judicious friend. I would not discourage you, my dear, from reading them," she was so kind as to add, "nay, I advise you to embrace the first opportunity to peruse carefully some of the best."

I replied that I should like much to do this under her guidance. This conversation became afterwards the germ of much pleasure and benefit to me when the subject was better understood, and her ideas, in a measure, realized in my own experience. The very next day, in fact, it being rainy, I began to act upon her suggestions, for, rummaging the shelves appropriated to books, in a cupboard in the corner of the spacious "east room," I came across an odd volume of Shakespeare, to my great delight, and spent most of the day absorbed with its contents.

My mind was, however, too scantily cultured at that time to be any more than amused, yet it chanced, oddly enough, that when, not long after, I visited the theatre for the first and only time, the identical play, with some modifications, was represented which I read that day.

The memory of the benevolent face of Aunt Brooks is still before me, and my visit to her home was one of the greatest pleasures I enjoyed while awaiting the coming of Mary and her husband.

This excellent and gifted lady, who appeared not to belong to the family or scenes around her, but to live among them a different being, and in another world—a world of her own, inspired in me love and confidence in a high degree, and I parted from her with regret.

CHAPTER XXII.

" MIDSUMMER NIGHT'S DREAM."

AUNT BROOKS proposed herself to drive into Boston with me at the conclusion of my visit, but on the day appointed, and just as we were ready to leave, her own married daughter rode up to the door, to make a visit of some days ; so I was obliged to take a seat in the daily hack plying between that place and Boston. I was the sole passenger, and being busy with my own thoughts, as usual, took no heed where I was going, and had gone several doors past the house, when the driver asking my destination, I told him, in my simplicity, that he need not be at the trouble to go back. He readily acceded to my gratuitous offer, and I alighted in the street, leaving my little bundle of clothing in the carriage. I was then quite fresh in the matter of public conveyances. My things were carried away to the other side of the city, though Aunt Hastings, with some trouble, procured them again.

Nothing of importance occurred to mark the remainder of my stay, except my visit to the theatre, which was brought about very unexpectedly to myself.

One evening Bessy had gone out to walk with a tall, grave, pleasing, and gentlemanly personage, who sometimes called, and with whom we now and then fell into company in the Mall.

· On these occasions, I had more than once seen the quick blush on Bessy's face, when answering his particularly kind and respectful greeting, and came to my own conclusions upon the subject.

Aunt Hastings and I were sitting in her chamber; I had been reading to her from the newspaper, till the softening shadows of twilight were gently falling around. I sat musing in silence by the window, listening to the ceaseless echo of footsteps on the pavement below.

"What are you in a brown study about, Anna?"

"I am thinking, aunt, about the notice of the theatre that I saw in the paper; one of Shakspeare's plays is to be acted to-morrow evening, and I should like much to see it. Do you ever go, Aunt Hastings?"

"We attended the theatre once, soon after we were married," she replied; "I have had no wish to go since. I should not object to any one's going for once, but the practice of attending the theatre is one of the most pernicious of habits."

"Aunt Brooks," said I, hesitatingly, "told me it was improving to read Shakspeare's plays, and to study his female characters."

"Oh, Aunt Brooks is a great reader, and finds something to admire in every thing; but though she may sometimes read them, she would by no means approve of going to see the same plays acted."

"Why not?" said I; "it seems to me it would only be the more interesting"

"Undoubtedly it would, and also for that reason the

more pernicious. The late hours tend to destroy all sober and regular habits ; half the night spent in a state of feverish excitement unfits both mind and body for every duty, as well as all calm and rational enjoyments, even were there no bad influences from the sentiments, which, not seldom, are far from being pure and wholesome."

"But, aunt, why could not the best of them be acted in the day, and thus avoid that evil ?"

"Few would care to see them performed, when stripped of all the illusion consequent upon the glare and dazzle of evening lights. The fascination is chiefly, not in the play itself, but in the music, the rich decorations, the display of dress and gaiety, the high-wrought excitements of the place and hour, by which one is carried away. The heated fancy still craves renewal of the alluring pleasure, till property is squandered, business neglected, and all the duties of life become a disgust and burden. Many promising sons, who might have been a blessing to their parents, and to society, have been thus ruined for this world and the next. The passion for attending the theatre has been the inlet to all kinds of vice. My own son," said she, "might have taken the same course, but for the judicious restraint of his father ; it was only just before his marriage that he saw the inside of a theatre ; and Bessy has never been, though I intend she shall gratify her curiosity on some fitting occa sion. I do not object to a single visit ; perhaps it is well for each one to judge for himself ; nor will one be apt to judge wrong the first time, if properly educated."

My aunt's remarks led to rather a revulsion of feeling in

regard to going to the play ; but the next morning it
chanced that Bessy's friend, before alluded to met us in the
• Mall again, and spoke of the subject, saying that he did not
make a practice of attending, but it was seldom that one of
Shakspeare's plays was represented ; and, in fine, he would
be happy to have us occupy a box with him, with the sanction of Bessy's parents ; adding, that he would call and
consult with them.

He did so, and a party was made up, consisting of
Cousin Joseph and his charming young wife, Bessy, her
friend Mr. Lansing, and myself. I felt quite ashamed,
afterwards, that all memory of the subject of the play, upon
which I had previously thought so much, was lost in a con
fused, dazzling cloud of images, so delightful, so intoxi-
cating to my senses, that my head was dizzy with pleasure
and excitement. For a day or two after, I was in a bewil
dered maze of sweet sounds and gorgeous scenes of beauty
The play was the " Midsummer Night's Dream," of which I
only recollect the descent of the fairies to their enchanted
ring, as they gently and softly floated down one after
another, wafted by some invisible agency, with the most perfect grace and elegance in all their airy motions, enveloped
by a light shadowy beauty, pervaded by a sort of haze
which enhanced the illusion, while music distant and uncertain, but wild and sweet, completed the enchantment.

CHAPTER XXIII.

A SEA VOYAGE.

MARY now arrived, with my new brother, Doctor Emery, on whom I too was, for the time, dependent for protection as well as happiness. No brother could have been kinder ; all care and anxiety were confided to my companions as freely as a child abandons itself to its joyous pleasures, trusting in a father's care.

The little preparation they had to make was speedily accomplished, and in a few days our passage was bespoken in a dingy schooner—albeit the best to be found—waiting for favorable winds.

We had no very sanguine expectations of pleasure, for Mary and I, it must be confessed, awaited almost tremblingly our voyage to Bangor, which seemed to me then a committal of life and safety, as vast, perilous, and formidable, as now to circumnavigate the globe.

Our friends talked most discouragingly of the prospect of going to the distant, dreary province of Maine, into the wild country and among wild Indians ; representing the rigors of the climate so great as to cause an average of six feet of snow, and a winter of six months' continuance. Dr Emery, however, though careful to give a moderate coloring to our anticipations, bore, from actual knowledge, a more favorable testimony. This region was already attract.

ing attention from enterprising men to its vast wealth of timber land, its majestic forests of almost ocean breadth, in which were already discerned the life of its traffic, and a broad basis of prosperity. Nor were inducements wanting in the awards of husbandry, to which the virgin soil, the pleasant aspect of the country, and above all, the low price of land, invited.

It was a warm, bright evening, when at length, all being ready, we stood upon the deck of the little coasting vessel that was to convey us to the new settlement of Bangor, our first destination. Sitting on a rude bench, we watched the slowly receding city, bathed in a flood of amber light, from the glorious setting sun.

"Beautiful city!" said I, "farewell to your sumptuous dwellings, and your scenes of magnificence and gaiety!"

"And farewell, too, proud city!" said Dr. Emery, "to your busy multitudes, your merchandise, your traffic, and your wealth; yet all this had a beginning—the rough cuttings of the unhewn block must precede the polished shaft —so *we* go to lay the foundation; the stern labor of commencing the edifice will be *our* part in the new region to which we are bound."

"Yes," said Mary, "less than two hundred years ago here the sea beat against a wild and solitary shore; the first settlers called it the beautiful Tri-mountain, and spoke of the soft verdure which covered its triple crown, rising with graceful swell above the blue waters."

"A few years later," said her husband, "the royal governor of Massachusetts Colony had a Fort Pownal in this bay, with truck-house for trading with the Tarratines; then there were forests all around, unexplored by the whites, and unknown except as the region and domain of the red man."

"Now a noble city has started into life and beauty," said Mary; "an enduring monument of the piety, wisdom, and enterprise of our fathers."

"Boston," said Dr. Emery, "is justly the pride of New England. She is yet in the morning of her strength—the race is before her."

Thus we conversed till darkness gathered around us; it was a clear star-light night, and I gazed, spellbound, on the widening sweep of waters as we rapidly passed islet and headland, the distant light-houses sending their friendly rays far over the heaving waste. Soon we were upon the open sea, that rolled continuous for thousands of miles, that had rolled unchanged for thousands and thousands of years!

What a grand, yet awful spectacle is the ocean! What hosts of human beings have its waves devoured! What treasures lie hid beneath its dark bosom! Its restless tide flows on, ever the same; generations may live and die, suffer or enjoy; races of men start into existence, and become extinct; cities may be settled, prosper, or perish; commerce, wealth, science, philanthropy, flourish or decline; the sea cares not—heeds not—it sleeps in calm, or it heaves and roars, it tosses, it dashes against the shore, all independent and alone.

We sat in silence and in darkness, while the gleam of the
10

dark waters shot up, ever and anon, like the fearful eye of
a giant thing of life, filling the soul with mysterious awe
and terror, as our bark rolled on over the heaving tide.
Ere long all sense and feeling were lost, save a troubled
consciousness of tossing, pitching, plunging, in a wild whirl
of confusion, and Dr. Emery could scarce attend us to the
cabin, ere himself needed assistance.

The passage was long and stormy, the little vessel rocked
from side to side most unmercifully : most unlike it was to
the rapid and smooth transit of our modern, commodious,
and elegant steamers over the same waters. Even danger
came near, for, after being tossed about for some days on
the open sea by the fury of the winds, when the storm at
last ceased, the night shut in cloudy and dark, and all at
once we were startled by an unusual noise and confusion, followed by a sudden crash, and instant rush of all movable
things into one mass. The vessel was thrown upon her
side, she having in the darkness "run foul" of a fishing
craft, making a most narrow escape from being capsized
and sent to the bottom. The next morning we were
rejoiced to find ourselves in Penobscot Bay, coming into
calm water. The crew and passengers were talking eagerly,
in high excitement, over the accident of the night, all agree-
ing that it was an almost miraculous escape, and the captain boasted the superior rigging of the schooner, to which
he declared our safety had been owing. Weak and miserable as I felt, I was forced to laugh heartily at the earnest
gestures of one man, an old sea captain, half intoxicated ;
he pressed eagerly up to each one, reiterating in a loud voice,

and in the queerest manner, " Oh ! I tell you we 'scaped a
great marcy ; we 'scaped a wonderful great marcy !"

Soon after this we were becalmed, and lay at anchor near
an island, where it was proposed to go ashore, as the best
remedy for sea-sickness. Mary was extremely timid on the
water, and would not trust herself to the frail-looking boat,
but I had no fear, and longed to set foot on land again,
even for a few minutes.

The gentlemen proffered their best assistance. The bluff,
good-humored captain said, " Yes, give her a smack of the
land breeze, and she'll get her color back again," and taking
me right up in his arms, he handed me over the side of the
vessel, as if I had been a little child. We soon reached the
long, low island, and finding some blueberry bushes, I
plucked some of the leaves, and ate them for very love and
longing for something from the green earth. No sooner
had I swallowed them than I felt instant relief, all nausea
was gone, I was a new being, and experienced at once the
"gladness that bathes the spirit in that one feeling of
health, when the flow of nature's vital flood is pure and
unimpeded !"

After rambling and scrambling among the rocks and
bushes for half an hour, proving with every step "the
vivid sense of what there is delightful in the breeze," I
returned, extolling the virtue of the blueberry leaves, but
Mary laughingly declared them without efficacy unless
eaten on land. She was now, however, quite recovered, as
well as I.

We lingered along for lack of wind, spending one entire

day on shore, in quite a social manner ; notwithstanding
the delay, the passage up the river was pleasant to us, we
were in the mood to enjoy everything now, the varieties of
the coast, the little villages seen from time to time, and now
and then the lone house on the shore, overlooking the broad
tranquil river.   We arrived at Bangor just at evening
and walked to the only tavern, a few rods distant, the
motion of the vessel making the ground appear to rise to
meet me at every step.

Dr. Emery had his few household goods and effects
stored in a small building, which stood alone on the landing,
and was, when the tide was in, quite over the water.   It
belonged to one of our fellow passengers, Captain Stephens,
a military gentleman of talent and education, who subsequently attained some rank in the United States' service

CHAPTER XXIV.

BANGOR.

THE next morning we looked around the new town, then almost a wilderness, but giving evident promise of future importance.

It occupied a low, level space near the shore, or rathe. on both sides of the wild, romantic Kenduskeag, here joining the main river, Penobscot, which making a bend round a considerable point of land, formed a fine harbor, already inviting a brisk trade in fishing and lumber.

The tributary stream was crossed by a small ferry-boat near where it emptied, and its course could be seen for some distance, deeply shaded by thick trees and overhanging bushes. The banks rising more or less abruptly, to a high hill on either side, were almost wholly covered with the primeval growth of the forest. Two or three comfortable houses, some small cottages and log-huts, together with a number of stores and shops, on the "flat" near the shore, comprised at that time, the whole of Bangor, even the limited space that was cleared being defaced by many an unsightly stump.

Dr. Emery left after two or three days, to return for us as soon as he should be able to arrange things comfortably in the new home, to which we were going.

Our landlady, good Mrs. Bolls, was extremely kind to us.

She was an admirable woman; kind, cheerful, prompt, and
efficient, she managed her large household with equal discre-
tion and good temper. I seem to hear her voice even now,
as she was wont to speak to her rough, unprincipled husband
in such a pleasant, lively way, yet with a touch of reproof
at his rude oaths or thoughtless words: it was the authority of goodness and not seldom he felt and yielded to it.

They had a daughter, Eleanor, about two years younger
than myself, a confident and forward girl, good-natured
withal and kind-hearted, quite mistress of herself on all
occasions: she would laugh and talk saucily with the young
men at her father's table, with the greatest ease and
assurance, while I could scarcely converse at all, but my
tell-tale cheeks would painfully betray my timidity and
embarrassment.

Miss Eleanor attached herself to me, and I was soon
quite at home with her.

Not a little attention was bestowed upon Mary and
myself. Dr. Emery's character and bearing commanded
respect, and Mary always won favor from her sprightliness
and charming agreeable manner, no less than the unaffected
sweetness of her nature. As for myself, I was but a child
in feeling or experience, innocent quite of any wish or
thought of particular attention from the other sex.

I could sing songs, laugh and frolic in happy thoughtlessness, wondering at the notice I received, not deeming myself
fit for the companionship of gentlemen so much older, so
accomplished, apparently, in all that makes up what is
called the " air of fashion " and " knowledge of the world ;"

for society then and there, was by no means without pretension to elegance, refinement and high breeding, and justly
too, though the numbers were so few, that every accession
was hailed with warm welcome. From the very paucity
of ladies, Mary and I were complimented with all the charming category of agreeable things, so that my poor, little
foolish head was in danger of being quite turned by the
attention and flattery I received.

One day, accompanied by our friend Eleanor and Captain
Stephens, before mentioned, we went out for a walk, wandering along the curving, irregular shore of the river, in
some places jagged with projecting rocks, in others smooth,
with here and there an old tree left standing alone. On
the opposite side, two or three log-houses were seen half hid
among the trees, and behind them appeared a wood-capped
eminence of broad, gentle outline ; further on, up the river,
the high bank, covered with dark green bushes, threw a
deep shadow quite across the water, contrasting finely with
the nearer view, which lay in soft sunshine, wrapped in the
hazy atmosphere of an autumn afternoon.

Around the landing, and at various points up and down
the river, groups of fishermen were engaged with their nets;
it was a lively, busy scene, to me as novel as it was interesting.

Near where we stood were two men on a rock in the
edge of the water, with a basket-like net held by two poles
as a handle, which they dipped in, bringing up each time
the struggling fishes, and throwing them successively on the
bank, high and dry.

"This is beautiful!" said Mary. "The dark shadow on the water, with the green bushes on the hill above, forms a perfect picture of repose and quiet. What can be more graceful than those tall pines and firs lifting their tops against the sky, as if guarding over the still river beneath?"

"The great number of evergreens adds much to the beauty of the forests of Maine," said Captain Stephens, "giving them a verdant appearance, even after the wintry frosts have dismantled other trees and lighter foliage."

"But," said Mary, my eye misses the bright, variegated tints of our autumn woods; this depth of green looks solemn and melancholy."

"It is true," he replied, "we have here very few of those beautiful trees which give such brilliancy to the autumn landscape in most of New England."

"I think," said Mary, "the dark blue tint of the fir is the most mournful-looking of all nature's infinite varieties of green, and the woods must appear sombre and dark, even in midsummer, with so much of the evergreen."

"Oh, no," he replied; "I have never seen more beautiful vegetation than in Maine. Nature is bountiful every where, and we have a sufficient sprinkling of bright green to throw into fine relief the deeper verdure; while the cooler nights and more plentiful dews give a soft and fresh aspect to summer landscape, seen only in spring in your own Massachusetts."

"See," I exclaimed, "what a quantity of fishes those men below us have just drawn up, and look at the bank above—it is covered with them."

"Those are alewives," said Captain Stephens ; "it is a fine day for them : not many more will be caught this season ; it is almost their last chance."

"Oh," said Eleanor, "I have had rare sport, many a time, catching them. We girls used to get a large handkerchief—sometimes our aprons—and dip it down by the corners : we often caught several at a time."

"What could you want of them ?" I asked.

"Oh, just as the fancy took us ; sometimes we carried them home, and sometimes put them back into the water. The sport was in catching them. But once I slipped in, and though I scrambled out again, it was a most thorough ducking, and frightened me from it awhile."

"They are loading those two vessels yonder," said Captain Stephens.

"Are there many," asked Mary, "employed in fishing as a trade ?"

"Ah, yes ; it is the life of our business. I have seen, in the height of the season, more than a dozen vessels at a time taking cargoes : many hundred barrels of fish are shipped daily, principally alewives, but great quantities of shad too."

"Are those delicious salmon caught in this river ?"

"Not so frequently as formerly ; they retreat before the face of man and civilization, and find refuge in quiet, lonely streams, unvexed by the noise of busy labor, and the creaking of saw-mills."

We were now on our way home, and being near the store of Captain Stephens, on the wharf, in the chamber of which our effects were stored, Mary and I went in to take some things from the chests. Among other articles, Mary took out and put on a satin cardinal, trimmed with fur, quite rich and stylish, which she had procured in Boston. When we came down stairs to our two companions, the increased air of consideration and deference yielded to the handsome furred cardinal was very perceptible, and caused us no little amusement; nor was that the only occasion on which honor was given to our "trappings" merely. The idea seemed very absurd to me then, for I was new to the world; I had been estimated in my own native Wayland by the actual knowledge of my townsmen, not measured merely by appearances.

Dr. Emery had been gone about a week, when we heard it mentioned at dinner that a clergyman from Massachusetts had arrived the preceding day.

We took little heed of the information, but in the course of an hour or two after a gentleman called, and on being summoned, to our great surprise and joy we saw our own beloved minister, Mr. Rice, of Wayland.

He informed us that he had accepted a mission to spend several weeks in this remote place, destitute at that time of any stated worship : he was now a guest in a private family across the " stream."

Oh! how delighted we were to see him—an old friend in a strange land! We had a long interview, conversing first upon our own private affairs, then upon the situation and promise of the flourishing little settlement in which we had so unexpectedly met. He spoke with much feeling of the want of religious interest, and of the immense importance that a right direction should be given to the influence of a place so promising, yet open to so many evil tendencies, from the diverse character of the inhabitants, brought hither from various places and by different motives.

Just as he was leaving us, he took me by the shoulder, and regarding me awhile, smilingly said, "It seems but a year or two since you were a little child, playing about under the trees; now you are a young lady. I suppose you will be getting married one of these days; possibly before you are again under the wing of your father; but remember one thing," added he, affectionately, almost solemnly, "be sure that you get a *husband*, when you are married; many girls marry, and do not find a husband, and much better had it been for them to have remained alone."

I was quite confused at this address, but thanked him, telling him I thought it wise counsel, and trusted I should remember it.

The next day our good minister came again, accompanied by his hostess, Mrs. Woleby. She invited us, most cordially, to spend the ensuing week at her house, in the company of our beloved pastor.

We gladly accepted the polite invitation, and thus formed a pleasing acquaintance with a most estimable family, who subsequently proved valuable friends.

CHAPTER XXV

THE VISIT.

" Be such, and only such, my friends,
Once mine, and mine forever."

. At our new friend's we were made to feel ourselves quite at home. Emilia, the only daughter, was a lovely, gentle girl, saying little herself, yet enjoying much the conversation of others ; she could sing some of my songs with me ; she loved to read, too, and many a good time we had together in her own little chamber, poring over the same book.

With Mrs. Woleby, too, we felt acquainted at once ; she was so essentially motherly in her every look, with a thoughtful, clear, grey eye—her whole aspect indicative of good sense, cheerfulness, and energy.

The house, one of the best in the village, was on the sloping bank of the Kenduskeag, a few rods from the river, which, opposite the house, was quite concealed from view by the thick trees on its banks ; a little further down, toward the ferry, Mr. Woleby's shop, made of new pine boards, stood on the brink of the water ; a road led to the ferry, but in every other direction mere foot-paths led into the yet uncleared forest.

Nothing more excited my curiosity and deep interest than the native Indians, who came frequently around, entered the houses familiarly, with baskets to sell, sometimes with fish or game which they had obtained, always anxious to trade, and very shrewd and grasping in making their bargains.

One morning, by chance looking from the window, I saw an Indian coming up the walk to the door, with all the slow gravity of their manner.

I took some work in my hand, and quietly seated myself in the kitchen, to which he was approaching, that I might gratify my curiosity in seeing and hearing this native of the soil.

His object was easily divined, for he had a large salmon supported on his crossed arms. He came in, took the chair offered him, with an unconcerned look, without speaking, or even looking towards any one in the room.

" Good morning, brother !" said Mrs. Woleby, pleasantly.

He murmured something in a low tone, still without raising his eyes.

" What money do you want for your fish ?" said she.

" Fish very big," said he, without the movement of a muscle.

" Oh, yes ! very good one ; but I have meat for dinner," said she, pointing to the pot over the fire.

He preserved a dignified silence of several minutes.

After a time she offered him what she deemed a sufficient price for the fish, which was a fine one, but he was not so easily satisfied ; he continued in the same posture, with the same unaltered composure of manner, making a remark from time to time, as—

" Me just catch him ; he fresh ; he very big ; me want

great piece of money ;" closing, after a while, with naming his price, which was exorbitant.

Mrs. Woleby was accustomed to deal with these people, and finally obtained the fish at a fair price ; taking care to pay him chiefly in pork, and other articles of provision, to lessen the temptation on his part to procure rum, the bane and destruction of the poor Indian.

While he sat there, Mr. Rice came in ; he was a man of commanding carriage, very tall, with piercing eyes, and black hair. The red man watched him awhile intently, then, as if surprised out of his usual reserve, he exclaimed,

" You a big man ; who made you ?"

This question from the poor untutored man, though so amusing, affected Mr. Rice, and he sought to enter into conversation with him, but could scarcely obtain a reply--- perhaps he felt his want of a command of words, and was too proud to show his ignorance.

Mary was quite taken up with our recital of the incident, and an excursion was planned to some camps a few miles up the river, but a heavy rain prevented our going, to my great disappointment. Mr. Rice, however, went to visit them at their station on a large island in the river, at some distance. He spent a day there, and had a long conversation with their chief, from whom he gained much knowledge of his tribe—the once powerful Tarrateens—whose sway extended so far westerly that they successfully coped with the fierce Mohawks in many a bloody battle. On his return, Mr. Rice described to us, most vividly, his talk with the old chief— the dark fire that glowed in his eye, as he recounted, by emphatic gestures, the stirring deeds of his fathers—his whole soul roused into intense excitement.

The delightful week of our visit quickly flew over our heads, and we repaired again to our lodgings and temporary home. Our excellent Mrs. Bolles seemed as glad to see us as if we had been old friends, and Eleanor was wild in her demonstrations of joy, capering about the room full of talk and glee ; but the kind welcome given us by the aged grandmother, Madam Bolles, was really touching.

She was quite infirm, and, with a deformed, sickly daughter, also advanced in life, occupied a chamber just across the passage from us. Mary had spent much time entertaining them in her own sweet way, conversing, singing, or ministering to their comfort ; for my dear sister, let me say, was tireless in every meek and sweet modification of womanly duty. The tears ran down the good old lady's cheeks, as she clasped her with trembling and withered hands, blessing her that she had come back again to comfort her.

CHAPTFR XXVI.

AN EVENING AT MRS. WOLEBY'S.

NOT many more days passed before Dr. Emery come, prepared to escort us to our new home; he could, however, take only one at a time, so I was to wait a few days longer till he could return again for me. Travelling was very difficult and dangerous, there being in that direction no roads except a mere bridle-path cut through the forest, occasionally trodden by a few ox teams.

The evening previous to their departure was spent at Mrs. Woleby's; the pleasure of seeing Mr. Rice being as great and unexpected to Dr. Emery as it had been to Mary and myself. We all enjoyed the evening much.

How forcibly memory recalls the pleasant room, the large open fireplace, the huge, slowly-burning logs—for it was cool autumn weather. The conversation, too, how distinctly it comes to my mind. Much was said of the wildness of the region, the difficulties and hardships of the first occupants of the untamed soil, with its resources and rewards for the enterprising.

But the especial interest of the evening was in the relation of a thrilling incident in Mrs. Woleby's own experience, which, as nearly as I can recollect, was in these words:

"One morning," she began, "in the early part of last June, I left home in fine spirits to pay a long-promised visit to an old friend and schoolmate, who lives on a newly improved farm about two miles up the stream, and on the opposite bank. To reach my friend's, it was necessary to follow the winding cow-path on this side for half a mile, to a place where the trunk of a large pine had fallen across the narrow stream. Crossing this primitive bridge, a walk of a mile through the woods led me to the opening in which stood the house. My visit was delightful, for we had been long asunder and had much to say.

"We lingered over the parting words till the sun grew low in the western sky, when I commenced my homeward walk, and though I hastened with quick step, the dark shadows that gathered around my path warned me of approaching night.

"When I emerged from the thick woods and came to the rude log bridge, the early twilight showed me a black object on the end of the log at the opposite bank, and a few minutes sufficed to confirm my worst fears—it was a large black bear. Agitation and terror at first deprived me of all thought; but lifting my heart to the God of the defenceless, and rallying my presence of mind, I began to think what I could do. To return to my friend's house, would not only be unsafe in the darkness, but my absence would alarm the fears of my family; to attempt to reach home in any other direction than across the fated bridge was vain, and not to be thought of.

"Finally, I sat down by a tree to watch my companion— the grim sentinel of the other side.

"I had heard that this animal did not, like wolves and
11

other wild beasts, prowl around in the night, and I hoped
that ere long he would retire into the deeper shades of the
woods ; so, with beating heart and the most feverish
anxiety, I awaited his movements. Almost an hour I
continued in this strange situation ; the summer night wind
cooled my face, and the ruddy twilight which shone through
the branches of the trees, and softened the bright verdure
around me, deepened into uniform dull shade, when at
length my straining eyes saw the black object move, and
presently Bruin, slowly rising, walked off leisurely into the
woods.

" I have no recollection of my passage across the log, but
I was soon traversing the woods with hasty step, not venturing a glance into the thicket around.

" Almost flying over the ground, I gained the more open
path among the low bushes ; here I overtook a boy driving
home some cows, and seldom has the sight of a human face
been more welcome."

We had listened with breathless attention to this true
story of startling adventure. Many praises were bestowed
on Mrs. Woleby's courage and presence of mind. An
animated conversation followed upon similar scenes, wit-
nessed or heard of by those present.

Mary related the account of our grandmother's encounter with a bear, which I have already narrated, and Mrs.
Woleby told us some of the peculiar characteristics of this
ferocious animal, of which I remember one was the tenderness of his nose, his most vulnerable point, to defend which,
he will instantly drop any booty he may have secured

The next morning, taking an affectionate leave of the friends who had shown us so much kindness, Mary left Bangor, on horseback with her husband for a tedious day's ride, though but twenty miles to their home, the settlement of Clemence.

The day passed rather heavily with me, for I did not relish being left behind ; but early the next morning letters came from home. Oh, how my heart leaped at the well-known characters, and how doubly impatient I was now to reach my destination, that Mary might read them too, for we had longed—oh, how much ! to know how all was going on with those dear ones, whose names were so often on our lips.

Grace gave us a lively picture of all that had taken place at home ; and Bessy, dear Bessy, with her anxious sisterly expressions of affection mingled many kind hints and suggestions modestly set forth, just like herself. One thought I remember was this—that in going among strangers it is very important to discriminate character, and not to yield implicit trust on too short acquaintance—a lesson of much practical value to one so ignorant of the world, and so unsuspecting as I then was.

CHAPTER XXVII.

THE NEW HOME.

" Around their hearth by night,'
What gladsome looks of household love
Met in the ruddy light."

THREE long days of expectation elapsed, ere a messenger appeared to conduct me to Clemence, for Dr. Emery could not leave. It was a dull, chill day, and a gloomy ride I had. The man walked by my side to assist in difficult places, for my horse stumbled frequently over stumps, roots of trees, and deep hollows of mud, in the miserable road through the woods.

So thick were the trees, and so dark, sad, and heavy-colored looked the autumn foliage, that the forest was literally black on either side the narrow path.

Before half the day was concluded, each thump of the rough road gave me a severe pain in the side, and when at last I arrived, about dark, I was fain to go to bed with head throbbing, without a look at my new home.

The next day I could not sit up without fainting, but " youth repairs its wasted spirits quickly," and I soon began to take a peep at the strange place in which I found myself, which I felt to be home, since it was with Mary and her husband.

She was most lively and cheerful, neatly arranging her simple furniture in the very small, unfurnished cottage, which, however, was the sole framed house in the settlement.

The settlement consisted of about a dozen houses, extending a mile or two along the narrow road, a mere uneven, muddy lane, the small "opening" of dun-colored, stump-ridden fields being closed in by lofty interminable woods.

Here was no graceful Pine-mountain lifting its friendly head, no picturesque valley or running brook, neither pretty groves, nor waving orchards, nor neat gardens ; nothing but dreary fields and half-cleared pastures, in which a few stunted cattle were gleaning the last scanty herbage.

There was the same sky indeed, the deep, serene October heavens now beaming down upon us, and again murky and troubled, tempestuous with warring winds, the gloomy presages of coming winter.

Yet in this little place, shut in by the blue overhead, and the wall of dark woods around, was abundant scope for the display of the ever-interesting actors in the drama of life, the fair and lovely in humanity, the kind and good, the curious and grotesque—all were represented, for there is everywhere a "something in all features, and all tones of voice, and all manners, betokening origin from one root," and creating a bond of sympathy between human beings, as such, wherever they meet.

Monotonous and dull as the place looked in the nakedness of autumn desolation, it was yet a ridge of excellent land, rewarding well the hardy cultivators of its strong, deep soil.

Fine crops of wheat and other grains were raised, but the difficulty of transporting their produce to market, and of obtaining other things in exchange, caused a scanty supply of the comforts the farmers could not themselves manufacture.

Nothing could exceed the beautiful simplicity, the unaffected kindness and warm friendship of those few, but most worthy families. Seldom has it fallen to the lot of mortals to receive more cordial sympathy and affection than were bestowed upon us by our neighbors. The most kindly feeling, deeds of love, and a sincere friendly interest in each other's welfare seemed to unite them together almost as one family.

We were especially welcomed by this isolated little community, for Dr. Emery was the only physician in a circuit of many miles, and his settlement among them was hailed with joy.

Our house contained one moderate-sized common room, and a smaller sleeping apartment, each closed up with pine boards, unpainted and unplastered, looking, it must be confessed, very much like a barn, or rude shop. My sleeping room was the low, irregular chamber, where between the huge chimney and the little square window was ample space for my bed, which Mary, with true sister's art to please, had arrayed in her prettiest counterpane.

She had also hung against the rude chimney opposite the bed, a pretty picture of Mary, Queen of Scots, a fine old painting, which had been given her in Boston. Indeed she had almost robbed the rooms below to give a cheerful, inviting aspect to my little loft.

The owner of the house, Mr. Asa Worth, who also owned a large farm with it, shortly after we came, added another sleeping room of rough boards, and took up his lodgings with us for the winter.

His presence in the house gave to Mary and me a feeling of security, in the long winter evenings when Dr. Emery was detained by a sick patient, and we should otherwise have been left alone. He was a man of upright character and dignified bearing, and we soon learned to respect and value him, as a friend on whom we could rely.

CHAPTER XXVIII.

Just across the road from us stood a new barn, partly finished, in a tolerably smooth field, which, with the farm belonging to it, had been recently sold, and the new owner was shortly expected to take possession.

This barn had been, during the summer, the appointed place for religious meetings, and I recall quite vividly my first Sabbath, only a day or two after I arrived, with the strange, queer, comical aspect that every thing bore to my eyes.

Rough board seats were laid across from side to side, and a motley group covered them. Old and young, with every variety of fashion and form in dress and appearance. Children, women with infants in their arms, dogs rubbing their noses against one and another as they ran about, seeking out every crevice and corner of the strange church, while children gambolled, and babies crowed and screamed.

But the preacher—oh! how unlike all our previous conceptions of

> " The holy man with rev'rent air,
> In decent garb arrayed."

He was a youngish man, almost boorish in aspect, coarse and illiterate in language. His long, yellow hair hung down his neck like strings, and he spoke in a sing-song voice, keyed to its highest pitch ; earnest and sincere, however, he seemed, and many of his hearers listened with devout and serious attention.

But, joined to his earnest words, his sincere exhortations, and Scripture aptly quoted, were innumerable blunders ; and at last, after many sudden turns and digressions, he began declaiming against human "larnin ;" stating, what none could doubt, that he never thought beforehand of what he should preach : to do so, would be sinful distrust of the Lord, who taught him what to say.

"Just think of Saint Paul," said he. "The Bible says he was brought up at the foot of Gamel Hill, which must have been in a barren, mountainous country, where he had no chance at all for larnin."

This was the climax : I laughed from sheer necessity, and Mary joined with me, though against her will, for we had been too well instructed to allow us to turn into ridicule any meeting for the sincere worship of God.

When we got home, Dr. Emery seated himself by the fire, and laughed heartily. "Here you have a specimen of our Sabbaths," said he, "and of our very instructive religious teachers ; and surely it requires an expanded intellect to receive his conclusions respecting Saint Paul's bringing up." We laughed again.

"Oh, Mary!" said I, "can it do one any good to attend such meetings as these ?"

"Certainly," she answered, "they are far better than none ; this preacher may be sincerely pious, unlettered as he is, and perhaps he and his hearers are more acceptable

in the eyes of our Heavenly Father than many of the great
and wise who meet in costly temples, surrounded with all
that wealth and luxury can bestow."

"But only think of his blunders," said I; "how can one
help laughing in his face?"

"These blunders," said Mary, "though ludicrous enough,
do not affect the heart, nor alter the Bible itself, nor its
truth."

"I wonder," said I, "that so many should be found to
come to hear such preaching."

"In these lonely neighborhoods," said Dr. Emery,
"where life is comparatively solitary and uneventful, every
occasion for mingling together the social human sympathies
is hailed with eagerness. The people come together to see
each other, especially the young folks."

"I thought there seemed evidence of deep religious
feeling, too, in many of those present to-day," said Mary.

"Oh yes," said he, carelessly—for at that time the subject was a matter of indifference to him—"the religious
element is strong in every human breast; man is ever
reaching after something higher than himself."

"I love to view this tendency in another light," said
Mary: "that God, in his boundless mercy, is reaching
down an arm of love to draw the wayward hearts of his
creatures to himself."

"That is truly a beautiful thought; worthy of you, my
Mary; and it may be so. I noticed the rapt interest
beaming in Mrs. Paul's face; that woman," said he, "came

not less than four miles through woods, where there is scarcely a path through the tangled bushes."

"Is it not dangerous?" asked I, recollecting Mrs. Wolcby's adventure.

"It might be, perhaps, to traverse it alone, but several go in company; trees are marked, from point to point, to guide in the right path; many come from that distance, whenever there is a meeting."

This conversation was just after the morning service, the preacher went on his way to another congregation, for the evening, and the afternoon meeting was "carried on" among themselves, several, by turns, giving "a word of exhortation."

One addressed us as "this intelligible congregation," and told us we were "born to trouble *as the sparks are that fly upward.*" Another, who stooped so much as to appear momentarily in danger of falling, and whose common appellation was "Broken-backed Josh," talked glibly a long while, repeating an indefinite number of times, "Let us pluck ambrosial fruits from life's fair tree."

Others, however, spoke in a manner to which no exception could be taken; all were, doubtless, sincere and conscientious in the discharge of duty, and thus were acceptable in the sight of Him who looketh on the heart; and their self-denying efforts to sustain religious worship were worthy of all praise.

After this, the meetings were transferred to the log-houses of the settlement, where they were held in turn through the winter, the barn, which had proved so commo

dious during the summer, being now called in requisition
for the temporary shelter of the family of its owner.

This family, consisting of his wife and two children,
shared with us our scanty accommodations for a week,
while the husband fitted up his barn-dwelling with a rude
chimney and some partitions.

Thus prepared, the dwelling was as comfortable and commodious as many of the other houses in the little village.

CHAPTER XXIX.

OUR NEIGHBORS.

" Think us no churls; nor measure our good minds
By this rude place we live in."

WE soon became acquainted with each family who lived near us, our new neighbors, visiting among them freely, and receiving visits in return.

No small variety of character was found in that narrow circle.

There was Mrs. Tibbs, tall and bony, with deep furrowed face, and grizzled hair, bristling out from under her cap, over her sharp little grey eyes.

She possessed a singular faculty for mangling and disjointing her words, distorting them in the most ludicrous manner. Scarcely a sentence of our mother tongue left her lips but it underwent a process of clipping and garbling.

She was a strange being—an exemplification of the truth that in actual life, individuals are found, who, if faithfully described, would be pronounced forced, unnatural characters.

This queer old woman was jokingly called " Aunt Kitty," from her partiality for cats, for she always had about her a goodly number and variety of the feline race.

She lived, with her daughter, in a little hut quite near us, professing the deepest poverty, though it was well known that her husband, an industrious, clever man, had left her a comfortable provision. She was penurious and grasping, and had once or twice been surprised in counting her money. On one occasion, Dr. Emery himself having dealings with her, saw her reluctantly produce some of her precious store from its singular place of concealment—the straw bed !

When any one bestowed a favor upon her, she was lavish in her praise and flattery ; but if called upon to part with her idol, even to pay a just demand, she complained bitterly of her destitution, and the unfriendly dealings of others.

I went to her hut once with some nice bit ; she loaded me with thanks and praises, declaring nobody was so kind, extolling the doctor to the skies, and Mary too, say-ing,

" She is a pretty critter, and she dresses as good as a queen ; but," she added, heaving a sigh, " beauty nor fine clothes can't pervent her life—she'll lies as low as any on us !"

Aunt Kitty never failed being present at the meetings, always with a Bible or hymn-book in her hand, and swaying herself backward and forwards. Then, during the whole time of singing, exhortation, and prayers, she kept her eyes riveted upon the good book, as if some potent charm pertained to it, while, in truth, she knew not how to read a word.

Her daughter Marcy, inoffensive and quiet, extremely limited in the range of her ideas, was a mere patient drudge to her mother. She was simple-minded and single-hearted, most conscientious ni her narrow views, living and dying one of Christs "little ones."

She had a delicate face, though skinny and freckled, with fine, reddish, light hair, which, she told me, she never curled but once, and that was when she "backslid."

At one time, with much circumlocution, and many entreaties that I should not be offended, she besought me not to wear a ruffle on my neck, because, as she said, it gave "so much 'casion."

Visiting once where she was present, we were, as usual, requested by the lady of the house to sing; Mary turned to her, saying,

"Would you like to hear a song, Marcy?"

She simpered, twisted about in her chair, blushed, and with a simple moral courage, worthy of more weighty cause, replied:

"If I should say I should, I should tell a lie."

Then there was our frequent visitor, a Mr. Tinney, whose love of the marvelous often constrained him to narrate most wonderful and incredible tales.

When any question was asked concerning the particulars, which might possibly lead to an exposure of the impossibility of truth of these "entertainments," his ready reply was,

"Well—that's a little more'n I can tell ye; I've asked Miss Tinney, and *she* don't know."

"*Miss* Tinney," as he called her, was his patient, kind, and forbearing wife, who ever tried to screen his faults, even when, influenced by the liquor he loved too well, he loaded her with abuse. She was a most pious, conscientious woman, who would not for the world exaggerate, or deviate in the smallest degree from the exact truth, yet he loved to throw upon her the responsibility of his ready-made falsehoods.

One family near us soon became our special friends. Their name was Campbell; the father was of Scotch extraction; was well descended, and born to wealth.

He had served in the Revolutionary War, with the rank of lieutenant, and like many of the noble men of that period, sacrificed to his whole-souled patriotism, all personal and pecuniary considerations.

Finding himself at the close of the war without resource, he plunged into the forests of Maine, resolved, with cheerful and strong courage, to win for his young family home and independence from the virgin soil of his country.

He had six children, of whom Margaret, or Maggy, the eldest, was about my own age.

She was truly a sweet girl, reminding me at first of my pleasant acquaintance in Bangor, Emilia Woleby; but while not less gentle and amiable, she had far more energy and spirit. Her circumstances called for exertion, and she cheerfully gave it; she spun, she wove, she tended the dairy, and she had the constant, and sometimes almost sole care of the younger children, for her mother's health was feeble.

Her step was lively, her face blooming with healthful exercise, and the beaming softness of her eye showed that its light was kindled at her heart.

I loved and esteemed this dear girl with my whole soul, and now, after nearly fifty years have passed away, as I recall the days when she shared my thoughts, and the happy hours we spent together, I still feel that she was one of earth's loveliest and best.

12

CHAPTER XXX.

COUNTRY VISITING.

THE first visit we made to Mr. Campbell's convinced us that we had met a family quite different from the ordinary stamp found in pioneer settlements.

I have lived in the most polished of our cities; I have been familiar, too, with places so retired as to be on the very verge and outskirts of civilized society; and everywhere have I found some of Nature's noblemen—noble in heart and soul—some person or family, cultivated in mind and refined in spirit.

Mr. Campbell was a man of fine, noble bearing, with a prompt, decided turn, a quick bend of his stout, compact frame, indicative not only of energy, but of unbending integrity of purpose. His wife appeared to me a mild, lovely woman, whose retiring virtues must be sought out, to be known.

We had been in the house but a short time, when Mr. Campbell came in to welcome us. After passing some compliments with Mary, he turned to me, and plied me with questions of all sorts.

His manner, both frank and polite, put me at ease with him, while he, no doubt, was reading me like a book, sounding my depth, and taking the compass of my mind, though I was then far enough from having such a thought.

"Is Mr. Warth coming?" at length he inquired.

I replied, that I did not know.

"Wife," said he, "I hope you did not forget Asa Wurth. He will hardly forgive you, if he is left out, where Miss Leland is concerued," he added, with a curious, searching look, which quite confused me. Observing it, he turned and called to him his little son, playing on the floor.

"Come here, Archie!" said he; but looking at him, "Ah, I was going to tell you to go and kiss the ladies; but I see you must have your beard off first. Go and find your razor, boy."

Maggy vanished with her little brother, and soon appeared with him again, his chubby face as clean and fresh as a dewy rose.

While we were there, two young men came from Bangor, on a journey further up the country, stopping at Mr. Campbell's for the night.

They were brothers, by the name of Green; one a lawyer, the other a land surveyor. I had met them in Bangor, and their presence on this occasion is brought to mind by the fact that, at their request, Mary and I sung a song upon the Sedition Act, which harmonizing with the political views of the company, called forth a shout of applause.

We were obliged to repeat it, and often sung it afterwards, though now I do not recall a word of it.

This was the beginning of a succession of visits, for the doctor and his family were favorite as well as honored guests, and in many of them I found much enjoyment.

We all went one evening, by invitation, to take tea at

the house of Mr. Spear, a very good, pious man, who occasionally preached or exhorted.

His family lived in a small, low house, built in the form of a shed, having a roof but on one side, entirely unfinished; the chimney and hearth were of rough stones, with a huge fire-place; the floor of split logs, with large cracks between, through which the cold air found easy admittance.

There was but one room in the house ; this was lighted only by a window with four panes of glass, having a wide shelf beneath, on which lay a Bible, hymn-book, and almanac. The good man being a minister, something of a library was indispensable.

In one corner of the room stood a turned up bedstead, apparently of home manufacture; a few basket-bottomed chairs, and a common wooden table completed the furniture. There was, besides this room, a very small entry, one side of which the good woman used for a pantry, and a small dark *place*, entered by a rough door, swung on leathern hinges, where was some kind of a convenience to lay away children, after they went to sleep at night, of whom they had four, the eldest not yet five years old.

It was a winter evening, and about dark, when we arrived at the house. A great fire was blazing in the old fireplace, roaring and cracking up the chimney.

The oldest child, a girl, lay stretched upon the floor, fast asleep, with her feet towards the fire.

Mr. Spear held the second child in his arms, rocking to and fro, from two legs to two legs of his rickety, creaking chair, invoking sleep to release him from his labors ; vainly enough, however, for the rebellious urchin continued to kick and scream most lustily, almost drowning our voices with his noise.

A little girl of eleven years, from further back in the woods, who was staying with them to attend school, had the third; while the mother, with the babe in her arms, assisted us to unrobe, laying our things high up on the posts of the bed, the only place in the room, in fact, where they could have been bestowed.

In the course of half an hour the children were quieted to sleep, and one after another were carefully disposed of in the dark "place" before mentioned.

Now were commenced the preparations for supper : a fine spare-rib and a sheet of biscuit were baked before the fire, potatoes boiled in the tea-kettle, the tea meanwhile steeping on the coals an hour or more ; a great store and variety of pies, cakes, pickles, and preserves were brought forth ; the little pine table drawn out and duly balanced on the uneven floor, and, about eight o'clock, a most excellent supper was served, according to the best knowledge and ability of our truly good and kind-hearted hostess.

After the onerous business of the table was dispatched, Mrs. Spear took her knitting-work and sat down, as if the visit was just now begun ; and Mr. Spear, freed from the care of his noisy boy, also made himself very sociable.

Their plain common sense, and real kindness of heart, covered, as with a mantle, the defects of their meagre accommodations.

No two people could have taken more pains to entertain their guests, to the utmost extent of their power, and we went home, feeling assured that they were among our valuable neighbors.

CHAPTER XXXI.

OUR LANDLORD.

> "—— who can tell
> The yearnings of his heart, the charm, the spell,
> That bound him to that vision?"

It is time, perhaps, to say something of Mr. Asa Worth, the owner of our house and almost from our first residence an inmate in the family.

He was a short, well-built man, rather good-looking than otherwise, of twenty-seven or eight years of age. Smart and enterprising, highly esteemed in the community, he possessed the fullest confidence of Mary and Dr. Emery, whose staunch friend he had ever been.

When it soon became manifest to them, that he had a special interest in me, it naturally enough met with their approbation.

I regarded him with great respect as an elder friend, and as nearly as I can recollect was just as frank and trusting in our ordinary intercourse in the family, as if he had been a brother.

Even after Mary began to talk with me about him and his wishes, I did not take the subject in earnest, and scarcely gave a thought to it; with a sort of girlish simplicity, I neither understood nor appreciated his hints and approaches, but laughed all off in a joke and light-hearted glee.

When, after a time, he spoke more plainly, and sought opportunity to find me alone, I parried all questions and attacks in one foolish, light way, or another, sometimes with a whirling dance round the room, by queer looks to make him laugh, or would make answer that it was a strange thing to talk about, that in eight or ten years I would begin to consider the matter.

Sometimes he carried on the joke himself ; once he wrote an obligation for me to sign, purporting that I should marry him or forfeit ten thousand dollars, to which I gaily put my name.

I think now, that my manner and treatment of him, with his knowledge of the feelings of Dr. Emery and Mary in his favor, deceived him as to my real sentiments, though I was most innocent of any such intentions.

But I was like some other silly young girls, so perfectly heedless and inconsiderate that I scarcely took a sober view of anything. I wonder he did not get weary and out of patience with my levity and thoughtlessness ; but thus it went on during that winter, and indeed much longer.

Mary, from time to time, tried to bring me to some serious thought and decision, or rather, to a favorable decision, but I still declined giving the matter much attention.

The time, however, passed happily along ; the few young people frequently met, in a familiar, social manner.

There was Jerry Withington, with his heavy shock of red hair, his long, freckled face, and longer nose, but otherwise not ill-looking, and passably agreeable, always very neat in his dress and appearance ; and Mr. Allan Ryler, rather short, with bushy, black hair, cropped close to his swarthy visage. He was intelligent, very well read, and a great talker.

These two, together with our friend Asa Wurth, were the gay gallants of the small settlement. Their kindly proffered service was ever ready to assist females to meeting on stormy Sabbaths, as well as to collect the fair damsels from one and another of the log houses, and convey them fleetly over the deep snow, in sled or sleigh, to the cheerful gathering on the long winter evenings—the time of leisure and enjoyment.

During the keen, sparkling, winter's day, all was stirring life ; the huge, slow-paced oxen were driven forth to their daily work ; sometimes to make roads through the new-fallen snow, so deep as well-nigh to come up to their backs, but usually drawing the almost endless piles of logs, for fuel in the cold, unfinished houses.

The voices of men urging forward the patient beasts, mingled with the jingling of bells, and the creaking of the crisp snow under the pressure of the enormous sleds, with their loads of fresh, fragrant wood.

Oh ! those winter days in the heart of the old woods ! when, for many, many weeks, except for an occasional fall of snow, the sky was without a cloud—its dazzling sheen reflected by myriad sparkles of pure, snowy crystals, its blinding radiance tempered and beautifully relieved by the surrounding forests of evergreen, resting against the clear, pearly sky.

No bleak, driving wind could penetrate through the thick trees, but the very stillness of the air seemed to indicate intense cold. A faint, white mist arising from the earth, like an icy grasp almost arrested the deep hurried breath, while the blood moved swiftly in the veins, and the whole system, wrought to unwonted exhilaration, was stimulated to new life by the clear, cutting atmosphere of those Borean skies. The very rigors of the climate gave strength and hardihood to the frame, energy and enterprise to the mind.

One bright, starlight evening, a jovial group were gathered at Mr. Campbell's ; in a family near them were three grown daughters—Estella, Polly, and Ruth Mudge. These girls, with Maggy and myself, comprised all the young females of Clemence, though occasionally others came from neighboring openings.

Estella, or Tella Mudge, had attained the mature age of twenty-two, and in virtue of her superiority in this respect, felt herself entitled to take the lead among us.

Besides, she was, in expressive Yankee language, termed a " smart girl"—bustling, energetic, dauntless, and capable.

Her eyes were black and piercing, her features large, and she had a snip-snap way of answering one which, perhaps, gave her some importance, but certainly was far from agreeable.

Polly was pretty, but insipid and tiresome, and for ever fingering her light, dangling curls.

Ruth, the youngest, was quite tolerable ; a lively, good-humored, ordinary girl.

The evening was spent with the usual amount of trifling small talk, petty railleries, and romping games and plays. I was called upon to sing, as usual, in which Maggy could join, but the Mudges could not sing, and I could not help thinking that many times Miss Tella, especially, felt spiteful and envious towards me on account of my songs ; I was never quite at ease in her company, for an ill-natured remark or question, or some covert sarcasm, was sure to make me feel uncomfortable.

Miss Tella had a grudge against me for another reason, as I afterwards knew ; she had "set her cap" for Mr. Wurth, as the most eligible match in the neighborhood, and she considered me in her way, no doubt.

All this evening he was quite devoted to her, evidently to her gratification. She was disposed to be pleased with every one, and I was in a gay and happy mood, entering into all the amusements with much zest.

When at last it was time to separate, we wended our way homeward with quick step, over the smooth trodden snow ; Mr. Wurth going with me, as was his common custom.

The transition from the warm room and murky fire-light into the clear, cold air, sobered my spirits.

I gazed in silent awe at the solemn cope above, with its million lights of heaven. How bright they shone out from their dark depths in that pure, keen air !

We had more than half reached home without exchang

ing a word, when my companion suddenly began, not in the pleasantest mood :

"It is a pity you haven't more agreeable company—if Allan Ryler was here, you could talk, I dare say, as fast as you did with him this evening."

"Certainly," said I, "I would try to entertain him."

"I shall know better next time," said he ; "I shall know enough to give place to more welcome attendance."

Not having much fancy for this kind of talk, I complained of the cold, saying I must try to shorten the road a little, and started into a fleet run, for I could run easily and swiftly.

He kept stiffly on, at his own pace, and I had time, not only to reach home, but to brighten up the fire, and slip off to bed before he came.

But my thoughts were anything but pleasant ; why he had been so crusty, I did not know ; or what I could have done to offend him.   I recalled the occurrences of the even-ing, recollected that he had scarce spoken to me, but had been very sociable with Miss Tella ; we did not go together, for I went early in the afternoon, to have a time with Maggy by ourselves—was this the reason ?

Or was it that Allan Ryler had conversed with me for some time about Boston, and Massachusetts, and the old times of the war ?

I felt quite sure that Mr. Wurth, by his movements, pre-vented Allan from accompanying me home ; and of this I was the more convinced, as I remembered his allusion to Mr. Ryler on our way.

After pondering a few moments, I resolved to take no notice of his moody manner, treat him just as usual, and care nothing about it—and so I fell asleep.

But that night was not to be given to tranquil slumber. I was awakened by the sound of voices earnest and anxious, and presently Mary called to me, saying that a fire had broke out in some of the houses.

The doctor and Mr. Wurth were just upon the point of starting to render assistance, telling us to remain quiet, and they would return with information as soon as they could.

We waited and anxiously watched the lurid glare from the burning house, rising in the black night, till near morning, when they came at last, bringing in their arms little Janet Campbell, a child of ten years ; she was wrapped in a blanket, and crying bitterly.

Oh ! how were we shocked and afflicted when we knew that it was indeed Mr. Campbell's house that was burned to ashes !

It must have caught soon after we left, for the flames had made considerable progress when they were discovered, about midnight.

Mrs. Campbell was ill, and was the first one awakened by the suffocating smoke.

None were near to help, and the father, rousing his faithful Maggy, consigned to her care the rescue of the children, who asleep in the chamber, were most distant from the flames; himself secured the safety of his wife, and by the aid of neighbors soon arrived, she was conveyed to the nearest house.

Then, with the greatest self-possession, he gave directions to the confused men around him, bending his utmost efforts to save from destruction the barn, where were his hay and his cattle, and which was in imminent danger of catching fire.

Dear, noble Maggy, faithfully performed her part ; she first tried to wake her eldest brother, a lad of twelve ; repeatedly she roused him, pulling him up by main force, while the boy, in his heavy sleep, would rub his eyes and creep back to his bed.

Meanwhile she carried little Archie and Stephen, next older, to an old cart that stood at some distance from the house. Janet and Nanny she partly dragged, partly carried, to the same place ; the oldest boy was at length sufficiently aroused to follow mechanically to their shelter.

There they all crouched, shivering and crying, while the agitated and breathless girl, scarcely knowing in her bewilderment whether all were safe or not, went back to the chamber and felt in each bed to assure herself ; then, without a thought of trying to save even their clothes, half dressed, and chilled by the night air, she returned to the little company to watch over them. There she found her father.

"My children !" said he, "thank God they are safe !"

Looking upon them weeping and half naked—the house now was one sheet of flame—his fortitude forsook him.

"Poor forlorn ones !" said he, in a broken voice, "without a shelter for your heads ! I have no house for you now !"

It was not till then that the doctor and Mr. Wurth reached the scene of disaster. The children were taken in charge by the neighbors, finding an asylum in different families.

Nothing was saved from the house ; the flames were rapid, and there were not means at hand, nor sufficient aid, to subdue them ; yet there was time to have saved many valuable articles, had all present been calm and self-possessed.

But the confusion and fright of many only impeded the movements of the few who knew better how to act in such an emergency. One man entered Mrs. Campbell's sleeping room, after she was removed from it, with intent to save something ; and looking round bewildered, he espied her cap hanging upon the carved top of the looking-glass. So, taking it carefully down, went and deposited it at a safe distance, instead of seizing, as he might have done, upon the glass itself, bedding, wearing apparel, or the many useful and necessary articles around ; but the precious moment was lost—all became the prey of the devouring flames.

Mr. Campbell, whose whole life had been a struggle with difficulties, and who had barely attained to a tolerable freedom from the rude grasp of poverty, now saw his family houseless, and destitute of even a change of clothing.

His was not a nature, however, to yield to discouragement and supineness, but was rather of that firm, elastic metle, that the harder it was buffeted the more it would rebound.

"God will provide a way for us," said he, with unwaver

ing trust; and, composed and cheerful, he began at once the work of repair and renovation.

And now were shown some of the noblest, loveliest traits of fair humanity, which, however overborne by selfishness, in the sordid sluggishness and narrow range of ordinary life never fails to assert its high empire in the breast, when roused to action by the power of sweet-stirring sympathy filling the heart with generous emotions. Our little neighborhood was busy, as with one heart and soul, in retrieving their losses: garments, clothing of all kinds, many things which could ill be spared, were freely, gladly offered, and fingers were nimbly plied to fit the gifts to the wants of the sufferers.

The men, too, with their stalwart teams, at once set about the labor of felling trees, and drawing the logs for building, and with so much vigor did they work, that in a few weeks a house was ready for them. Small, indeed, it was, and with but one finished room, yet a welcome shelter. Their friends, for the distance of twenty miles around, brought offerings of bedding, furniture, and provisions; while from Bangor came generous donations in various forms, till comfort again smiled in their dwelling, and their grateful hearts felt almost oppressed with such generous kindness.

CHAPTER XXXII.

SPRING-TIME.

THE winter passed on : spring came with tardy, unwilling step, and seemed to linger long on the threshold.

If a bright March sun, in its genial warmth, settled the level of the snow, and made glistening pearls drop from roofs and windows, the succeeding day, perchance, brought fitful winds and lowering clouds to usher in a storm of driving snow or sleet.

Not a speck of ground was to be seen for many changeful weeks. And then, instead of soft showers and warm sunshine, "the uncertain glory of an April day," light falling snow, mud, and rain seemed striving for empire on the bare, brown earth. But the tall cedars waved their green tops to the jolly, careless wind, and the sun shone out upon the many-fleeced, over-floating clouds, with just as much fervency of good-will as though their bright visages looked down upon scenes which could return their glances of beauty and joy.

When May-day came, a few of us, emulating the delights of more Hesperian climes, were intending to search the fields and woods for early blossoms, peeping from their cold beds of moss ; but, during the night previous, a few inches of snow noiselessly fell, spreading a pale sheet over the open

13

land, and lodging its soft burden upon millions of pendent boughs.

The mild morning sun looked out placidly through a veil of mist, as if conscious of his power to dissolve each tiny, feathery flake into grateful moisture for the opening buds.

Our promised excursion was changed to a May party at our house, of "the girls;" that is, my friend Maggy, and the three Mudges, with good Mary Tibbs, who, though much older, was a favorite with me, for her simplicity and kind-heartedness.

Youth, in its freshness and fullness, has little need to borrow its happiness from pomp and luxury : we sung, we twined our wreaths of evergreen, we read a new book together, as light-hearted in our homely room, as if wandering in orange groves under Italy's fair sky.

No small amusement, we derived, too, from watching a party of children, who, not to be baffled of their sport, went off "a Maying," through the snow and mud, "rollicking and frolicking," their joyous spirits and overflowing happiness condensed into musical little pellets of merriment, rebounding and ringing as they lavishly scattered them round.

Towards noon we saw them return, draggled and weary, yet protesting they had had rare sport ; displaying, as their reward, a few handfuls of checkerberries.

At evening I stood with Mary, in the open door, watching the retreating forms of my companions, as they warily picked their way over the yielding mud.

The sun had just set in glory, the air was mild and balmy,

and through the thick net-work of leafless branches glimpses of the bright sky gleamed, as if beckoning to some fair, peaceful region, far beyond.

Mary was softly singing, as she awaited the return of the doctor, who had been gone all day. He was soon seen coming, on horseback, at a slow pace, to accommodate the tardy progress of a pedestrian at his side.

A few moments' scrutiny, sufficed to show me that the stranger was Allan Ryler, who, being now employed at some mills, four or five miles distant, was spending that day on a visit to Clemence.

It instantly flashed into my mind that his name had been mentioned at dinner by Mr. Wurth, with an allusion that plainly pointed to me as the object of his coming.

Thinking only how to escape the encounter, I gently slid my arm away from Mary, and, going up stairs, sat down, half trembling, yet resolved not to be seen.

Snatches of the conversation soon came to my ears through the open door, and after a time my name was called ; but, quickly undressing, I retreated to my little cot.

I heard Mary say she thought I would soon come, and wondered where I could be. Presently she came to seek me, and was quite displeased, though she could not help laughing, to find me snugly ensconced in bed.

She endeavored to persuade me to go down, urging the incivility, and even rudeness, of such treatment, since he had specially inquired for me.

But I persisted, and she reluctantly reported me as hav ing retired

Allan Ryler no sooner heard this, than ne started up, walked with rapid strides across the room, and said, in his sharp, quick manner, "What does that mean?" Then taking his hat, he abruptly bade them good evening.

I was blamed, rallied, and bantered, without mercy, for my conduct, which was indeed foolish enough. Mr. Wurth, however, was extremely pleased, chuckling and delighting himself on every allusion, till I felt really uncomfortable about it.

CHAPTER XXXIII.

MY SCHOOL.

"There's music in the forest leaves,
When summer winds are there."

EARLY in summer, Clemence was visited by a missionary, who was on a tour of exploration to the new settlements, with some means contributed by the benevolent, to be bestowed in aid of public worship and schools in the more destitute places.

The small "opening," before mentioned, was a little neighborhood of but five families, and having never had any schools for their children, they received five dollars from the missionary, who applied to me to teach for them.

I consented, and they, encouraged to greater efforts, made up a small additional sum.

The older children sometimes attended school at Clemence, and had done so the past winter, for Dr. Emery had taught the young people, assisted by Mary, in his absence on professional duty.

I was not a stranger to the dwellers at Green Briar, and I entered upon my new vocation very cheerfully, "boarding round" in all the families, all in log-houses; in some the bare ground was the floor; in some places I ate potatoes boiled in a birch bark sap trough, and bread baked in an open iron kettle over the fire, which was also the sole utensil for frying meat, heating water for tea, and various other purposes.

In one place the wash-stand was a barrel covered with two pieces of board not very closely matched, and when one day at table a dish of salt was wanted, I noticed that the supply was obtained from this barrel.

Still, I was as happy in my little shed of a school-house as the birds that sang so merrily around me, and I remember to this day the names and faces of my few scholars.

Mr. Paul's was the chief family; they were of Scotch extraction, and friends of the Campbells.

Mrs. Paul was a pious, excellent woman. She had been often at our house. Her young people, too, I frequently saw, as they all attended meeting in Clemence. The oldest daughter was a buxom lass of twenty; the next, about my own age. There were two sons, of seventeen and eighteen; and five smaller ones, who were among my pupils.

Another family lived quite near, in a mere hut of one room, but enjoying the distinction of having attached to it the only barn in the neighborhood.

In the rear of this barn, itself furnishing one side, was the frail tenement of a school-house, composed of a few posts, boards, and beams, laid together, resting against the barn for support.

The floor and benches were of rough boards, and in the side opposite the rude door an aperture was cut for a window.

A very small space around was cleared of the bushes

and trees, and closed in by woods, whose deep shadow almost reached the open door, as each morning found me, with light step, tracing the dewy path to the daily charge of my shy little flock, while the melody of countless birds ceased not the livelong day.

How peaceful and quiet were those long summer days deepening into high noon, and fading in the ruddy west !

The marvelous loveliness of June is lovely indeed in the pure temperature of that northern latitude, where vegetation is so rapid that its growth can almost be discerned from hour to hour.

The first tender freshness of Nature's green robe is everywhere enchanting in its sweet budding luxuriance, its balmy odors, and the subtle harmonies of a thousand blended influences.

Then, too, the long, soft twilight—for there scarcely four out of the twenty-four hours are not tinged with some faint gleams of day—like the summer nights in Norway, where the delicious half hour after sunset, which seems like the smile of earth and sky, is prolonged throughout the whole night.

Those twilight evenings—the sweet "gloaming" of the Scotch—devoted to recreation and rest ! their retrospect is bright, yet mingled with regrets.

To my pleasure-loving youth, nothing came amiss ; and when the young Pauls and some others besought me to teach them to dance, I agreed to their plan—nothing loth

Dancing had been a very common amusement with the young people of Wayland, the comparatively few pious parents permitting it in their children : even the sons and daughters of Mr. Rice, our minister, partook with us in all our gaiety.

Perhaps some will recollect the time when there seemed to prevail, in New England, a general conformity to the world ; even Christians of undoubted piety, not heeding the command, "Come ye out from among them, and be ye separate."

In consequence, there was much lack of earnest, active piety ; the distinctive doctrines of religion were scarcely recognized, either in profession or practice.

It was usual then, upon marriage, or when somewhat past the hey-day of youth, to join the church, as a decent and proper show of respect for religion, with little said regarding the momentous question whether the soul had indeed " passed from death into life."

I had always danced in Wayland, and saw no harm in doing so in Green Briar. There was not convenient space in the house, so the lads brought some boards, used for threshing, and made a floor upon the green grass. There, evening after evening, in the open air, under the sunset sky, we plied our nimble feet in this animating pastime, till the stars twinkled, while the " old folks " looked out slily upon our sport from some obscure corner.

I well knew, though I did not heed it then, that good Mrs. Paul was grieved in her heart because of our dancing ; her children overruled her objections, but her conscience was troubled that the inmates of her family should engage in this vain amusement. Her scruples should have been respected by me, and I have ever since been pained by the remembrance of this portion of my giddy, thoughtless youth.

The period of childhood and youth is generally deemed the most favored and happy portion of man's life, and many a fond sigh of regret is cast back upon those early years.

Childhood is, indeed, most lovely and gladsome, the bright impersonation of innocence and love.

The golden morn of youth is, oh, how precious ! as the germ and type of all after life. But childhood, with its smiles and tears, who would recall ? Its sunny gaiety is like the frisking of lambs on the lea, or the gambols of the playful kitten—the soul is not there.

And youth, free-hearted, joyous youth—its memory is, indeed, like the glad murmur of the running brook, like the gushing melody of the birds in spring—but is happiness found there ?

That is a fountain still and deep, welling up from the in most heart, and comes only with the matured intellect, with the full flow of the tried soul, conscious of its strength— nay, it is only truly attained when the chastened spirit finds its infinite treasure in its Almighty Creator.

The memories of youth are, with most, shaded by the sorrowful recollection of follies committed, golden opportunities wasted, willful errors, ignorance, and waywardness.

So true it is, that memory has both its lights and its shadows, and with the bright train of the one comes ever alas ! the sad procession of the other !

CHAPTER XXXIV.

"THE HUE OF DEATH IS CAST O'ER EVERYTHING."

SAD scenes awaited us in the succeeding autumn.

The summer had been extremely warm, with great drought, and a malignant fever prevailed.

Dr. Emery was hurried from patient to patient, often to a distance of several miles, riding all day and all night, returning home for a hasty meal, or to snatch a few minutes' repose.

In one case he went twenty miles, over wretched roads, being gone from home nearly a week.

At length, a family of six were all sick at the same time, having the fever in different stages.

The disease was deemed contagious, and a great panic prevailed, mastering for the time all impulses of humanity in the one instinct of self-preservation.

Scarce any one could be found willing to watch by night, or even attend upon the sick by day, and Dr. Emery, faithful to his charge, was both nurse and doctor to his patients He stayed with them day after day, till, by the blessing of God on his skill and unceasing exertions, all were convalescent ; then, utterly overcome, he was himself prostrated by the fever.

Mary was alarmed, and sent at once to Bangor for medical aid ; two physicians came, but, alas ! their utmost skill could not avail ; his exhausted frame was the easy prey of disease. He rapidly sunk under it, and his life was the price of his generous devotion to others.

He died at the post of duty, a brave, unflinching soldier !

My poor sister ! She made no loud demonstrations of her sorrow ; she meekly bowed her head to the stroke, and in the secret silence of her soul sought consolation at a Father's hand. He who had smitten, He alone could heal.

Our neighbors were struck with double terror to see their physician and helper fall before the Destroyer, and even at the funeral, scarcely were there enough collected to bear his beloved remains to their last resting-place.

But we heeded little then that we were left almost alone in our affliction ; the one great grief swallowed all smaller ones. When the panic of fear had subsided, proofs were not wanting of the most tender and deep feeling for our bereavement Many tears were shed with us, and for us— tears of sorrow for the dead—tears of affectionate sympathy with the living.

Mr. Campbell, as soon as he was able, for he, too, had been one of the sick, acted the part of a true friend towards us. Mr. Wurth at once took upon himself the care of the doctor's business, all his out-standing accounts, bills, and liabilities ; managing everything in a most faithful and able manner.

Our friends at Bangor sent letters of condolence and kind messages of sympathy. I had kept up occasional correspondence with my two friends, Eleanor Bolles and Emilia ·

Woleby, and new cordial invitations came from both families for Mary and myself to spend as much time with them
as suited our convenience, with the assurance that we should
be most welcome to pass the ensuing winter at Bangor.

But our thoughts turned to our own home, far away,
and the dear ones there.

Our father urged our immediate return "to those," he
said, "who shared all our griefs, and who would strive, by
the cares of love, to lighten them."

Mary's stricken heart yearned for her childhood's home,
and its comforting endearments, but difficulties were in her
way. It was now too late for a passage by water, and to
return by land was a journey, at best, long and expensive,
and that, from the state of the roads, could only be performed in winter by sleighing. There was then no stage
east from Portland, and the expense of hiring private conveyance, with proper attendance, was not to be thought of.

Dr. Emery had possessed nothing but a thorough knowledge of his profession ; free-hearted and generous in his
feelings, he often refrained from making charges against
those who were struggling along for the mere necessaries of
life, as was the case with many in that region.

Yet his practice was so extensive, that, had his dues been
promptly paid, there would have been ample provision for
our present wants. The past season had been an unfavorable one ; many were straitened still more by sickness ; so
that some who had kind hearts and just intentions failed
altogether in meeting their engagements. Besides, all had
been in the practice of paying their doctor's fees in produce

from their farms, but now it was needful that the arrears should be paid in money. Where all are poor and struggling together, the selfish instincts are constantly excited, and long-continued poverty is apt to blunt the edge of the nobler feelings of humanity—the just, the generous, the humane.

CHAPTER XXXV.

It was no small addition to Mary's troubles, that her situation was so perplexing, it being utterly impossible to collect a sum sufficient to defray the expenses of our return home.

But a kind Providence sent relief, when least expected, Mr. Campbell came one day to inform us that he intended going in his own sleigh to New Hampshire, to visit his brother, and that he could carry one of us as far as that on our way home; at the same time inviting the other to remain at his house till the following spring.

He advised Mary to stay, alleging that her affairs might then be better arranged. Dr. Emery had purchased some land, just before his death, and he thought that might be sold the ensuing spring, and her other bills collected.

I saw the change that passed over Mary's face, at this proposal; I saw the struggle in her mind, and felt that she needed the ministrations of home—the kind, cheering voices of kindred—to soothe her wounded spirit.

I resolved, at once, to be the one to stay; and I urged so many cogent reasons in favor of it, that so it was decided.

With the first deep fall of snow Mary went, taking with

her the very few things that could be packed into the sleigh. Her journey was favorable, and immediately after her arrival at home, a letter was sent me from them all, full of love, counsel, and cheering encouragement.

Captain Stephens, of Bangor, agreed to take charge of the remainder of our effects, and ship them to Boston. Maggy aided me in preparing the various articles for transportation by sleighing to Bangor.

It was the first time I had been in the house since Mary left it, for it seemed so lonely, I could not bear to enter it.

The day was dreary; the wind came in gusts against the bare windows; snow fell at intervals from the sullen clouds; a sense of desolation came over me, and it required all my self-command to keep back the tears.

Mr. Wurth was there too, assisting us in removing and arranging. I was oppressed with his kindness, and longed to speak of it, but could not trust myself to talk, lest the flood-gate of tears should be opened. I almost wished I could find it in my heart to repay him in the way he desired.

At length all was packed, except Mary's bureau, which, it being inconvenient to remove, I requested Mr. Wurth to keep for himself. He was at first unwilling, and said sadly, as we were standing together, "I do not want it; I shall have no use for it," then sinking his voice lower, "If you would but take possession here, accept the house and its owner; it is all I would ask in this world!"

I felt, in the depths of my heart, that I was not worthy of such regard from him. I told him so, amid raining tears; called myself foolish and ungrateful, and spoke with earnest

sincerity of Maggy's loveliness and worth of character. I
know not why, but I had a feeling that she would not refuse
him, would he but appreciate her many excellences, and
seek her favor. He did not reply. We soon separated, and
I only saw him once afterwards. But my instincts were
not at fault ; Maggy eventually became his wife.

CHAPTER XXXVI.

RETURN TO BANGOR.

ABOUT mid-winter, I accepted the invitation of my Bangor friends, though with some reluctance, for I longed for seclusion, and shrunk from mixing in company.

At Mr. Bolles's, I knew I should be in the midst of gaieties and excitement, and I had no longer any heart for such scenes. The various sad experiences of the last few months—my loneliness—all wrought a total change in me.

Dr. Emery's death was an ever-present reality to my mind. He was gone—he had made the fearful plunge—but whither?

This awful glimpse into the unseen world greatly affected my spirits; all else seemed vague, unreal, and of no importance. The Campbells thought me low spirited, and advised my going to Bangor, that I might have change of scene, and some amusement.

Instead of that, most happy would it have been, if my softened feelings and salutary seriousness had been cherished by fitting influences, and that the tide of worldly pleasure and vanity might then have been rolled back.

I was drawn into the giddy round, at first reluctantly, in compliance with custom, and to avoid remark, often with a conscience ill at ease; but company, and flattering attentions, had their influence.

14

I found that the past year had made great changes in this thriving place; the number of dwellings was more than doubled, new stores were added, streets opened, and there was great increase of business, as well as of fashion and gaiety.

I was soon noticed as a pretty dancer, and was quite sought after at all the parties. On one occasion, at a gay gathering, one of the toasts given was, "To the lass of Clemence." How confused I was! I scarcely knew where I was or what to do; and my head was actually dizzy as I caught the word passed from mouth to mouth.

It must have been by mere accident or caprice that I received so much attention at this time; there was nothing in me to call it forth; there must have been much which needed to be excused, on the ground of my youth, timidity, and inexperience. My appointments in dress, too, though I thought little about it then, must have been meagre enough, for my means were literally nothing.

I remember once, when returning late from some walk or visit, one of my shoes was lost by an inadvertent step; the next morning a packet of shoes was brought me that I might choose from them a good fit; and I took them, simply, without any of the scruples of delicacy I might have felt a few years later, in such a case. No doubt I needed them, for I had little or no money; indeed, I scarcely recollect having any during this period.

Among the boarders at Mr. Bolles's was an English sea-captain—Captain Hamlet.

His vessel had been accidentally frozen in. late in the preceding fall, and he, consequently, spent the winter in Bangor, amusing himself as best he could. He, was somewhat past his youth, tall, rather haughty in his bearing, but perfectly well-bred, very fond of gay scenes, and quite chivalrous in his gallantry and polite attentions to ladies.

I saw little of him except in company, for, being quite at home at Mr. Bolles', I was in any part of the house with Eleanor, seldom going to the public table with the numerous boarders.

After a time he began to distinguish me with his notice, and finally, when he chanced to encounter me alone—for Eleanor and I were seldom apart—he asked me if I would be his wife, and go out to Liverpool with him.

"I want to show my mother what America can produce," said he, protesting, as I hurriedly made my escape, that his "intentions were honorable."

I do not recollect that I made any reply of any sort; I only remember feeling very much frightened and very foolish.

However, in this instance at least, my "*gaucherie*" served me in as good turn as the most approved rules for behavior in such cases. I kept out of his way, never even speaking with him again, though I had a high opinion of him as an accomplished gentleman, and was flattered by his admiration.

It was well for me that my fancy was not caught, for some after developments of his character proved that neither his honor nor his principles would have been a safeguard for my inexperience. He made high pretensions, however; I saw him once, in the midst of a large party, suddenly march across the room, with a flushed face, and demand the import of a whisper between two young men, who thus violated the rules of good breeding by some trivial remark.

A part of my time was spent at Mr. Woleby's ; there I was much more retired, and, as I now know, in a situation much more proper and safe for an unprotected young girl. But Eleanor Bolles was quite pertinacious in exacting my stay with her ; and in her father's open house I felt more at home, less as a guest receiving hospitality from comparative strangers.

My heart beats with gratitude in recollecting the generous, motherly kindness of Mrs. Woleby to a poor stranger.

Many times have I looked back with astonishment, as well as with deep, thankful reverence, that my Heavenly Father so provided for my need, and put it into the heart of so many to show me kindness.

Mrs. Woleby ever welcomed me to her house ; she often called me daughter, and it was with the feelings of a Christian mother that she exercised a guardian care over me.

Her gentle Emilia was a favorite with all.

Unlike some who are caressed and admired abroad, and called sweet, obliging girls, but who are at home selfish, indolent, and ill-humored, her good and lovely character shone brightest there. She was kindly attentive to her parents, and always ready to minister to another's happiness, not with professions and promises, whose fulfillment was ever in the future, " as the manner of some is."

There was one boarder at Mr. Woleby's ; a young lawyer, who chose a more retired, or, perhaps, a more exclusive residence than at Mr. Bolles's, the usual resort of the young men of the place. This young man, Otis Gibbs, was called peculiar ; he was so, in his personal appearance at least, being shorter than most women, with a very large, white face, his shoulders broad and high, while his lower limbs were so slender that it apparently required an effort to maintain the centre of gravity.

He was extremely nervous and excitable, and often have I seen him, at a sudden meeting or at an unexpected occur-rence, reel and totter from side to side, with difficulty pre-serving his equilibrium.

Yet he was a young man of superior mind and excellent character, albeit deformed by various littlenesses, set notions, and weak points of temper.

He aspired to Emilia's favor, and would have won it, per-haps, could he have condescended to mingle more freely with others, and to unbend from his reserve and inflexi-bility.

At least, my reflections convinced me that his true worth and fine qualities, if but unfolded in fair light to the gentle, considerate girl, would have eclipsed in her mind any lack of mere external attractions. Certain I am that we both did him great injustice ; I, especially, made him the subject of many a jest.

He said of me, that " he should like me well enough, if I was not always either laughing or singing "—over which remark we had much girlish merriment.

Could he have seen me a few years later, he would probably have formed a very different estimate of my character.

My friend Emilia some years after this married a gallant sea-captain, and after a few brief years of domestic happiness, was successively bereft of her husband and four children.

It was just before the death of the fourth, a lovely and accomplished girl of eighteen, that we met again, for the first time since these scenes of our youth just narrated. It was after a lapse of thirty years—we had each been tried and shaken by deep affliction—we had each fixed our hopes and affections beyond this world.

We spent together one precious day—a day of. tearful reminiscence—of mutual experience—gratefully recognizing the hand of our Heavenly Father in all the dealings of His providence.

"For who the backward path hath scanned,
But blessed his Father's guiding hand."

Emilia has long since passed to her home in the skies.

Her mother, the last remnant of the once flourishing family, died a short time since, full of years and honors, having lived to see the rude settlement around her become a large, thriving, and beautiful city.

The homestead, though changed, and occupied by strangers, still stands upon its site, overlooking the Kenduskeag, now hidden from view, not as of yore by thick trees, but by long blocks of lofty dwellings, stores, bridges, wharves—all around instinct with the life and stir of business.

CHAPTER XXXVII.

NEW FRIENDS.

It was not long before the breaking up of the ice in the Penobscot, that several of us took an excursion up the river some six or seven miles, to visit at a Colonel Butler's.

The ride was not without danger, for though the trodden track on the ice was still safe, the least deviation from it might lead into thin places of greater or less extent, and horses and riders be precipitated at once into deep water.

We were to return by moonlight; but just as night came on, snow began to fall, soon obscuring the path so as to have required the utmost caution to keep in the track, even by daylight, and a return by night was not to be thought of.

To accommodate ten or eleven guests, called for strenuous exertions on the part of our hospitable host and hostess. The house was a common-sized cottage. There was a square entry in front, with a room on either side, one of them quite narrow, and containing the "spare bed." This, with two small bedrooms and a garret, comprised all the sleeping apartments.

The family consisted of father and mother, a hired man, three grown-up daughters, and a group of younger children

How were the eleven guests to be provided for ?

No difficulty at all ! The utmost hilarity and good

humor reigned among all parties, and the most thorough pleasure was taken in pairing off the company, making numerous partitions, with the aid of forks and nails, and plenty of coverlets and blankets ; the large common room being thus divided into four curtained compartments.

The beds were then shifted and shaken, separated and multiplied to the best possible advantage ; all lending a helping hand, amid much mirth, and the cracking of jokes, greatly enhancing the enjoyment of both visitors and hosts.

But this was not all the pleasure, as respects myself, for Colonel Butler taking occasion to inquire about my friends and home, I was both surprised and delighted to find that he had been an old neighbor and friend of my own mother.

He, on his part, was equally well pleased to see the child, as he said, of his fair schoolmate, Bessy Lyle, and he plied me with questions about my uncles and aunts, of whom for many years he had lost all knowledge.

"The last time I saw your mother," said he, "she was just about your age ; you resemble her some, but she was handsomer than you are. Oh," added he, smiling, "you look well enough. I dare say you are vain of your good looks now ; but Anna and Bessy Lyle were two of the finest girls on Roxbury street."

" Ah !" said he, "it was a sad time for that family when the father died ; your grandfather, I mean. Both parents were taken within a few months, and in the prime of life, too, for he was not more than forty-five years old ; not older than I am now. He died in his full strength—a portly, handsome man—and he looked, in his coffin, just as if he had fallen asleep in the full flush of health."

Colonel Butler informed me of many particulars respecting my grandparents and their children; made minute inquiries concerning the present situation of each, and of my own brothers and sisters, as well as the time and circumstances of my mother's death.

He regretted much that he had not known Mary and Dr. Emery; the news of the sudden death of the doctor had reached him, "but I little thought," said he, "that his wife was the daughter of my old friend Bessy Lyle."

He interested himself in my welfare, and warmly invited me to make his house my home, until I returned to my friends in Massachusetts.

I gladly accepted his proffered kindness. He came for me, in a few days, and I was quietly established in his pleasant but lonely cottage home, close upon the bank of the dark and rapid Penobscot.

Here I assisted the daughters occasionally in their household employments, and enjoyed many an hour with them in paddling up or down the river, in a little open boat or canoe, which I learned to manage with ease.

But their house was overshadowed with a great sorrow, during my stay there. That insidious destroyer of the young and lovely, Consumption, laid his inexorable grasp upon the second and fairest of the daughters; he placed his mark upon her blooming cheek, and at his icy touch the wan girl faded away like an April snow.

The family were long blind to the progress of disease,

unwilling to admit the possibility of danger, and even to the last they never mentioned death in her presence, or intimated their fears on her account. They were not religious people—seemed never to think of God, or the eternal world.

I was not utterly thoughtless; the voice of conscience was not altogether silent within me. I knew that I had no interest in the Saviour's pardoning mercy. I had sought none, nor cared to seek reconciliation with God. I was deferring the matter.

How wonderful the rich mercy of my Heavenly Father, that I was not left to my own chosen way! But though so regardless of my own best good, I was deeply anxious that poor Celia should realize her danger, and seek the salvation of her soul, ere it should be too late.

My lips were sealed; I could not bring myself to speak upon the subject, especially before the family; yet, whenever I was left alone with her, I would have my Bible with me in the room, to read in, if she desired it, till, by a sort of tacit consent, that became the only reading when she was left in my charge.

She would sit reclining on the bed, propped up by pillows, her bright, glassy eyes fixed on mine, as I read to her portions that I selected; answering her questions, and explaining the meaning in a manner surprising to myself, and as I could not have done, had I not, from early childhood, heard the Bible read, and been instructed in its truths, by my father.

The first day of May was the Sabbath. I do not recollect how it happened, but I was alone with her most of the day. I read to her several of the last chapters of the Book of Revelation—a singular selection for one so ignorant as myself; yet I was powerfully impressed by it—and as we conversed earnestly upon the mysterious import of that sublime portion of Holy Writ, we were both in tears.

At length she said, in a subdued tone, "You have done me a great deal of good since you have been here."

I could not speak ; and as some of the family now came into the room, I walked out by myself, desiring to be alone. I passed along the river's bank, through a clump of cedar trees and bushes, where all seemed a lonely wild—for there was neither house nor living object in sight—indulging the mood of my feelings ; sad, yet soothed.

The wood-thrush whistled ; the frogs croaked ; the open land had a drab and cadaverous complexion ; the mottled hue of the wooded wilderness around me, and across the river the dark tops of the firs, tinged with the yellow-green of the beech and the juniper's red-barked boughs ; the poplars' white trunks and spangled limbs spotting the whole with a faint glare ; while the jetty black, glittering stream, like a huge serpent, crawled along at the foot of the whole. All this, seen through thin clouds of mist as a veil, had a softened, indescribable effect. My thoughts reverted to Dr. Emery and his lonely grave—to myself, away from my home, and dependent on the hospitality of strangers—then, to poor Celia, just my own age, sinking into an early grave! for I knew she could not live, though she had for a day or two seemed better, and quite free from pain.

How strange appeared now my former thoughtlessness and light-hearted gaiety! how mad and foolish to live on, heedless of death and the dread realities of another world!

Resolutions were formed, and thoughts and feelings registered, that I was sure would not be again disregarded; but I knew not my own strength, or rather my own weakness, against the power of sin in the heart, and the fascinations of the world.

I returned to the house, to find all in confusion and wildest sorrow—Celia was gone!

She had been taken with a fit of coughing, not worse than others, but had suddenly fallen back and died, without a parting word or look.

I must not dwell on the sad scenes that followed—on the pall and gloom of burial—on the void that is felt in a house when the pleasant voice and sweet smile, so like sunshine to the heart, are quenched in the silence and darkness of the grave.

What can cheer the mourner's heart, if the peace of religion be wanting?

CHAPTER XXXVIII.

GOING HOME.

THE ensuing summer I was engaged, by Col. Butler's means, as teacher of the school in his neighborhood, the avails of which were most acceptable.

I visited Clemence, too, once more ; Mr. Wurth came for me at the instigation of Maggy. But it was a painful visit, awakening sad associations, and was the source of regret rather than of pleasure.

The Mudges were invited by Maggy to meet me at her father's. Miss Tella seemed more than ever sarcastic, and even unkind. Mr. Wurth was then a boarder with them, and I think she was vexed that I came there again, fearing the defeat of her own designs.

I bore, without appearing to notice them, several cutting retorts in the course of the afternoon, till at length she said something which quite broke down my self-command, and I burst into an uncontrollable fit of weeping. Nor could I get over it, but was obliged to leave the room, filling the family with concern, troubling Maggy extremely, and spoiling the pleasure of all.

The next day I returned, taking a long farewell of my kind friends the Campbells. With Maggy I kept up an occasional correspondence, till some time after she became the wife of Mr. Wurth; but our paths in life have been widely severed. Once again we met, but it was not until both had passed from the spring-time to the autumn of life.

At the close of my school, in accordance with my earnest desire, Col. Butler, and my Bangor friends, secured a passage for me to Boston, with Captain Gilpy, whose trusty and excellent character was well known.

At first I was the only female on board, but the captain's family residence being upon one of the small islands in the bay, he anchored his little vessel, and spent the first night on shore, taking me with him to his rock-girdled cottage. The next morning his niece, who lived with them, concluded to go with me, and visit some friends on Cape Cod.

She was a self-satisfied, bouncing girl, freckled and red haired, and rejoicing in the euphonious name of Marcy Toothacher; but she was one of my own sex, and I was glad of her company. I confess I did not feel particularly pleased when she proposed to accompany me to my Uncle Hastings's, in return for her uncle's hospitality to me; but I could not decline the honor, so, with some secret misgivings, I escorted her to my uncle's handsome house, and introduced her as a guest to pass the night. In addition to her ungainly person, she was coarse and repulsive in manner, and essentially verdant in everything pertaining to good-breeding.

Bessy was immensely diverted with her, and, though treated with perfect civility while there, the actions, looks, and name of Marcy Toothacher called forth many a witticism, and became the standing subject of raillery and mirth;

Bessy declaring that I deserved a premium for bringing them such a natural curiosity.

My cousin was busy in preparation for her marriage, soon to take place. Aunt Hastings kept me employed in answering questions and giving her an account of our life while we had been in Maine.

I had one day quite an animated discussion with Uncle Hastings upon the character of those Eastern people. He thought them mean and over-reaching in trade, with very lax ideas of truth and honesty, as well as coarse and profane in their language.

I warmly defended them from what I knew to be an aspersion of their character, and wondered that he could be so prejudiced and unjust towards them. I had, indeed, mingled with a refined and elevated class of people, far from being such as he represented. I did not consider that I was entirely unacquainted with the many fishermen and low craftsmen whom he chiefly saw, and who at that time probably fully justified his opinion.

My stay in Boston was prolonged two weeks, much against my wishes, but my father had no means of sending for me, and could not leave his farm-work sooner to come himself.

Ah ! that was a joyful meeting with my dear parent after so long a separation !

How I enjoyed the long, quiet ride of two days, every moment bringing me nearer home, and in which I seemed to have more close and affectionate intercourse with my father than ordinarily in many weeks.

It was a day or two after my arrival before home again shone out in its home-like aspect. How strange, yet familiar was every object !

Bessy was gone to her husband's home, and at first I missed her. Mary was there, looking hopeful and happy, and as lovely as ever.

Grace had, perhaps, a slight shade of dignity superadded, a sort of womanly bearing that sat very becomingly on her. Hester I had left an unformed, dumpy girl of fourteen. She had attained the rounded grace and composed air of the young woman ; short and full-formed, she had fair, round arms, a pretty neck, and a face of clear white and red, though with little pretension to beauty of feature, for her head was too large, and her square, broad forehead projected over her light blue eyes, injuring somewhat the symmetry of her face.

Hester was always in good humor ; quite too obliging, for she could never keep anything for herself that another wanted. She was constitutionally timid and fearful, and ever ready to blame herself on the slightest grounds. I have seen her so agitated during a high wind as to be nearly convulsed, yet making the utmost effort to conceal her sufferings, because ashamed of her want of self-control.

Her talent at mimicry furnished no small amusement to her friends, and she was quite distinguished among the young people for her fine voice in singing.

The younger children were so changed by the lapse of two years, that I felt myself quite a stranger to them.

Willy had always been remarkably small ; now he had

shot up into a tall boy, with a bright eye, a bold front, a ready jest, and the frequent witty repartee.

Little Rhoda, the youngest, the petted darling of her mother, was the imperious little queen of the household. She was a child of faultless beauty, but capricious, exacting, and self-willed ; not so much in natural disposition as through over-indulgence, and the ill-judged fondness of her mother. In her childhood and haughty youth she was almost disliked by her sisters, whom she quite looked down upon, but in after years she became lovely in character as in person, and greatly endeared herself to her family and friends.

At eighteen she was a bride, and beautiful as a dream. Queenly grace was in her elegant figure, and a spell of loveliness in her fair face.

She gave her hand to our young cousin, Mark Leland, the son of Uncle Harry and Aunt Kathy, the same who in his babyhood so won my childish admiration. He lived at some distance from us, and when he carried home his beautiful bride, there were few happier men, I ween. He was captain of a military company, and a great favorite, and, when dressed in his epaulets, he looked indeed a fitting match for his peerless bride.

High-spirited and generous, he had an ever-ready purse, which, unfortunately, was too soon empty, and Rhoda's subsequent life was a struggle with poverty, sickness, and deep affliction. She died, while yet in her prime, shortly after following to the grave her only son, a youth of great promise.

15

Poor girl! she had, indeed, many sorrows; but she nobly bore them!

Royal, our brother, next older, was a pleasant, quick-witted little fellow, a great favorite with us all.

It was not long before I felt quite at home with my brothers and sisters again, and the time of our separation faded into the past like an uncertain dream.

CHAPTER XXXIX.

SISTERLY CONFIDENCE.

" The tones
Of a most pleasant company of friends
Were in my ear but now."

ONE day, soon after my return, Mary and I had a long talk upon our life in Maine, and our friends there, each one passing in review, and old scenes lived over again.

Speaking of Mr. Wurth, she acknowledged she was in the wrong, in having felt so anxious that I should accept him.

"I was trying," said she, "to shape out your course myself, in my short-sighted ignorance, instead of viewing, as I ought, all events in the hands of God. How wonderful are the ways of Providence, and how little are we disposed to heed them! Aunt Hastings used to say that 'we walk as if enveloped in fog, not seeing the path that we take; but if we will look back, and scan closely the way we have come, we shall find it illumined in light.' One year ago, how dark and mysterious seemed the path my Heavenly Father was leading me! Now, all is clear. How wonderfully, too, you have been guided, led, and cared for, in your need, while a stranger in a strange land!"

After much similar conversation, she said, rather hesitatingly, "Sam Lyman has rented his farm, and opened a store in Westmead."

"Ah," said I, after scanning her face a moment, "he visits here again, does he ?" She nodded assent.

"Where is the family ?" said I.

"Oh ! didn't you know that Madam Lyman has married old Deacon Dudley, of Dudleyville ? He is quite wealthy, you know."

"Where are the sisters, Mary and Abby ?".

"Mary, as gentle and retiring as ever, is soon to be married to Samuel Dudley, the deacon's only son. Report says that Madam Lyman found means to break up an attachment between this son and a worthy girl living with them, on the plea that it was beneath him to marry one in the position of 'help.' Whether this is true or not, the match between him and Mary is now decided on, and she is worthy of him. He is a fine man, but some years her senior."

"And Abby ?"

"Abby has been a year or two with her sister, in Boston, and has altered so much, you would hardly know her. She is soon to marry Moses Chaplain, and be the lady-mistress of that large house and farm in Valleybrook."

"What ! Moses Chaplain, that used to be called the Western bear ?"

"The same. He is very rich, and that suits Mrs. Lyman well. It is said she had some hand in bringing it about, but Sam is not very well pleased with the match ; he thinks Moses's habits are not good, and that he thinks of nothing higher than raising fine cattle, and increasing his stock, which, he says, to make the main business of life, is quite beneath the dignity of man."

I smiled; for I recollected Sam Lyman's old way of speaking, and thought it precisely what he would say upon such an occasion.

Mary confessed that she was already engaged to her old admirer, saying she could not help feeling a grateful regard for him, because she had been his sole choice, though she had discarded him and married another; and that her feelings pleaded powerfully for him from the first renewal of his attentions, which had now been some months.

"Do tell me, Mary," said I, "what mother meant this morning, when she told Grace she was so nice, nobody was good enough for her?'

"Oh, she was referring to David Hill. He visits here sometimes, and though Grace likes him well enough as a pleasant acquaintance, that is all; and mother says she holds herself too high; that if she cannot be satisfied with David, and his nice house in Valleybrook, she hopes she will have to take up with a poorer chance, or none."

"David Hill is too shallow and ignorant," said I; "he knows nothing beyond his shop, and some pretty things to say to the girls. Grace would get tired of him, if she had to pass her life with him."

"So Grace thinks. She happened to speak of 'Paradise Lost,' when he was here one day, and he wished to borrow it. The next time he called, he brought back the book, saying that 'somehow he couldn't get the hang of it.'

Grace says she must be able to look up to a man, before she cau have sufficient regard for him to marry him.   David calls only as a friend, but he evidently admires her, and is probably hoping, in time, to gain her affections in return."

CHAPTER XL.

MASTER HOWARD AND CHARLES COKE.

" I knew there was a rival in the case."

My object is to give a plain, unvarnished recital of occurrences as they took place—a simple, true picture of fire-side scenes.   Life as it is, is made up of trifles, not of great events, therefore many minute and trivial details must enter into the story of this portion of my life—the short, remaining period in which we were all together—a band of sisters under our childhood's roof.

One, indeed, was already removed ; but our beloved Bessy was near by, an hour's walk would easily bring us to her wedded home ; nor were our visits there wont to be brief or seldom.

We were four happy sisters still at home, the youngest just sixteen.   The ensuing season was one of much gaiety.

Wayland boasted a numerous and goodly company of young people, and it was so easy to find occasions for meeting together.

There was the paring bee, and the quilting, and then the young men must have their husking match at the gathering in of the yellow corn, when the presence of their sisters was quite essential, to prepare as well as to partake in the social cheer of nuts, cakes, and apples.   In winter the singing school, sleigh-rides, and parties, filled up the time.

My relish for these scenes of gaiety was happily kept somewhat in check by the purpose I had formed to devote my time to improvement in some branches of knowledge; not only for my own benefit, but that I might be the better fitted for teaching.

Our "school at the brook," as it was termed because the little, square-topped school-house stood on the brink of the stream, was taught this season by a young gentleman, called, par eminence, "Master Howard," on account of his fine tact and success in teaching, as well as his excellent education.

He was about twenty-six years old, tall and spare with very light, thin hair, and small, deep-set eyes. Refined and gentlemanly he certainly was, yet not to my eyes prepossessing. However, he became a frequent guest at our house, and I was always happy to see him. He excelled in conversation, and was so enthusiastic in respect to the progress of his pupils, that to assist them at all times and seasons was his great delight.

I knew that he was pleased with me as a scholar; he expressed his pleasure at my improvement, and praised my readiness in mastering difficulties.

We were very good friends, and I thought of nothing further till one morning, near the close of the school term, happening to go unusually early, I found myself alone with the master. I was quite confounded when, after sitting by me a few moments aiding me in my lessons, he suddenly requested my permission to visit me occasionally.

I suppose my fright and confusion had the appearance of

an assent, though I scarce made any reply.   I was in a sort of maze all day, and in truth not very happy in the thought of the new relation in which he had placed himself towards me.   He had won my respect and regard as my teacher and friend, but I felt at that time no answering chord to a closer and deeper sympathy.

There was another who had, since my return home, made frequent visits at our house, whose presence always brought a thrill to my heart, with an undefinable intuition that I was the subject of his thoughts and the object of his calls.

This was Charles Coke, my old schoolmate, whose kindness I had often felt when a little girl, for he was ten years my senior.   He came at first only occasionally, with David Hill, then more frequently, until my acquaintance with "Master Howard," since which he had entirely ceased his visits, though I did not suspect that to be the cause till long afterwards.

The next season I spent in teaching, at a retired place called "Pudding Hill," about ten miles from home.

It was a neighborhood at the foot of a long, low hill, which rose in one spot to a round, bare summit, whose form suggested the name.   The road, lined with houses, orchards, and cultivated fields, skirted its base.   A bye-lane led to the little school-house, high up on the slope of the hill, deeply shaded by a grove of chestnut trees, whose branches waved close upon the windows, and to whose cool shade I repaired at the accustomed hour of "nooning," with my book and dinner, for the cousin with whom I boarded, lived a mile distant from the scene of my labors.

My friend, Mr. Howard, wrote me several letters while there, which I answered. These were mostly a mere friendly exchange on ordinary topics, for I had found courage to come to a sort of explanation with him, declining at present anything more than a friendly intimacy.

He still wished a correspondence with me, alleging that it would increase our acquaintance and be a means of improvement.

To this I willingly assented, for I was penetrated with gratitude for his preference, and felt myself honored by it. I well knew, too, who would be the gainer in the proposed "mutual" benefit of writing.

But I was not happy nor at ease ; Isaac Howard was not a man to be lightly rejected by any girl ; I could not deny that he was everything that I could ask, in his superior acquirements and excellent character ; much more, certainly, than I had reason to expect. I was now nineteen, and ought, surely, to be influenced less by mere fancy than by sober judgment.

Time after time I resolved to bring myself to the point, and settle down satisfied with the honorable, manly regard of one so unexceptionable ; but after making such conclusions a terrible oppression would come over me, as if something was irrecoverably lost, and I would again resolve still to defer the matter. I knew that my father desired to see his daughters well married ; he was poor ; could but just struggle along and provide for those dependent upon him ; and I may add—what was the simple truth—it displeased and vexed my stepmother to have us all at home.

I pondered much on the position of my sex, in respect to that which, of all things earthly, most affects their happiness. Having no freedom of choice but in rejection, did it then often occur that the secret preference must be ignored or quelled, and the sole alternative be, a single life with all its loneliness and dependence, or a union in which interest or expediency take the lead, leaving sacred, holy, deep affection in the background ?

Some such, doubtless, eventually become unions of souls, as well as legal bonds ; but how many ill-assorted couples we meet, who " worry along " together through life—both, perhaps, weary of their yoke !

I was annoyed, too, by the unwelcome attentions of a young man living near my cousin's—the agent in procuring my services as teacher. He made himself very officious during my term, in virtue of his office as director of the school, and manifested a most benevolent interest in my pupils.

A few days after my return home he came to visit me, but I treated him so coolly that he took his leave the same night ; being overtaken by a heavy shower, he lost his way, and after riding most of the night, arrived home dripping wet ; this furnished the subject of a witty letter from my cousin, affording us all some amusement.

One afternoon, shortly after the close of my school, Grace and I went, each on horseback, into Valley Brook ; whether for pleasure or upon some errand, I do not now remember ; but we chanced to call on our friends, Olive and Linda Coke, the sisters of Charles, who was standing in the door and took charge of our horses. I had not seen him for a long time, and a barrier seemed to have sprung up between us as if we had been strangers.

Somehow it was proposed by the Cokes to join us, and ride down the valley to Western, the next town. We con sented, all was soon agreed upon, and David Hill, their next door neighbor, made one of the party.

When starting off, I tried to manage to get between tho girls, Olive and Linda—partly to relieve Grace from David's exclusive attention, and partly wishing, I hardly knew why, to escape proximity to Charles ; but a movement of some of the rest brought me up close beside him and behind the others.

Wishing to say something in my embarrassment, I began to rally him upon his riding-stick—an extremely crooked one, which I had seen him select and carefully trim.

I asked him, " Why he did not cut a straighter stick ?"

He looked down a moment, then, with a peculiar sort of meaning smile, he answered,

" If I should have ever so nice a one, somebody would be getting it away from me."

" Perhaps not," said I, " unless you like to give it up."

These were trifling words, not weighing, apparently, more than straws, but in their effects, had a world of meaning.

The whole current of things was changed, and it seemed as if a veil was raised, not only between our hearts but on all the world around. I can look back on few scenes of my life with such unalloyed happiness as on that ride.

When we came back and parted at Mr. Coke's, Charles

came up to me, and said, in a low tone and with a glowing face—" Perhaps I shall be up your way to-morrow evening."

I bowed without meeting his eye, and rode swiftly away.

Reader—I was happy ! Not with the light-hearted, free, girlish gaiety of past years ; the source was deeper and broader ; the feeling more still—more profound.

My father was well pleased with my prospects ; my sisters full of good-humored raillery.

Charles Coke was what is called "well to do in the world." He was very ingenious in the construction of mills and all kinds of machinery, and he possessed, independently of his father, a pretty little cottage and some lucrative mills.

He was rather below the middle size, but finely formed, erect, and graceful, with clear, deep blue eyes, and fine features ; an expression at once grave and gentle, and a smile singularly sweet and winning. Such, at least, he appeared to me ; and as excellent in character as engaging in personal qualities.

He was quite commonly styled " Captain Coke," though far enough from being military in person or habit ; but the title that was at first given in sport had become a usual designation. Hester, in her mirth, used to call him " Captain Forehanded."

Meantime, Mr. Howard's last letter remained long unanswered ; and one morning late in the fall, I was surprised by a call from him. He appeared to be in haste, and, after sitting a few minutes in the common room, conversing, though not in his usual happy manner, he requested to see me alone.

We had but two other rooms below, one appropriated to our parents' use, the other a sleeping-room, in which Hester was now shaking the beds, all in the thickest confusion.

This was, however, the only place where I could speak with him in private, and, full of embarrassment, I ushered him in, much to the discomfiture of Hester, who speedily made her escape.

A single question sufficed for his errand. " Was I engaged ?"

I felt that fránkness was due him on my part, and I answered in the affirmative.

" To Captain Coke ?"

I bowed assent—he expressed a wish for my happiness, and immediately took his leave.

This was at the time a most unpleasant occurrence, and I wished he had fixed his thoughts on some one of the many others more worthy of him.

. How far distant from my imagination were the events yet with the secrets of the Future !

How wonderful the ways of Providence, seen in the light of the Past !

CHAPTER XLI.

NEW TROUBLES.

"MASTER Howard" was again teaching the winter school at "the Brook," and Charles Coke, though several years his senior, became one of his pupils.

Owing to the peculiar views and character of his father, Charles's early education had been neglected. The elder Mr. Coke thought nothing so desirable as the driving'forward, to the utmost extent, of the various branches of his business. His children he kept busy, the sons on the large farm, at the grist-mill, saw-mill, or in the clothier's establishment; the daughters, in the dairy, at the loom, or the spinning-wheel.

Charles had good native powers, and, in pursuance of his favorite mechanical arts, he desired greater knowledge of mathematical principles. In this Mr. Howard excelled, and therefore he was not ashamed, though verging on thirty, to apply to him for instruction. I esteemed him all the more highly for this. I was proud of his course, and loved him, if possible, still better for it.

Two things occurred, however, this winter, to mar my happiness, and disturb the fullness of my content.

I should before have said, that Mary and her old friend, Sam Lyman, were married early in winter, and went to reside at Westmead, a town some thirty miles distant, on the west side of the Connecticut.

Grace accompanied them, to spend the winter; so that Hester and I alone were left at home.

Hester's fine singing led to constant occasions for going to one place and another. Almost every day she was called for to meet a musical party, practice some new piece, or join some social company, and she, on her part, was always ready to go, for music was her delight. Her frequent companion in these gatherings was a young man named Albert Fayon, who lived in a remote part of Wayland, and with whom we had been little acquainted till now that his superior tenor voice became a sort of necessary accompaniment to Hester's fine treble. It was the time when the old fugning melody was so prevalent, the different parts chasing each other through the tunes with almost endless repeats.

Albert Fayon thus became a frequent visitor at our house, and very attentive to Hester. It was evident they liked each other well, and, indeed, for some time they had kept, according to the expression of the day, "particular company" together.

At length days passed, and he did not come—two weeks and more—and Hester went moping about the house, spiritless and heavy-eyed, dull and silent. She was usually talkative and lively, and accustomed to tell me every thing; but I waited in vain for her voluntary explanation of this mystery.

I finally sought, and at length obtained her confidence.

It appeared that, a few months previously, this young

man had been for some time a boarder in the family of Mr. Homer, the father of little Nabby mentioned in the former part of my story. She had grown up a tall, dashing girl, bold and hoydenish in manners, and quite free in the company of the other sex.

Now, to be brief, she found herself in trouble. Her parents were no longer in ignorance of her shame, and Albert, knowing the truth must soon appear, came to my sister and confessed his guilt, entreating her to overlook it, saying that the blame rested not altogether with him ; that his affections were still Hester's, and that he wished to marry her, if she would but accept him. Hester decided at once ; and, with a true womanly spirit, as well as according to principles of justice, urged him to make the atonement within his power to Nabby, by a speedy union with her.

She wavered not a moment in her decision ; she did not betray her feelings to him, but she was sorely stricken, Nor was the wound less deep because it was secret, and unsuspected to the eye of the world.

Hester never loved again.

She is living still in her maidenhood—a fair, cheerful, serene old lady. To want, sickness, and sorrow she has ever been the ministering angel of comfort. For these many years a devoted, humble follower of " Him who loved her and gave himself for her," who " went about doing good," she is looking forward, in the assured hope of being, ere long, transplanted to the heavenly garden, where the plants do not wither, nor the flowers fade.

Far happier has been her quiet lot than the stormy life
16

of Albert and his unprincipled wife ; for social crime not
seldom receives, even in this world, its own peculiar punish-
ment.　A union, necessarily lacking the foundation of
respect, could hardly be expected to, attain the super-
structure of affection ; and though they kept up the show
of domestic happiness, there were those who knew too well
that it was but a hollow pretence, and that the angel of
peace was almost a stranger in their dwelling.

I said there were two things that troubled me ; the
second recalls to mind that saying of the colored preacher,
"If you know any thing that will make your fellow-man
happy, *run quick* and tell it to him ; but if you hear what
will cause him grief, or trouble, keep it locked close in your
own breast."　Much sorrow would be spared, did all act
from this direction ; but, unhappily, an unwelcome report,
or an unkind speech, is sure to reach its object : some one
"feels it a duty" to repeat it.

It was intimated to me, about this time, that the Coke
family were not pleased with Charles's choice.　They said
I was "too lively, too fond of company and gaiety ; that I
should make him an unprofitable wife, drawing heavily
upon his purse-strings, instead of helping him forward in
life ; and withal, that, though proud enough, and fond of
appearing well, I was a poor girl, without a cent to do
with, and that Charles might have done much better."

I could not but feel that, from the genius of the family
and their habits, some such thoughts of me would naturally
arise in their minds, and I was deeply grieved at the idea of
appearing in such a light to the parents of my affianced

husband. Besides, if Charles heard such things said, would they not affect his own feelings towards me? This was a bitter thought, and I brooded over it some days, with a heavy heart, and swollen eyes.

Not wishing to meet Charles in this state of mind, I went over to Bessy's home, to open my heart to her, and seek her counsel. I told her all my wounded, resentful feelings, and that I had almost resolved to tell Charles we must separate, for I could not enter his family against their wishes.

"No," said my prudent sister, "do no such thing. Conquer your pride, and look calmly at the matter; it is best to look things fairly in the face, and then they often put on a brighter aspect."

"I have been thinking of little else for the last three days," said I.

"No," she answered, "you have only been looking on one side of it—the one reflected from your own wounded spirit. Very possibly you have heard more than was ever said, for you know a story loses nothing by being repeated. How did you hear it?"

"Sally Green told me; she stayed at our house one night last week, and we slept together, and she told me, because she thought I ought to know it. You know her brother Josiah's wife is Mr. Coke's eldest daughter, and she heard it from her."

"Sally Green loves to talk, too well," said Bessy. "It was not acting the part of a friend to tell you remarks that were never intended for your ear, if, indeed, they were ever made."

" I know it would not grieve her much to break off our engagement if she could ; she wants Charles herself. I have never reckoned her among my friends, still I think there must be some truth in it."

"Truth in it ?" said Bessy ; "certainly there is, and in the widest sense, too ; probably they have said something of the kind, nor do they ever say more than they feel ; but have they not reason for it ? You cannot deny that you are a poor girl, that can bring no dowry to your husband, and we must look at the light in which they view things, in order to judge correctly. They are all for work, and getting rich, and think it absurd to lay aside any business for visiting, or what they call frolicking ; dress they despise— and they never think of opening a book, for reading with them is a waste of time. We are different. It is then no wonder that they dislike to see their eldest son, so promising and well to do, in danger of ruin, as they think, from gaiety, company, and extravagance."

This was but probing the wound, and, with a pang at my heart, I looked up reproachfully, saying,

" Then we had best separate at once, for I could never please them, and should only make Charles unhappy."

" It is Captain Coke you expect to marry," returned she, " not the family. He is a man who thinks deeply, and observes well ; all this is known to him, and has doubtless been duly considered. I mean," said she, smiling, as I made a motion to speak, "that he is aware of the points of difference between his family and ours ; not that he sees just as his parents do ; his mind takes a wider range, and he looks at life—its purposes, duties, and enjoyments—in a different light."

"But I do so want to please them, for they are his friends."

"I think you will be able to do so in time. But even were it otherwise, it should be the same to you. Charles has chosen you as his life-companion—he values and seeks you for the qualities you actually possess. Therefore it only remains for you to stand up in your place with a modest self-respect, and act your part as well as you can ; complying with and conforming to the habits of the family as far as you deem consistent with duty and propriety."

" But, dear Bessy, is not this rather humbling advice ?"

" Humbling ? Perhaps it is ; but pride never makes us happier. The truest self-respect comes from a just appreciation of ourselves, and this constitutes real humility. He who is humble, in the true sense of the term, will always possess a certain dignity of character, an essential nobility."

I was at first but half satisfied, but a little reflection placed the whole matter in a new light, and, contrary to my first intention, I returned home the next morning, having a secret hope that I should see Charles in the evening at home.

He came, and our conversation turning upon the cultivation of the mind, I heard him, with not a little pleasure, express his views of its importance, of the value of good books, and of the benefit to be derived from reading and study. I had the sweet assurance that no misgivings arose in his mind as to the fitness of his choice, but that his estimation of me had the full consent of reason and judgment.

I was married the next spring, just before my twentieth birth-day. My husband was the man of my choice ; he was the handsomest and most wealthy young man of Wayland, and he was universally respected and beloved. My home in Valley Brook was a neat cottage, separated from the main road by a square lawn, bordered with trees ; lilacs and rose bushes were under the windows and about the doors. Another road crossed at right angles, and passing by the common entrance, ascended the steep hill-side, having on the left our blooming orchard, and on the right a green pasture, sprinkled with fine old chestnut trees, while further up the hill were our upper orchard and a plantation of sugar maples. The road winding along and over the rugged ascent, descended on the opposite side to the banks of the Connecticut, and to the pretty town of Dudleyville, spread out upon its fertile meadows, only five miles distant.

In front of our house this cross-road led down the gentle slope to the brook, there widening into a mill-pond ; and the sound of the blacksmith's trip-hammer, early and late, mingled with the ceaseless dash of the water. Skirting the mill-pond, on this side the brook, was a large, round clump of trees, like a verdant crown, on which the eye loved to rest. Beyond, the land rose abruptly, and far up, beyond a piece of woodland, a rocky pasture, and a strip of mowing, could be seen through the opening trees a glimpse of a red cottage, which was situated on a road near the brow of the hill, running parallel with the valley ; this was Bessy's home, less than a mile distant by the foot-path (kept well worn) through the woods and up the steep ascent. In plain sight from our cottage door, peeping through the trees, was the large, square-roofed mansion of father Coke ; rising in the background was the dark Pine Mountain, while close to us was David Hill's pretty house, neat shop, and trim garden. His young wife, Eunice Cotting, the sister of Bessy's husband, had long been one of my most intimate and loved companions.

As to earthly blessings, my cup was full. Rapt in a blissful dream, I was as happy for the next few years as any one can be who looks no higher than earth for her portion. Secure in the gift, I had forgotten the Giver. It seemed that my Heavenly Father, who had once and again spoken to me by the warning voice of His Providence, to lead me to Himself, was now proving me with the boon of earthly happiness—more pure and unmixed than often falls to the lot of mortals.

Alas ! Ingratitude and total neglect of my bountiful Benefactor was the base return !

CHAPTER XLII.

"IT WAS A DREAM, AND WOULD NOT STAY."

NEARLY five years had passed. Winter had set in early, and there was a deep fall of snow, though not yet quite December. The sleighing was excellent in the bright, keen, frosty air, and it was Thanksgiving Day, the great festival of New England.

Let us take a peep at my home, and the treasures there.

My husband was sitting near the fire ; his clear, manly brow lighted up with a look of serene content, as he gazed into the wondering eyes of the. tiny babe he held in his arms, whose little life had wakened into being scarce four months since. A little girl of two years, rosy and dimpled, stood at his knee. Her deep-blue eyes were the reflection of his own. She was full of childish prattle and gleeful ecstasy, to see her baby sister laugh and crow to her.

My precious boy, not quite four years old—a straight, chubby-cheeked, manly little fellow—was helping his happy mother to remove the breakfast things, with no slight sense of the valuable aid he was rendering.

We were to have a small but joyous gathering in our cottage that day, and I was busy in preparation. Fires were lighted in the two square rooms, the furniture furbished and arranged- in the best manner possible, and the bare, white floors freed from soil or dust. The turkey was ready for the spit, the great plum-pudding was in the oven, and long rows of pies, of diverse sorts, were set forth in goodly array in the pantry.

In due time the jingling bells announced the arrivals. First came Mary and her husband, now residing on his farm in Wayland, with their two little girls, Xenia, three, and Mary, one year old—sweet little children, with dark, curly hair, and witching black eyes. Next came Bessy and Brother Cotting ; he so grave and silent, yet laughing at the corners of his mouth with much quiet fun, when the joke went round. What he said was in a low, steady tone, scarce audible across the room, yet always replete with sense.

Two little sons had Bessy. Sammy, three years old, was quite a little miniature man, and both sober and roguish. Alger was a baby of a few months. Grace, too, was there, and with her a tall, dark man, of noble, engaging mien, whose name was Cunningham. He was a wealthy young farmer of Westmead, and he had won my beautiful sister's hand not long after Mary's marriage, and very proud of her was he. She, too, had a fair, blue-eyed baby-daughter, just able to toddle about the room. It was the first time Grace had been with us since her marriage, three years before. All marked a change in her : a still greater delicacy of form and feature. She was very pale, yet, with the least excitement, a warm flush would brighten her cheek, and an almost unnatural lustre would sparkle in her eye. She said she was well, and was all vivacity and happiness ; yet I trem·bled, for I thought of that insidious foe, consumption ; still my fears were much allayed by her assurances, and her evident enjoyment of life.

Hester completed the family group. She was to stay some days with me, and she now found ample employment in watching and admiring all the pretty ways of the little nephews and nieces. She was extremely fond of children, having her favorites among them, whom she would caress with a warmth almost amounting to rapture.

After our substantial dinner had been duly discussed, the gentlemen went together to visit the respectable inhabitants of the barn-yard and the sty, and to inspect their horses; returning to sit over the kitchen fire, discussing politics, farm, and town affairs; while we, the sisters, were by no means silent. Questions were asked and answered, laughing reproofs administered, jests retorted, and advice asked and given. We talked of our children, unfolding to each other all the particulars of our separated lives—our pleasures and perplexities, joys and sorrows.

Two weeks after this happy meeting a very different group were gathered in the same place. There were low tones, hushed voices, faces that were pale, and hearts gathering despair: it was the chamber of mortal sickness. In a corner near the fire stood three physicians, talking in subdued accents, and glancing from time to time to the bed near the middle of the room, on which lay the sufferer, tossing wildly—his strong, well-knit frame convulsed with agony. Anxious friends were about his couch, and his young wife bent over him, in anguish of soul, praying for life—only life!—praying against hope, with all the might of despair, that this sickness might not be unto death.

That anguish, that despair, was mine! That cup was given to me to drink!

My husband had been ill a week, the fever increasing every moment in violence, and baffling all the skill of the physicians. They said there was no hope! Late in the evening he became quiet; the intensity of suffering had spent its force, and exhausted nature was giving way before it—or, was it the crisis between life and death, and might he not rally again—the vigor of life within him triumph over the strength of disease? No! the cold dew was on his brow—he was dying! His eye all at once steadied, fixed, and settled on mine with earnest meaning—"Anna!" said he, "we must part!"

"I cannot have it so!" I cried, with a burst of anguish. "You must not die, and leave me! you cannot be spared!"

He closed his eyes, as if wrestling with his feelings. Forcing myself, at length, to be more calm, I asked the fearful question, "Are you willing to die?"

He paused a moment, with eyes still closed; he was summoning all his strength of spirit to the dread encounter. "I am willing," he said, at length; "all must meet their doom."

Oh! the bitterness of that hour! Even at that awful moment came a flash of conscious guilt into my mind, as if a mocking spirit said, "You have cast off your God, broken your resolutions, lived as if there were no death—no here after—and now He will not heed your prayers!"

Our little son was brought to his bedside. "Love your mother," said he, "and take care of her." He stopped—a violent paroxysm of pain came on—the struggle was terrible—and ere midnight he was no more.

Ah! that day of sorrow! Utterly prostrate, helpless, impotent, and desolate—my idol, my life, my all was snatched away! My sky was dark, the star of hope clean gone—the bright sunshine was a fierce glare—clouds and storms the angry scowl of defiance! Even my children, before my joy and treasure, at first only seemed to add weight and poignancy to the blow.

Thousands there were who lived on as I had done, in total neglect of God; walking in the light of their own eyes, and after the counsels of their own hearts; yet they were not smitten—their sun went not down at noon—their idols were not cut off!

Such was the daring language of my rebellious heart; thus I arraigned the justice of the Disposer of all!

CHAPTER XLIII.

"BEHIND THE CLOUD IS THE SUN STILL SHINING."

BETTER thoughts came—the promptings of the spirit of Grace. I learned to look up to God—blessed be His name! with sweet submission—to recognize His tender love even under his afflictive rod.

But it was long ere the bitterest drop of all was taken away. I knew that he who was gone had lived-not only thoughtless of God, but profoundly ignorant of His word and His will. His parents professed a belief in universal salvation, but lived literally "without God in the world." They never went to meeting ; their children spent the Sabbath as they listed, frequently attending church because other young people did, but were entirely heed- less of their obligations to their Creator. This had troubled me occasionally ever since my marriage, but now the thought was a constant leaden weight upon my heart, with a keen sense of my own guilty lack, for I had been religiously in- structed from childhood. I knew my duty, but I did it not. Who could know what the effect might have been of my example and influence on my Charles, ever so kindly obser- vant of my wishes, so ready to listen to me, even to solicit the expression of my inmost feelings.

My tortured mind dwelt on the parting scene. I strove

to fix on his words, " I am willing," as an anchor of comfort ; but my soul saw too clearly now—all mists were rolled
back ; the spirit could indeed nerve itself to meet that
which could not be shunned—with no alternative ; the body
wrung with pain might choose death rather than life ; but
was this the Christian's hope—the believer's trust ?

But after a time this, my heaviest burden, was mercifully
lifted, and I was enabled sweetly to commit all my cares
and sorrows to Him who is mighty to save. A God glorious in Love and Mercy became the great subject of my
thoughts, seeming to fill my whole being and the whole mea-
sureless universe around me. The world was as nothing.
I wondered at my past life ; it seemed such an amazing
state of blind selfishness and ingratitude.

I thought of myself not as a child of God, but as one of
the least of his creatures ; yet my mind was calm and peaceful, and I even felt a sort of serene joy in the thought that
my earthly happiness had been yielded up at His sovereign
fiat, as if immolated on His altar. I repeated continually
in my heart, " the Lord loveth a cheerful giver"—and the
words brought refreshing comfort. My feelings at this
time were all within my own breast ; none spoke to me of
the state of my mind, and though the words were ofttimes
on my lips, a shrinking reluctance prevailed, and I opened
my heart to no one. Gradually light shone upon my path,
and my duty to my God, and to my children, began to stand
out to my view; it became my great purpose and desire first
to confess Christ before men, then to nurture for Him the
precious souls he had entrusted to me.

My soul thirsted for some communication, sympathy, and counsel, upon this subject. My father, to whom I longed to unfold my anxieties, was ill in health and I saw him but seldom, never alone. About this time my Uncle James Lyle accompanied me to the shiretown to see the judge on the business of settlement. He being " first deacon " of the church, as well as a revered relative, it seemed a favorable opportunity to speak upon the matter nearest my heart. Accordingly, with much diffidence and hesitation, I commenced, saying that my thoughts had been of late much exercised upon the duties of religion—that I had a wish to unite myself with the people of God.

He answered at once, in a quick, careless manner,

" It will be a very good thing. You had better join the church by all means."

I cannot describe how I was chilled and thrown back upon myself by this indifferent tone and manner, as if something most dear and sacred to me had been rudely handled and treated as of no moment.

Uncle Lyle was, I truly believe, a good man—a follower of the Saviour—and was looked upon as a model of piety ; but religion at that time seemed veiled and hidden—a candle under a bushel—not upon a candlestick, giving a light to all around.

But my Heavenly Father provided for my need—sending to me, from a quarter where I least expected it, that great blessing—a true Christian friend.

Mrs. Chaplain, in the former part of my story mentioned as Abby Lyman, now the wife of Moses Chaplain, lived about half a mile from my dwelling, further down the valley on the main road. Their house was, however, just within the boundary of Western, the next town, where she attended meeting, and I was ignorant of the great change Divine Grace had wrought in her, taking hold of all the strong powers of her soul. She knew nothing of my religious state, for we had had but occasional intercourse.

Quite unexpectedly, early one morning, she came, bringing her sewing in her hand, to sit and talk with me. She said it had been in her mind to come, from day to day, ever since my affliction.

"And now, my dear," said she, "is it all right between you and your Father above, whose hand is laid so heavily upon you? Can you look up?"

My answer was a burst of tears, and an earnest impetuous cry broke from my lips,

"I can say from the depths of my heart, 'just and merciful are all His ways.'"

Then followed between us a long, unrestrained conversation; the flow of mutual experience, of the dealings of God with us. It was as a fountain of cold water to my parched soul.

Mrs. Chaplain had had many and severe trials. Her husband, who inherited a large and valuable farm, was a coarse, illiterate man; a hard worker and a hard drinker; hurrying and driving upon his farm-work, and giving heed to nothing beyond; withal bitterly opposed to what he was wont to style, with an oath, "religious ways."

His wife was a large-souled, noble woman, of great independence; by which I mean, that she was fearless in doing what she considered to be right. When she felt it her duty to profess her faith in Christ publicly, she did so, without consulting or informing her husband, for he never went to the house of worship ; she would not risk his refusal ; he had forbidden her to attend any religious meeting except on the Sabbath, and instead of aiding her to go then, he would place every obstacle in her way, and often she would take the horse from the stable or pasture herself, and ride off alone to the little church four miles distant.

Her little son, instead of being permitted to go with her, was many a time taken by his father to some scene of revelry, to witness drinking and profaneness in his own parent, learning ways which wrung the heart of his mother.

At home, if her husband chanced to find her engaged in reading the Bible, his anger knew no bounds. Coarse and vulgar language, even personal abuse, were then her portion, yet she bore it all with exemplary patience.

Nor was she exempt from sorrow of a different nature. Sickness visited her family, and death once took from her tender embrace an infant of only a few days by a distressing accident. Her nurse had been called away, and the child was for a short time entrusted to the care of a young housemaid. By some unpardonable awkwardness she let the little thing fall upon the stone hearth, dislocating its tiny limbs in a most shocking manner. I was soon sent for, and found all my sympathies called into full play between the grieving mother and the horror-stricken girl, who could not forgive herself for her blundering carelessness.

17

Death soon relieved the little sufferer from its anguish, but the mother at first "refused to be comforted."

Still, in this as in all her sorrows, she "went and told Jesus," and from the rich supplies of Heavenly comfort which she received at His bountiful hand, she was enabled to dispense to others.

Her trials taught her to feel for the woes of the afflicted, and many a lesson of resignation and trust did she teach to me by her example and her counsel.

CHAPTER XLIV.

MRS. CHAPLAIN.

" A perfect woman, nobly planned,
To warn, to comfort, and command;
And yet a spirit still, and þright
With something of an angel light."

" Her noble deeds leave 'footprints on the sands of time,' and her good works,
'such as become those who profess godliness,' find record in the Book of Life." ·

THE remembrance of my friend, Mrs. Chaplain, awakens in my mind many interesting reflections. I love to trace the threads of her checkered web of life, and by the recital of her subsequent course, and the fortunes of her children, recall her history, and note the manner in which the many trying passages of their lives have been conducted by an overruling Providence to such happy issue.

" Evil men," we are told, " shall wax worse and worse." The conduct of Moses Chaplain to his workmen and neighbors became more and more surly and overbearing. His downward career was a rapid one. Through frequent drunkenness and nightly carousals, his business was neglected, and his property wasted, till, from the accumulation of debt, he was forced to the sale of his large farm and handsome house, for the satisfaction of the reasonable demands of his numerous creditors.

Abby Lyman had been induced to become his wife by the

persuasions of her ambitious mother, Madam Dudley, in whose eyes wealth was the highest qualification, overtopping every other characteristic, whether of mind or person.

To her imperative sway Abby was ever accustomed to yield with unquestioning deference ; and, affectionate in her nature, she no doubt thought she loved the wealthy young suitor on whose advances her mother evidently looked with so much favor. Her after-life proved that it was a cruel sacrifice upon the altar of Mammon : her best feelings were outraged by coarseness and cruelty ; the common rights and amenities due to a wife—to a woman, sensitive and refined— were rudely trampled upon ; she was reproached and ridiculed on account of her religion, and constantly annoyed by acts of petty tyranny. It is written, "that all things work together for good to them that love God," and doubtless the severe trials of Mrs. Chaplain, under the disciplining hand of her Heavenly Father, thus wrought out good for her, strengthened in her soul the upright purpose, made her spirit pure, patient, lovely; and calling forth the nobler elements of her character, fitted and prepared her for the arduous work she afterwards accomplished, that of providing for her young family, and training them up, unassisted, save by the blessing of God, for stations of usefulness and honor. When, by the bankruptcy of Mr. Chaplain, his family was left without a home and penniless, the mother roused her energies and took upon herself the burden of their support. With courage and resolution, she looked at her position and formed her plans. Some distant relatives of her father, Colonel Lyman, who were wealthy, resided in

Boston : to them she made known her situation and wishes, and, by their favorable aid and patronage, she was eligibly established as mistress of a boarding-house, in a central part of the city.

There, in arduous and severe labors, no less than in judicious plans and efforts, her ample energies were successfully applied to the maintenance and education of her children. There were deep struggles with poverty, there was the breaking down of pride ; for, in her country home, hers had been a commanding position ; but these things she endured and overcame, in the humble spirit and with the strong faith of the Christian. The younger children were sent to the excellent schools so justly the pride of Boston, and the services of the elder made available in different ways. Two sons were, after a time, placed with a goldsmith, and became masters of that lucrative trade. The two daughters wrought with their needles, with industry and ingenuity, and were soon able to provide for their own wants; and availing themselves of the advantages of education within their reach, subsequently became accomplished teachers. Charlotte, the elder, a girl of strikingly fine appearance, was in her childhood unlovely in temper, and, like her father, sometimes peevish, and frequently overbearing and selfish. But these faults of her natural disposition she was enabled, by divine grace, to conquer so fully, that as a young lady she became as truly engaging in character as in person, and united in a rare degree the sweet, lowly virtues and graces with a fine queenly bearing and noble dignity, peculiarly charming. She became the wife of a man of eminent worth and respectability, and, surrounded by her lovely young family, deservedly enjoys no small share of earth's richest blessings. The younger sister, the gentle and lovely Emily, ever, from early childhood, the darling of the household, was always delicate in constitution and health : she died young, and died most happily, leaving behind her a sweet savor of the power and blessedness of the religion of Christ. There were two younger sons : of these, one fills a professor's chair ; the other lives, a prominent and useful Christian, in the city. Thus, during all these years, this heroic mother had struggled on, patiently meeting and overcoming every obstacle, till she saw all her children pious, honored, and happy. In words describing another, " her good sense, assiduity, tenderness, and vigilance overcame every obstacle ; and as the richest reward of a mother's solicitude and toil, she had the happiness of seeing her children come forward with a fair promise into life, filling the sphere allotted to them in a manner equally honorable to themselves and to the parent who had been the only guide of their principles, conduct, and habits." What greater reward for a mother !

The besotted husband and father she supported, mainly, from their first removal. He hung as an incubus on her steps, a constant source of grief and mortification. At first he obtained a little stall in the market, and purveyed somewhat for the comfort of the family ; but old habits and fresh temptations subjected him to their debasing thrall, and bound him in a willing chain, until at length he was arrested for debt. By the exertions of his family he was soon liberated, but again he plunged into excesses, and, for some offence against the law, was lodged in the common jail.

After some years, Mrs. Chaplain obtained a divorce from her unworthy husband, and his children subsequently placed him in the household of a poor cousin in his native Wayland, amply providing for his support and comfort. There he still lives, the decrepit wreck of his own vicious habits, a mournful monument of the evils of self-indulgence. A proper control first of his temper, then of his appetites, might have prolonged to him health, wealth, and loving friends; but the adage is thus again verified, "A man's worst foes are often within himself." After the toilsome pilgrimage up life's rugged hill, Mrs. Chaplain's evening is spent upon its tranquil summit; for,

> " Rightly it is said
> That we descend into the vale of years;
> Yet I have thought that we might also speak,
> And not presumptuously, I trust, of age
> As of a final eminence, a throne
> That may be likened unto his,
> Who in some placid day in summer looks
> Down from mountain-top."

Respected and beloved by many friends, and tenderly cherished by her grateful children, she resides in the luxurious homes of her prosperous sons, whose names are well and honorably known.

In the shifting turns of life, my early friend, Abby Lyman, and myself, have at different times enjoyed much pleasant companionship, not only in Wayland, but in Boston, in which place I, too, in the providence of God, afterwards

found a home.   It is now many years since we have met ;
we shall not probably meet again on the shores of time, but
a future communing will, I trust, be ours, when we shall
"sit together in heavenly places," in a world of blessedness,
peace, and love.

"Blessed are the pure in heart,"

CHAPTER XLV.

SOWING AND REAPING.

> " All ye who run in Folly's race,
> To win a worthless prize—
> Learn from the simple tale we trace,
> Where true contentment lies !"

In connection with the Chaplains, whose story has been narrated in the last chapter, another family rises to my recollection, also neighbors, who lived at about an equal distance from my home in another direction. To my mind, the different fortunes of these two families, contrasted, form a history both marked and instructive. Let me briefly trace that of the Rosses.

At the time of which I would speak, both families were rich, and exerted much sway in their immediate neighborhood. Esquire Ross was a tanner, and had a large and flourishing business. He possessed a wonderful facility for making money flow into his own coffers, and had acquired a handsome property in Valley Brook. Some points in his character, as well as circumstances, resembled those of Moses Chaplain, whose churlishness, even when young, gained him the appellation of the " Western Bear." Esquire Ross, too, was not unfrequently stern in manner, surly and curt in words, and overbearing to those in his employ. When seeking to secure some end, however, he could be bland, even facetious and merry. He was strictly temperate in his habits, passably intelligent, and possessing much natural shrewdness, he wielded no small influence in town affairs ; but he was regardless of principle, and his heart was utterly steeled against the necessities of the poor, or the interests of others, when in conflict with his own.

In spite of these dark shades in his character, however, he was better than his wife ; for, with equal lack of right principle, and, if possible, greater selfishness, she was ignorant, little-minded, and excessively vain, constantly exacting the homage of others to their various displays of wealth. The absence of a moral sense of right, and the felt obligation of duty as a principle of action, was lamentably apparent in the guidance of her household. Their eldest was an idiot, but they had several fine children, who, with the early influence of right motives, might have been trained up to good and noble impulses, and have possessed a strength of moral character able to defy the seductive temptations of youth. Lessons of some kind, children will inevitably learn; habits of mind, either good or bad, will surely be formed— while we think not of it, impressions may be dropped into the mind of a child like seed in a fertile soil. The teachings of Mrs. Ross, both by instruction and example, fostered pride of heart, and frivolous ostentation of wealth, and contempt and supercilious demeanor towards others less favored in fortune than themselves. We mingled more or less in the usual social and neighborhood courtesies ; our children went to the same school, and played together, and in such limited circles the influence of each person is correctly rated, and usually tells, too, in its effect upon the others.

She would say to a child when going from home to visit, or even when going to church—

" Now, hold up your head ; you are dressed like a pink, better than any other little girl, and your father is the richest man in town."

Such teaching, from a parent, brought forth its fruit in the ready soil of the heart.

She was a fond and careful mother in respect to the outward comfort of her children, and especially as to their appearance in the eyes of others ; but while their bodies were fed and clothed sumptuously, evil and noxious weeds were early nurtured in their too pliant hearts. " Bad habits are the thistles of the heart, and every indulgence of them is a seed from which will spring up a new crop of weeds." A natural consequence was, that the young Rosses thought their own opinions, their own dresses, their own possessions of whatever sort, superior to those of any or all of their associates. A ludicrous instance of this was shown in the expression of one of the little boys while one day visiting a playmate. The graveyard was near, and they had gone to amuse themselves by reading the lettering upon the stones, when some trifling altercation arose, and little Master Ross ran pouting off by himself, and taking his seat astride upon a tall stone, he exclaimed,

" I don't care—my grandfather's gravestone is bigger than your grandfather's gravestone is."

Almost a caricature upon the absurd points upon which superiority is often claimed in older circles.

The Sabbath—that moral safeguard—was with this family a day of pleasure-seeking and idle roaming. To church, indeed, they usually went, and experienced the gratification of attracting much general notice ; but the remainder of the day was devoted to riding or visiting—their children being left to follow such amusements as their fancy dictated. In fruit time, their apprentices and workmen, young men and lads, with their sons—a noisy company— would frequently on Sunday pass my cottage, on their way up the hill, to regale themselves with some choice fruit from " Widow Coke's orchard," making no secret of their purpose, nor deigning to ask permission.

The conscientious observance of the Sabbath, I have ever noticed, acts as the strong bulwark of morals and religion, and as a wall of defence against temptations to evil. On the contrary, let the obligations of holy time be disregarded, and the day be given up to idleness and recreation, and a gate is opened to vice and irreligion in every form. Thoughts on Sunday should be the best and most effective of any during the week ; good thoughts enter the heart most easily and most deeply then, and with least disturbing influence from the world.

Few minds are unobservant of the many wonderful turns in human life—unthought of—unnoticed, perhaps, by the busy actors in the scene—by which the Sovereign Arbiter of great and small among men, disposes of families in the working of His providence.

The dealings of God in the history of families and individuals, as well as of nations, are often mysterious to us, inscrutable in purpose, and as if governed by chance ; yet a retrospective view shows us a clear and constant connection between character and destiny. The family exists, as such, only in this world, and although personal accountability is to be referred to eternity alone, yet who can doubt that parents and children, brothers and sisters, are dealt with here, according as they have severally met their mutual relations and obligations. In the subsequent career of the children of Esquire Ross, this may be distinctly noted. For some time all went prosperously with them ; their wealth enabled them to flourish in pomp and splendor, equally feared and caressed, though truly loved and esteemed by few. But a change came : Pamela, a sweet child, the youngest and loveliest of their blooming circle, and not long after the youngest boy, also an uncommonly fine child, were both removed by death. Their idiot son, always a source of great mortification to the parents, became, on reaching adult age, very troublesome and unmanageable, displaying extremely low and brutal propensities, so that he was the fear and terror of the neighborhood. There were two sons besides ; the elder of these disgraced himself by effecting the ruin of a poor servant girl in his own father's house, and when exposure came, denied his guilt, and, abetted by his haughty family, traduced the girl and left her to her fate The younger son, while a mere lad, plunged into the worst and vilest excesses, and became notorious as a common thief and vagabond, and in early manhood died miserably, no one knew where, even his own family apparently taking no notice of his death, for his name had ceased for some time to be mentioned in his father's house. I well remember him as a lively, high-spirited, and handsome boy, the favorite of his mother. She did not live to know his sad career and miserable end. She fell into lingering ill-health, without herself apprehending any danger ; while others marked her as the victim of consumption, she shut her eyes to her increasing weakness and hectic symptoms, still cherishing the hope of returning health ; her portion was in this world, and she could not bear the unwelcome thought of death. At the very last, she died in her chair, almost with the words on her lips—"I can not die now ; I *will not* die ; save me, doctor !" As the words floated away on the air, a paroxysm of coughing stopped her breath for ever !

Three daughters were left ; Mary, the eldest, was a showy girl, with a brilliant complexion and fine eyes ; she had, too, many superficial accomplishments, and possessed good natural powers, with some shrewdness like her father ; but the lack of moral principle led her into a fatal mistake in respect to that matter justly considered of greatest moment to woman, and which, perhaps, more than any other, displays her true qualities of heart.

She had gained the affections of a young physician, an honorable, high-minded man. They were pledged in marriage and the preliminaries arranged, when she chanced, at one of her gay visits, to fall in company with a dashing young merchant from a distant village, reputed as wealthy.

He was attracted by Mary's beauty and lively manners,

and his attentions being well received, he pursued them ; his vanity was gratified by her evident favor, and with a mischievous desire to supersede her love, and exhibit his own superior attractions, he continued his assiduities, and became a regular visitor. The designing girl blinded the eyes of her affianced lover by various deceits and subterfuges, for some time receiving the visits of both gentlemen. On one occasion, the two were at her house at the same time, she adroitly managing to share her company, alternately, with each. At the close of the evening, the unconscious dupe of her treachery took his leave in good. faith, and with full confidence in her affection ; the ensuing day he received from her a short, unfeeling note of dismission ; thus she ruthlessly cast away the true affection of a noble-hearted man.

She soon after married her new lover, and in little more than a year she found herself the wife of a ruined man—a spendthrift, dissolute and worthless ; his wealth was wasted by excess, and he had no longer money or character, while her life was embittered by his ill treatment ; for as their union was not founded on mutual respect and esteem, neither was it cemented by enduring affection, and her life passed in a vain struggle of wounded pride to keep up the appearance of gentility, and maintain a precarious and doubtful position among the gay and fashionable. Her sister, nearest in age, Martha, a small, dark-complexioned, black-eyed girl, was by far the most estimable of the family ; she was early united to an old schoolmate of her childhood, a well-meaning man, with whom, indeed, she lives happily, but his inefficiency and feebleness of character and purpose, led to their frequent removal from place to place, each time becoming poorer, till at length they went to a manufacturing village, and there the daughter of the proud Mrs. Ross, with her husband—they had no children—became daily operatives in a cotton mill. One other daughter remained —the sparkling Julia ; she most resembled her mother in person and character, and coming upon the stage after her father had acquired large wealth, full scope was given to her vain pride and love of display.

Lively and witty, the youngest of the family, petted and caressed, she deemed that the ascendency of wealth and station screened her name from the effect of each folly and extravagance, and after a giddy course of gaiety, she gave her hand, while yet quite young, to a man of equivocal reputation, a broker of the city, one of those characters who always have money to spend, but no one can divine by what means. And now, with an establishment in a style of lavish profusion, in a fashionable quarter of Boston, the gay Julia thought herself highly favored, and like the silken butterfly, lived only in the thoughtless present ; her associates were the very froth of the heartless and corrupt city circles of gaiety—the mere devotees of pleasure, and their baneful influence took effect ; in two or three years from their marriage, it began to be whispered abroad that Julia Ross and her husband had separated ; soon it was known that she, with her child, had sought a home with her dressmaker, and was ostensibly supporting herself by her needle. Vague rumors there were, of visits, evening rides, and costly presents;

but the particulars of the sad story of shame, no one knew; her thoughtless levity, and the gratification of early-fostered vanity, opened a too ready avenue to the seductive approaches of vice.

Henceforward she held no communication with her sisters, nor ever visited her father's house, and not long after she went far from her friends, and the scenes of her girlhood, to a southern city, and her fate is involved in obscurity.

Esquire Ross still lives, as grasping and worldly as ever, soured in temper—an unhappy old man. His large, empty house, is not enlivened by the cheerful presence of dutiful children, nor by the happy voices of grandchildren.

The garden has fallen into decay, the house looks weather-beaten and gloomy ; it is as if the frown of God rests upon the household who " acknowledge not Him in all their ways."

18

CHAPTER XLVI.

"NOT LOST, BUT GONE BEFORE."

"The life which is, and that which is to come,
Suspended hung in such nice equipoise,
A breath disturbs the balance."

IT was not many months after the death of my husband,
when time, the healer, had but just begun to subdue the
poignancy of my bitter grief, that I was called to a new
sorrow.   Grace—our beloved sister, the fairest of the flock—
was soon, we plainly saw, to exchange her earthly home for
a heavenly one.   She had always been delicate in constitution, and after her marriage she had gradually faded, till at
length consumption was written on her pallid brow and
flushed cheek, in unmistakable characters.

Her kind and indulgent husband, Mr. Cunningham, strove
by every means in his power to avert the threatened blow.
By the advice of able physicians, he took her to the sea-
shore, accompanied by the loving Hester, whose gentle ministrations were ever grateful to the languid invalid, in the
fond hope that the invigorating breezes might renew the
wasting strength in her feeble frame.   But all failed of the
desired effect, and she longed to see once more her native
hills.

She came home by slow and easy stages, and for a few
days she rallied, and our hopes were again raised for her

recovery. Again she sank, and then we knew it was too late to hope. We watched her sadly, but at last she said, "I am content to die," and left her sorrowing husband with the care of two motherless babes. While yet in apparent health, she had made her peace with God, and we felt that now the tired spirit had gone home.

It has been said that when Death enters a house, he takes care to leave the door upon the latch, that he may be able to come in again before the close of the year. Soon after our darling Grace was laid in the tomb, we were hastily summoned home to see our father for the last time. For some years past he had been partly deprived, by paralysis, of the power of speech, and, unable longer to perform the arduous labors of the farm; he had spent much time at the homes of his married daughters, in whose children he took a lively interest.

He did not, like some aged persons, turn away in disgust from all the concerns of life, because no longer able to be a prominent actor upon its busy stage. There is sometimes a species of self-deception, it is to be feared, in the apparent love of solitude, the silence, the seeking of retirement, in which to fit for heaven, after the best years have all been spent in the service of the world. Is it not often the result rather of selfishness and dissatisfaction, an unwillingness to see those younger, and possibly less wise and worthy, standing in the place once theirs? My father felt that there was still a good which he might perform, though small, not unimportant, and in the endeavor he no doubt found a reward. He was the consoler of the sick and distressed, the friend and instructor of the young, to whom he was ever ready to impart, with cheerful kindness, the many lessons he had learned by long experience and observation. His counsels were bestowed, not chidingly, not with harsh reproofs, not in a dictatorial or arrogant manner, but with a look and tone that left no room to doubt that his only motive was to benefit those whom he addressed.

Latterly, his increasing infirmities had confined him more closely at home, and in our frequent visits we usually found him seated in his comfortable arm-chair, with the Bible upon his knee, or lying upon the little table beside him; ever cheerful and placid, his face expressing in every lineament the peace of heaven.

At the mournful summons now, we gathered around his couch. We were all there. Willy and Royal, now tall, athletic youths; Bessy and Hester, Mary and I; while Rhoda, now almost as lovely as had been our Grace, held the hand of the dying man.

With a blessing for each, spoken in faltering accents, he gave us one more look of affection, then closed his eyes, and we stood, the living with the dead.

"A beauty fair and deep lies around the hollow eye and the sunken cheek, breathed from the calm air of the untroubled spirit that has heard, *resigned*, the voice that calls it away from the dim shades of mortality."

CHAPTER XLVII.

PARTINGS BY THE WAY.

——— " A shadowy band
Rise, like remembered music on our ears,
And vanished hope, whose arch of promise spanned,
The coming years."

IT was at about this time that we heard of the death of our aunt, Lois Pettys. The elder sister, Aunt Grizzel, had some years before paid the debt of nature. She was of a full, plethoric habit, and was suddenly carried off by a violent congestion on the brain. But the spare frame and light, elastic person of Aunt Lois seemed to resist alike the encroachments of disease and the infirmities of age.

After the death of her sister, she confined herself almost wholly to the precincts of her antique, and now nearly dilapidated, dwelling ; her spectre-like figure scarce waking an echo as she wandered, restless and disquieted, through the vacant and gloomy apartments, till gradually sinking, she faded away like a summer cloud, and died peacefully in the arms of her maid, the kind and faithful Sally.

There were many heirs to their ample and well-hoarded property, and at a cold and formal meeting of the distant relatives concerned, the sale of the old mansion and its surrounding lands was determined upon, on account of the otherwise insuperable difficulties in the way of an amicable and equitable distribution of the effects.

Had the farm, however, been left undivided, a few more years would have enhanced tenfold the amount realized, the adjacent city having steadily extended street after street, until now the ample grounds are occupied by closely-built tenements, and the house itself replaced by dwellings of more modern structure, and the only glimpse of nature afforded is by a trim garden here and there.

My mother, their niece, received her portion partly in antiquated dresses and household gear ; yet a sufficient amount fell to her lot, in more available form, to yield her a pretty little income of her own. After the death of my father, she took up her residence with her daughter Rhoda. The defects of her character, before delineated, were not amended by age, but, on the contrary, they were augmented by her infirmities and decreased mental vigor ; for if there be a lack of proper self-control, and an habitual yielding to the impulses of selfish feelings or passions in the prime and maturity of life, there will exist little power to curb the violence of temper, or to restrain the bent to self-indulgence in the waning strength of advancing years.

The husband of Rhoda, often annoyed and fretted by the petulance and meddlesome disposition of his mother-in-law, was once heard to declare to one of the family friends that the property she had brought into his hands would weigh lightly indeed, in comparison with the daily petty vexations of her troublesome ways.

I have as yet hardly spoken of the course of events as relating to my two brothers, Willy and Royal, during these intervening years, and I will here refer more particularly to

their history. Of Royal, indeed, I can give but few items
of interest, as he was for many years so separated from
the rest of his family, that we could know but little of him.

He had a roving disposition, and a great desire to see the
world, and left Wayland at an early age, determined, as
the saying is, to "seek his fortune."

Of course he went first to Boston, and finding a good
opening in a ship-chandlery, was for a time employed in that
establishment; but becoming tired of the drudgery and
confinement, he soon left the business, and shipped as a common seaman on one of the European packet-ships. After
the vicissitudes common to a seafaring life, but always main-
taining a character of strict honor and probity, he became
master of a sloop coasting on our own shores, and acquired
a comfortable competency. He never married, though
when, in his later years, he used to visit the homes of his
brother and sisters, he would often declare that he meant to
give up going to sea, and settle down as they had done.
But though upon his first return to the comparative ease
and quiet of a life upon shore, the contrast gave him delight,
yet the power of habit was strong, and again and again prevailed—with his love of the excitement of the sea—to draw
him away for "just one more trip," as he would say.

Poor fellow! the future of which he dreamed never came,
for, in a violent gale off Cape Hatteras, his vessel was
wrecked, and he met a watery grave, while yet in the
strength and vigor of manhood.

Willy was always a favorite, not only with his partial
sisters, but with all the young people, as he grew up. He

had a quick, ready wit, a jovial and social disposition, and was withal a most excellent singer ; in this resembling our Mary and Hester, with the latter of whom, as nearest in age, he was always most closely associated.

In those days the cup of exhilarating drink, by which so many bright hopes have been laid low, was freely passed at every convivial gathering. Willy's agreeable qualities in this, his early youth—that turning period so important, so perilous often, before manhood stamps itself upon the brow—led him into imminent danger from this cause. A round of singing-parties, sleigh-rides, and balls, during the winters, placed before him temptations frequent and strong. My father became exceedingly apprehensive for his safety, and added to his prayers faithful counsel and advice, earnestly striving to disentangle him from the web of the destroyer seemingly gathering around him. He sought for Willy, too, the added influence of his elder sisters, confiding to Bessy and me his fears for the gay young man. Bessy wrote him a letter, full of sisterly affection, but strong in its warnings and entreaties that he would in time take heed to his steps.

Willy never alluded to the letter, though we knew, that he received and read it. I, too, sought and found an opportunity, in private, to plead with him his duty to our father and to himself, and that the long-cherished hopes so fondly placed on him might still be realized. I besought him to turn with manly decision from any use of the deadly beverage so universal then, and so destructive in its effects upon every thing good and noble.

These efforts were not in vain. Before unconscious of his peril, he now woke in some measure to the insidious nature of his dangerous habits ; and when, not long after, our revered and beloved father was laid in his last resting-place, our dear brother stood forth a man in his strength. He was now the representative of him who was gone, the stay and support of the diminished household.

From the jovial, gay, and pleasure-loving young man, careless of consequences, seeking no worthy aim in life, he stepped forth, as it were, at once, from the influence of his merry companions. Standing upon the threshold of active life, he entered upon its duties and responsibilities eminently fitted for usefulness by true moral worth, joined to his really fine mental powers, and above all, by intelligent, devoted piety ; for through the rich mercy of God, the loss of an earthly father was the means of leading him to an Heavenly one, through faith in the Redeemer of men.

About this time he became acquainted with a beautiful girl who had recently come among us, and in a year or two after our father's death he brought her, a lovely bride, to our paternal homestead. Alas ! beauty, youth, and love, could not avail to shield her from the shafts of disease, and in one short year Consumption had secured his prey, and deprived her infant son thus early of the priceless blessing of a mother's love. But he was welcomed to a warm heart, and was not left to know the full magnitude of his loss. Hester, as I have before intimated, had no family ties save those connected with her childhood's home. To Willy she had ever been as a guardian angel, and to her care he now confided his child.

She loved the little stranger with a warmth of feeling only second to that of a mother, and as he passed from infancy to youth and manhood, he well repaid her for her care and kindness, by his almost filial respect and affection. She was soon his only guardian, for our brother never recovered his health or spirits after the loss of his beloved companion, and at the age of only four years the little Joseph was an orphan.

Thus, again and again, did death visit our household, taking from us the darling sister, the loving parent, the brother with whom we had enjoyed so much domestic and fraternal intercourse, the youthful wife and mother.

> " So star by star declines,
> Till all are passed away—
> As morning high and higher shines,
> To pure and perfect day.
> Nor sink those stars in endless night,
> But hide themselves in Heaven's own light."

" Call not the mourner unhappy who lays his dear ones below the earth, and returns to the home where their voices are to be heard never more.

" That affliction brings forth feelings unknown before in his heart, calming all turbulent thoughts by the settled peace of the grave."

CHAPTER XLVIII.

" It is true, there are shadows as well as lights; clouds, as well as sunshine; thorns, as well as roses; but much *happiness*, after all."

SOME events in the life of our sister Mary now awakened all our sympathy for her and her husband ; for life is made up of alternate good and ill fortune, "clouds as well as sunshine," and Mary, who had been so severely disciplined in her youth, was not without lesser, but very painful anxieties, in her later marriage.

On the marriage of his mother with Deacon Dudley, Sam Lyman had taken the family homestead, and assumed the payment of his sisters' portions. Finding this difficult from the slow proceeds of the farm, he sought the more lucrative and available profits of trade, and accordingly established himself in a store in the flourishing. village of Westmead. The old farm, once so productive, being left to the management of tenants and hirelings, rapidly diminished in thriftiness and value, and his mercantile transactions, after some years' trial, proving disastrous, he was forced to return to Wayland. For a few years he struggled with debts and pecuniary difficulties, extremely embarrassing to his high spirit and nice sense of honor ; but he bent his every effort to the satisfying of the just demands of his creditors, and though his dwelling was for the time being the abode of poverty, and his family subjected to many privations, yet he manfully persevered in his course of industry and self-denial, until his object was attained, and he was again enabled to give them the comfort to which they were earlier accustomed.

Mary's character shone out brightly during this period. She had always the sunshine of hope in her heart, a cheerful smile on her face, and words of encouragement on her lips. She shunned no toil ; she was ever ready to aid her husband by doing what was in her power, however unwelcome the task.

I remember a little incident, trifling in itself, but illustrating the annoyances of this part of my sister's life.

She was accustomed frequently to take the grain for the family use, herself, to the mill ; and on one of these occasions—it was a warm, bright day—was slowly tracing the road through Valley Brook to Father Coke's gristmill, not far from my own dwelling.

She was seated, with old and faded dress, in a rickety wagon, partly filled with the bags of grain, when she saw approaching, an elegant looking man with a handsome equipage. As he checked his speed, while the jaded and plodding farm-horse toiled painfully by, she suddenly recognized him as William Homer, the dashing beau of her lively girlhood. He stopped short, exclaiming, in his surprise,

"Can this be Mary Leland ?"

Her face flushed, but with a sudden burst of wifely pride, she answered,

" No, sir ! it is Mrs. Mary Lyman !"

He looked earnestly at her, with a half sorrowful expression, and passed on.

When my sister came, shortly after, as was her custom, to my house, to wait while the miller was performing his task, the tears of bitter mortification too plainly showed, as she told me of the rencontre, that poverty had thus again made her feel keenly the pressure of his iron grasp. But she soon recovered her usual equanimity, and, indeed, such a yielding to the feelings of wounded pride was a very unusual occurrence with her. She was by no means unhappy, even in her privations, for so steadily did she look at the bright side of every circumstance of her lot, that the darker shade was in great measure hid from her vision.

In their five rosy-cheeked little girls, both Mary and her husband felt themselves rich indeed, in the midst of their pecuniary trials. She used to say to them, in their childish perplexities—" Keep up good heart, girls, nothing comes of crying "—and her husband would add, in his peculiar tone of seeming pomposity—" Yes ! be cheerful, my daughters ! ever be cheerful ! Cheerfulness is one of the cardinal virtues !"

After these many clouds and adverse winds, their evening sun shone out bright and clear, and in later years, when Mary recounted to her beautiful daughters more of her earlier sorrows than even her sisters had ever known, she could also point them to a Heavenly Father's guiding hand as the constant and hidden source of all her strength.

They grew up a most lovely family—in the hope and

brightnes of their youth becoming humble, faithful, devoted Christians. Their early experience of privation, toil, and self-denial, formed habits of self-reliance, while it nurtured in them the germs of all else that is most truly excellent, for idleness and self-indulgence not only blunt the powers of intellect, but deaden in the heart the better, nobler sympathies of our nature—" all the sweet charities of life."

In after life, they have proved themselves capable of rising above the petty thoughts and aims of inferior minds, of filling with dignity exalted stations, or of adorning or elevating those more lowly.

CHAPTER XLIX.

THE WIDOW.

"So well is the harp of human feeling strung, that nothing but a crash that breaks every thing can wholly mar its harmony."

MEANTIME I had many cares and labors, but I accepted with cheerfulness the burden laid upon me. Little by little the grace and mercy of God roused up in me what I had before seemed not to possess, the sense and wisdom to comprehend my arduous duties and responsibilities, and to act as the necessity of the case required.

My husband's property was entangled with that of his father and brothers, and Father Coke urged that the estate should be settled without reference to strangers.

Distillery, carding, saw-mill, and farm, all were at loose ends ; my very home was in the hands of my father-in-law, for no deed had been given by him. He loved to retain in his possession whatever had once been his. There was much cupidity and grasping, but it was overruled by my kind Heavenly Father, so as even to work to my advantage, for it excited an interest and care for me with all my friends and neighbors. One man—with whom I had little acquaintance—self-moved, sought a favorable opportunity of conversing with Father Coke, and obtained from him statements which secured the title of my home to me and my children.

An old Quaker, from a distance, after liberally settling his account, inquired of me, " Does thy rich father-in-law deal justly by thee ?" with so much feeling and kindness in his face, that the tears rose to my eyes.

It had been my desire, from the first, to enter my husband's family as a daughter and sister : one with them in interest and affection. I had been successful in allaying prejudices, and winning their confidence and esteem, and the five years of my married life had passed most pleasantly in this regard.

Now, more than ever, was I desirous that the delicate matter of settlement, with its complicated business and conflicting interests, might be happily completed, without disturbing these pleasant relations between us.

Some two or three years were occupied in adjusting the various interests involved in the estate, small as it was ; and previous to the final disposition of affairs, a trial came which I little expected.

The Coke family were extremely reluctant to suffer the mills to pass out of their hands into the possession of strangers : many turns and shifts had been proposed to prevent this result, and much discussion of the subject had taken place at different times. Father Coke alleged that he could not purchase the property of me, because he had made recent investments in a new enterprise just commenced in the town ; neither were any of the younger brothers able to assume such obligation on their own account.

They accordingly desired me still to retain the property in my own possession, subject to their control, proposing to share the proceeds equitably in common. But during the past year the mills had been carried on for me by one of the brothers, and the profits—before a considerable revenue—had been almost wholly absorbed in the management of the concern, and I was convinced that the sale of the mills, and consequent separation of interests, alone could render the late flourishing business of my husband of any avail for our support, or, indeed, secure harmony of feeling with all parties.

While these things were in progress, Mother Coke came to see me one morning. With Mother Coke, especially, I had been, since my marriage, on the most kind and cordial terms. She had many admirable qualities; she was entirely sincere and straight-forward in all her ways, with great activity and energy; ready for any and every work of kindness or necessity, and was quite notable in the various appointments of her large household, with its arduous duties and labors. Not gifted with the nicer shades of feeling or perception, she was yet high-spirited and ambitious, the aggrandizement of her family being her chief aim. It was she who had desired a more wealthy connection for her son Charles; but whatever feeling of that kind she might once have cherished, had long passed away.

Her visit at this time surprised me, because, unlike her usual short stay, and hasty conference on some domestic concern, she sat almost silent for a time, and then entered into the discussion of business affairs, in which, indeed, she was quite competent, although seldom interposing her opinions unasked. She now spoke of the settlement of the estate, enlarging upon the fact, that Father Coke had been the original sole proprietor of the mill-seats of Valley Brook, and wishing they could still all be retained in the family.

I replied, as I had expressed before, that it would suit me well, if Father Coke, or one of the sons, would become the owner of the property, paying me as might be convenient, to aid in the support of myself and my children. I then reminded her that I had as yet received no avails from the mills, though they were in good repair and unencumbered. She answered, that "the business had been poorly managed, and the dues not promptly collected," which was true enough ; "but," said she, with a meaning smile, " there is a way in which you can keep the mills and secure the profits, and your children be well provided for. Cannot you guess?" continued she, in answer to my questioning look. " You and Reuben can make a match of it. He proposed the plan to me yesterday. He is anxious for it ; and I will be bold to say, if he is my son, that he will make a good husband, and be a kind father to the children."

I felt as if struck by a sudden blow.

"Does Reuben know of your speaking to me of this, mother ?" said I, the tears filling my eyes and almost choking my utterance.

"No ; he has gone away to-day, but I thought I would tell you about it, so that you might have time to think it over before he saw you."

The first quick feeling of resentment had passed away, and there only remained the wish to annihilate the thought, if possible. I hoped Reuben would never come himself upon the errand, and, with more emotion than I would willingly have shown, I said, "Then do not let him know I ever had such a thought brought to my mind."

Mother Coke seemed much surprised at the feeling I betrayed. She had no doubt supposed I should view the subject in the same business-like way as herself. Little more was said—what, I hardly knew—and she soon took her leave. When I was left alone, my tears flowed long and unrestrained ; they wrought relief. After the troubled waters subsided, my mind became calm, and I sought to enter into the feelings—natural enough, perhaps—of Mother Coke ; not, indeed, with any less repugnance to the point proposed, but that I might fairly and honestly view the motives that prompted it—motives of kindness to myself, as well as desire for the promotion of the supposed family interest.

CHAPTER L.

Reuben Coke was some years younger than was my Charles, and resembled him somewhat in form and features, though little in his general bearing.

Good looking, in truth, he might be deemed, yet he had a sort of stolid air, and a sluggish, heavy manner, too plainly marking that the finer and higher attributes of soul were wanting—were overborne by the more sensuous qualities, or at most by that lower type of intellect which has its compass and scope centering in self.

His kindly good nature, steady habits, and honest, upright character, I could value and respect, but a hallowed, endeared union with my husband's brother—with Reuben Coke! The very idea was odious! as discordant as were our sympathies and taste, our aims in life, and especially our views in reference to the things of religion.

As the subject recurred to my mind through the day, I began to fear I had not been sufficiently explicit with Mother Coke to preclude the repetition of the disagreeable topic; nor was I wrong in the apprehension. The next morning I had but just dispatched my little son, with his companion Energine (of whom more hereafter) off to school, when Reuben Coke made his appearance. My brothers-in-law were familiar guests at my cottage, coming and going with entire freedom and without ceremony ; but now Reuben's constrained and hesitating manner left me little difficulty in divining that he had come with an unusual errand. I was finishing my few household avocations, and nearly ready to inspect the contents of my workbasket ; my little ones were playing around me in the long family room which opened directly upon the small plat of grass separating the house from the road.

My visitor sat for some time saying little, but fondling my two little girls, and listening to their prattle.

After a while he began to speak of the contemplated sale of the mills, the disposal of the property, and then of his own circumstances and present plans. Full of his own thoughts and wishes, and seemingly unconscious of all else, he rose and stalked backwards and forwards across the room, apparently intent on seeking the most fitting way to unfold the purpose of his visit. There were some long poles suspended from hooks near the ceiling at the top of the room, on which were hung some strings of apples and sundry long strips of pumpkin, in process of drying for winter use. Reuben, as he rose from his chair, had donned his high, bell-crowned hat, and this just reaching up to the drying apples and pumpkins, at each turn dislogded some of the pendant fruit, and brought it to the floor as he paced up and down the long room. I picked them up successively, till all the hanging contents of the poles were at length transferred to the table at the side of the room. He was wholly uncon-scious of what he was doing, and I was myself too much engrossed by the unpleasant topic of our conversation to pay much note at the time to the ludicrous performance or to the fate of my goods ; but afterwards I laughed heartily at sight of the confused heap of dried edibles which burdened the table.

At length our painful interview was ended ; and let me do him the justice to say that, in all sincerity—and he was incapable of dealing otherwise—he did not propose a union and offer his hand as a convenient joining of interests merely, or as a sordid scheme for the securing of a mutual advantage ; but he told me in his own plain, blunt manner, that he " was sure he should like me better for a wife than any one else he knew "—that " I had long stood very high with him." On my side, I endeavored to meet him on his own ground, treating the subject in a sincere and very practical way. I tried to show him the undesirableness of such a connection on various grounds, and succeeded in making clear to his mind the utter impossibility of my acceding to his plan ; softening my decisive assertions, from regard to his feelings, as much as I could consistently with perfect sincerity and my determination not to be misunderstood.

He displayed no anger, nor, indeed, much emotion of any kind, beyond his first embarrassment. The subject was dropped, and the trifling constraint and unpleasant feeling arising from it soon passed away. The mills were sold, and all our affairs were amicably settled, with the continued kindness of the family, who were ever after ready to aid me in every emergency, especially showing the greatest tender·ness for my fatherless little ones.

CHAPTER LI.

THE HEIRESS.

> "Fy! let's a' to the wedding!"
>
> OLD SONG.

"She is so young, my son!"

"Yes, mother, but she is so pretty!"

"She knoweth not how to do work, or to guide the house, or to leave off her girlish plays!"

"Yes, mother! but she sings so sweetly, and laughs so merrily, I know you will like her!"

"You think every one must like her, because you do; but I fear me! I fear me!"

"Well, mother—but she is rich!"

"Is she rich? Art sure of that? Well, well! my son! have thine own way! I dare say she will learn to be a very proper wife!"

> OLD PLAY.

SHORTLY after the visit above described, my brother-in-law, Reuben, was abundantly consoled by a sudden turn of fortune, by means of which a lucky prize, apparently, was thrown into his hands in the person of a romantic girl, both pretty and rich, not yet quite out of her teens, who came with her invalid mother to Wayland, and was spending some time with an aunt. Reuben first met her by accident, and the pretty, innocent-looking face, and frank school-girl manners of the young lady, solicitous to please, at once fascinated his simple, honest heart. His courtship sped well, for the managing aunt—our old acquaintance, Mrs. Golding—thought the son of the rich Mr. Coke no bad match for her niece, now just from boarding-school, and ready to make her fortune in the world. The young lady herself was by no means averse to the so devoted attentions of a veritable lover—her first conquest. I first heard of the matter from Mother Coke; she came over with her knitting—a rare occurrence—to sit with me one afternoon. "Have you heard any reports about Reuben?" asked she, thus introducing the subject. I replied that I had not. "Haven't you heard of the Widow Lovell and her daughter? The mother is a sister of Mr. Golding. She has come to stay there awhile for her health."

I was quite ignorant of the existence of any such persons. She continued: "Her husband died two years ago, and left her a large property. There is only one child; her name is Angeline. She has just finished her education, and is handsome as a doll, and a real heiress."

"And what about Reuben?" said I, beginning to guess at the drift of affairs.

"Why, he has begun to pay his addresses, and we think it will be a match," she replied.

"The mother or the daughter?" I half mischievously asked.

"Oh, the daughter, to be sure! the mother is always sick, and the most notional person you ever saw; but Angeline is a very pretty girl. Reuben will not try for a widow again," she added, with a peculiar smile.

I told her I was very glad—as, of course, I was most sincerely so—to hear of Reuben's good fortune; hoping the youthful "heiress" would prove a fitting companion for him. The circumstance of her reputed wealth touched the weak point with Mother Coke, and she was highly gratified with the golden prospects of her son.

Angeline Lovell was indeed pretty and interesting as a young miss, "but half a woman, half a child." She gave her consent for an early day, and became a wife, thinking, no doubt, far more of lovers' vows and bridal favors, than of future cares, duties, or responsibilities. I looked upon my new sister with a feeling of sympathy almost akin to pity, light-hearted and pretty as she was ; for I saw in her a character at once weak and immature, which greatly needed the development of careful culture, and earnest, serious preparation for the humble and prosy, yet indispensable occupations of every-day life. She might thus have been fitted to bear her burdens easily, and might have passed smoothly along on the common current, filling her place usefully, and with happiness to herself and others.

Poorly adapted, as she really was, to the practical duties and homely cares devolving upon a wife and the mistress of a family, her temper, naturally amiable (so far as it could be said to have any character at all), became peevish and irritable.. Her health failed, and she grew nervous and weak-spirited. She lacked both energy and capacity to manage her household, and everything suffered neglect and went to decay.

Little by little their comfortable property wasted away. Her husband, never very enterprising or active, grew dispirited and indolent, until he who had married the " heiress " became the poorest of the family. Not only destitute of outward means of comfort, they were poor in health, poor in a spirit of active exertion, and poor in hope for the future—theirs was poverty indeed !

·I have before alluded to the investments of Father Coke which had employed his available funds in a new enterprise As these outlays were the means of some important and disastrous results, I will explain them more fully. Olive Coke—the one nearest in age to my Charles, and a very dear sister to him—had married a physician, Dr. Blake, one of those restless men always full of schemes and new enterprises. Olive herself was a gentle, loving girl. I had often heard my husband say that amid all the faults and follies of childhood, or the waywardness of youth, he could not recollect a single instance of disagreement between them. This endeared her to me, as well as her own loveliness and excellence. Her husband was beginning to secure a good practice, but was not contented with his slow gains, and at length started the plan of a glass factory, which he declared would soon raise the quiet and obscure town of Wayland into a village of some importance, boasting at least one branch of flourishing business.

As usual, he entered upon his project with the utmost zeal, and pursued it with unremitting ardor and activity, inspiring many of the staid people of Wayland with a portion of his own confidence and enthusiasm. Money was invested with large hopes of success, and the flattering promise of liberal returns. Fortunes were to be made in a day by taking shares in the new enterprise of glass-making.

· No one, save the originator of the scheme, Dr. Blake, enlisted in it more warmly, or invested more largely than Father Coke. There was an auspicious commencement, and for a time all went on swimmingly ; but a few brief months of actual experiment conducted the too sanguine projectors to utter failure, as might have been predicted from their total want of experience in the business, and the difficulty of procuring competent workmen. Father Coke's loss was several thousands, and Dr. Blake's little all was swallowed up. He soon after removed to the State of New York. This separation of our dear Olive from her friends was a very sad one to us all. They were going in utter poverty to encounter the hardships of a new region then little known, with two little girls, the eldest not yet three years old.

But Dr. Blake soon, fortunately, found a good location near the pleasant town'of Kingston, on the Hudson, where, rendered wise by experience, he steadily practised his profession, and in time gained a competency, and was able to surround his now large and flourishing family not only with comfort, but with all the appliances and refinements of domestic and social life.

Father Coke could not be reconciled to the disastrous issue of his unfortunate speculation. He was deeply mortified that he had so foolishly adventured his carefully-kept gains, and was perpetually bemoaning his loss, wondering at his rashness and the blindness which could not have foreseen the result. His health began to suffer through the uneasiness of his mind, and he became so ill as to be unable for some weeks to attend to his ordinary business, but sat silent and gloomy, brooding over his misfortune.

His sons, who at first had been quite cast down by the

loss of the property, began to be still more troubled that their father took it so much to heart. Mother Coke endeavored to divert his mind by company and visits, hoping that by free converse with his friends and neighbors his thoughts might revert to their accustomed channels, so that he might find interest as usual in his various plans of business ; for he was by no means a ruined man in worldly affairs, but possessed still a very considerable property. He consented one day to visit with her a family living some three or four miles distant. It was near the last of February. The snow was deep and gently falling, though the day was mild. Father Coke seemed in tolerable spirits and conversed with some cheerfulness ; but scarcely had they proceeded more than a mile, just as they were entering the deep gorge at the foot of Pine Mountain, he appeared to be faint, the slackened reins dropped from his hands, and he leaned heavily against his wife. She quickly turned the horse about, to return home, speaking to him meanwhile and seeking to revive him ; but in vain—he was dead !

Without a moment's warning, in the sleigh alone with his wife, on the highway, his spirit had taken its flight, his soul passed for ever away from scenes of earth.

In indescribable terror and agony of mind, Mother Coke supporting the lifeless body of her husband, herself drove home in the quickest possible time, each moment seeming an hour ! When I arrived at the scene of distress the dead husband and father lay on his bed with overcoat and boots still on ; his children were weeping around, in all the confusion and dismay of sudden grief ; the stout young men, the

grown-up daughters, sobbing unrestrained as the utter hope-
lessness of restoration became evident. It was, indeed, a
most mournful spectacle !—to me most solemn and affecting. What now to him who was gone were all the trifling
concerns of earth ! Where was now that spirit so wrapped
up in the interests of the world, so suddenly ushered, naked,
into another sphere, poor indeed, without other and more
enduring riches !

CHAPTER LII.

LITTLE HELPS.

AFTER the sale of the mills, the income of my farm, increased by my own exertions in different ways, afforded us a frugal living, while the care and training of my dear children was my great concern and object.

Soon after my marriage, we had received a little orphan girl in charge to bring up, named Energine, of whom a more particular account will be given in a subsequent chapter. She was soon able to assist me in various ways, and well did she afterwards repay my care, by a devoted affection on her part scarce ever exceeded by a daughter.

As time wore on, my little Charles, too, became able to help. He was a strong, manly little fellow, very capable for his age, and many a time I have, with a fearful heart, sent him to perform labors well fitting the strength and judgment of a lad of twice his years.

In the pasture were many fine chestnut trees, and when the frosty nights of autumn had begun to scatter their fruit, I would go with the children to gather the brown nuts, that their avails might procure for us some needed little comforts.

My stout, active boy—a mere Lilliput in stature—would climb the tree, venturing out to utmost limb, while Energine and I stood with a spread sheet to catch the nuts as they fell ; my two little girls meanwhile filling their tiny baskets, and thinking it rare sport.

We had, too, a fine plantation of sugar maples, at some distance from the house, high up on the hill-side ; this also was made a source of profit.

First, a man's services were requisite to "tap" the trees and prepare the vessels for receiving the sap ; then, in the keen, bright March days, Energine and my trusty Charles would be dispatched to empty the sap-troughs, and to kindle a fire under the kettle for boiling.

The rude fire-place was ready made, and seemed one of nature's freaks. A large layer of rock, smooth and level, projected horizontally, resting upon a smaller ledge for support, while at the extreme end of this natural floor two similar ledges lay transversely against the steep hill-side, leaving just space enough for a large kettle to be suspended. Above the whole were two or three birch trees and other shrubbery, forming a shelter somewhat from the winds. Here the sap was boiled, the two children watching and tending it day after day, while I repaired frequently to the spot to overlook them in their labors.

I remember one day in particular, when Energine was gone to stay with a sick neighbor, and Charles was tending alone upon the hill—he may have been nine or ten years old—I had been very busy in the house, and had not visited the scene of operations that day, but had sent my youngest girl, a child of about six years, with a warm bit for her brother's dinner, and permission for herself to stay with him through the afternoon.

It grew late, and the children did not come home ; but I knew my little son would stay to ever so late an hour, if the boiling syrup was at a point unfavorable to leave ; for it was his way to finish whatever he undertook before leaving, if it was possible to do so.

As night shut in, cloudy and dark, I provided myself with a lantern and proceeded to the place.

Ascending the hill in part by the road, I entered the pasture by a narrow path, and passed through it. Then crossing a small rivulet, I began to climb the steep ascent, and soon perceived the fire lighting up the rocks, the bare trees, and patches of snow beyond, and I saw the little forms of my children flitting back and forth before it.

Keeping carefully in the shadow, I gained the further side of the ledge, concealing my light under my cloak, and stopped near a large stump, a rod or two from them, to see whether they would observe me. My little Anna was capering from side to side of the rude floor, calling it her house, and full of lively talk and play, as was her wont.

It was not long before her notice was attracted to my dark, still figure, and she said to her brother, " What is it that looks so much like a black man standing out there ?"

He scarcely looked up at first, so busy was he in replenishing his glowing fire with brushwood, or adding sap to the boiling liquor in small quantities to temper its heat, his thoughtful young face showing in the firelight that his whole mind was absorbed by his trust.

My little girl kept uneasily watching me, and when at last I opened the folds of my cloak a little, so as to suffer the light to shine around me, she became really alarmed, and urgently called her brother's attention.

"Oh!" said he, after a moment's scrutiny, "perhaps there is a little snow on that stump that makes it look light."

But, not satisfied with his own explanation, he continued to look, and at length descended his platform of·rock for a nearer examination. His sister cried out, "Don't go! Charles! don't go!" but the brave little fellow approached, and fairly touched, before he recognized me.

"I meant to know what it was," said he, when I asked him why he came to me; "but, mother, why didn't you come and let us know you were here?"

"I wanted to see how much courage you had," I answered, "and to see how you were at work here all alone."

Great was the joy to see "mother" in the dark and loneliness, and soon, putting out the fire, we wended our way home, and I, with a happy and a thankful heart, laid down to rest beside my tired children.

In simple pleasures like these, and in the cheerful performance of the little duties that filled up the course of my retired life, I found a quiet comfort, and even joy, seldom realized in a more brilliant and showy sphere, and which could hardly be imagined by those whose whole existence has been spent in the "giddy round" of amusement and festivity.

20

CHAPTER LIII.

PINE MOUNTAIN COTTAGE.

" What mournful tragedies are ever around us, flowing on unseen, with the per-
petual under-current of human life, each hour laden with mystery and sorrows,
with floating wrecks, we see, but cannot snatch from the darkening tide."

" A little child
That lightly draws its breath,
That feels its life in every limb,
What can it know of death ?"

THE history of my own branch of " our family " would be
quite incomplete, did I fail to say something more of my
little orphan Energine. Her origin and subsequent varied
life might form the basis of a most romantic tale, could it
be skillfully delineated in the delicate and fanciful style of
some imaginative writer. But a more plain and prosaic
account must suffice the less favored readers of my humble
story. Energine's parents removed to Wayland a short
time before her birth, and with their little son of four years,
lived in a house belonging to farmer Gibbs—a little brown
cottage standing just at the foot of Pine Mountain. The
thick chestnut grove which almost surrounded the base of
the mountain, cast a deep shade upon the roof, and gave the
dwelling an air of seclusion—almost of gloom. There was
a mystery about Mr. and Mrs. Harlow, for that was the
name of these people, which, while it served to keep their

neighbors from any great degree of familiarity with them, rendered them the more frequent subjects of conversation and conjecture. They had arrived by stage, and, as the driver affirmed, from "York city," and after a few days' stay at the village tavern, they quietly sought a home in the obscure dwelling of Mr. Gibbs.

Little was known of them even after some intercourse had worn off their first reserve.

There were some marvellous stories told of rich dresses in their trunks, of which, now and then, a sight had been obtained ; of some trinkets of value in a little box of rare and antique workmanship, which stood upon the little table in their bed-room ; but beyond these glimpses of former wealth, and the shrewd guesses to which they gave rise, nothing was apparent of their past history. None could fail to observe the contrast, however, between the delicacy and refinement of manner and language of Mrs. Harlow and the blunt good humor of her husband ; but all saw that there existed between them the most perfect, confiding affection, and that each was to the other a whole world in *one*. In a country town each person is individualized, and the history, thoughts, and opinions of each, become, in some sort, the property of all.

A tax is levied upon the social, moral, and intellectual wealth of every member of the little community, that thereby the whole may be mentally and socially enriched and gratified. They who are totally unwilling to contribute to this tax should not attempt to live in the country.

Those larger objects—those topics of general interest and

excitement which occupy the thoughts and attention of city neighbors, sufficing to employ the activity of their minds, cannot, in the nature of things, be removed to the country town ; while there the same activity and curiosity will find its aliment in the doings and sayings of associates and friends.

But to return to my story.   Mr. and Mrs. Harlow gradually won upon the confidence and respect of their neighbors ; but it was very evident that Mrs. Harlow was unaccustomed to the primitive habits of a retired country life, and though she strove to accommodate herself to them, so as not to appear singular, yet it could plainly be seen that many things which to others were only trifling inconveniences were to her real hardships and privations ; and though the tender care of her husband left no room to doubt that in her marriage she had found all she expected, it was still easy to see that some secret and weighty sorrow pressed down her spirit, and at times left the traces of tears upon her pale checks.

It was not long after the birth of Energine, that her health began to fail, and after lingering two or three years, it became apparent to all around her that she must die. Still she clung to life, and, day by day, cherished every faint and flattering hope.

Kind Mrs. Gibbs besought her to write to her friends, but she always declined with a quiet dignity which effectually forbade inquisitive remarks.

But she grew weaker and weaker, and one morning, after a severe paroxysm of pain, she requested pen and paper, and with some difficulty wrote a few lines and gave the note to her husband ; he added a brief postscript, and the letter was sent. In a few days, a carriage stopped at the gate before the little brown house, from which alighted a lady richly dressed, and of most haughty bearing, accompanied by a gentleman as stately and haughty as herself. It was the sister of Mrs. Harlow, with her husband. They arrived only in time to see the poor sufferer breathe her last—too late for recognition or word. The sad event appeared to give them but little pain or concern ; on the contrary, they appeared desirous that the funeral preparations should be hastened, that they might immediately return home. But a startling and mournful event awaited them. While Mr. Harlow was, next morning, caring for the wants of their mettlesome horses, a sudden kick from one of them, as he was stooping down, felled him to the ground, and he was carried into the house a corpse ! At first, even this appeared to produce but slight effect upon the proud, unfeeling lady ; but when she went to view the bodies dressed in the habiliments of the grave, and lying side by side in their last slumbers, the icy fountain at last gave way, and she gazed long, and with bitter tears, on the pale, cold faces before her. No word was spoken, until after some moments, by a strong effort controlling her emotion, she wiped the unbidden tears, resumed her proud look, and coldly remarked to her husband,

" My sister was handsome, but he was a very common man."

Alas ! for the evil in the human heart ! The presence of death itself cannot check its pride nor soften its hate !

The two who had manifested the most tender attachment in life, were not separated in death, but were buried in the same grave. Ah ! many a bereaved mourner has craved that blessing, to whom it has yet been in mercy denied ! Their children, the little George and Energine, were now, indeed, objects of compassion—orphans at so early an age, and with no friends, as it soon appeared. The brother-in-law, after ascertaining that there was nothing left which would maintain the children, declared he should do nothing for them ; a decision in which his wife fully acquiesced. Giving to Mr. and Mrs. Gibbs a small sum of money, they recommended them to have the two orphans placed in good families, if such could be found to receive them, and then take for their trouble whatever was left in the cottage. Thus summarily disposing of affairs to their own satisfaction, the haughty couple again entered their elegant carriage and drove off.

CHAPTER LIV.

THE ORPHAN.

"But is it not a happy thing,
All fetterless and free,
Like any wild bird on the wing,
To carol merrily."

"God ! who gavest
Into my guiding hand this wanderer,
To lead her through a world whose darkling paths
I tread with steps so faltering—leave not me
To bring her to the gates of heaven alone !
I feel my feebleness."

THE just indignation of the people was at once excited at such unblushing outrage of the commonest feelings of nature, and it was soon resolved that the children should be befriended by their neighbors, since thus cast off by their unfeeling relatives. Mr. and Mrs. Gibbs, having no children of their own, adopted the boy, who afterwards studied the profession of law, and practised successfully as an attorney for many years.

After some hesitation and reluctance, lest I should fail in so weighty a task (for my husband left the decision of the matter entirely to me), I acceded to the urgent solicitation of the selectmen of the town, and the little girl became an inmate of our family. The relatives never appeared in Wayland again, and I soon came to regard the little stranger with much affection.   She was a child of excellent disposition, though somewhat peculiar in temperament ; always kind and loving to my own little ones—all younger than herself—and most affectionate to me, there was yet wanting in her mental constitution a balance-wheel, a regulator, rendering her liable to great extremes in her feelings.   Sometimes exalted to a high pitch of perfect good humor and gaiety, she would, perhaps, the next hour be cast down, dissatisfied and sad, with no apparent cause sufficient to account for the change.   This wavering tendency caused me no little trouble and anxiety for her.   I constantly strove to cultivate in her a more equable and placid disposition, though with but partial success.   Yet she rarely failed to engage the kindly interest of those who knew her intimately and saw the really good impulses of her heart ; while the clear brunette of her complexion, the bloom of her red cheeks, and her twinkling black eyes, lighted up with liveliness and joyful good temper, made her by no means unattractive to strangers.

To myself she became very dear, though my patience was often sorely tried with her fitful waywardness through the years of childhood and youth.   I instructed her, to the best of my ability, in the usual avocations of household labors, in most branches of which she became quite expert, though there were some few specialities to which she took and ever retained a most unaccountable dislike ; such, for instance, was the making of a bed, and also the suitable preparation of some of the most common articles of daily food, I was never able to teach her, with my most patient and persevering efforts. These peculiarities annoyed me exceedingly, until I fully made up my mind that they were idiosyncrasies which I could never overcome, and, with this conclusion, I gave up the useless endeavor. At the district school, to which she was regularly sent, she was always esteemed bright and apt scholar ; but here, too, the peculiarities of her mind and disposition manifested themselves in various ways. While she loved her book, and was usually prompt with her lessons in the branches there taught, there was this single and marked exception : she could never be persuaded nor compelled to pursue the study of arithmetic beyond the four simple rules. Not only did she evince an unconquerable dislike to the study, it seemed utterly impossible for her to attain a distinct comprehension even of its plainest principles. Many a time did she come home from school at night full of grief, and shedding floods of tears, at the reproofs and the severities, sometimes, of teachers who had striven to overcome this strange aversion and determination.

They always strove in vain ; for, after all her grief and tears, and my own persuasions and arguments—for in this thing I never resorted to commands—her repugnance was still strong as ever ; and after a few such efforts, the victory was reluctantly yielded to her invincible will, and her equally evident incapacity.

To add and subtract, to multiply and divide, was all, she used to insist, when she was older, that a woman need ever know of numbers ; and why then puzzle her brain and tax her memory with the complicated and practically useless rules requiring a deeper mathematical insight than she either possessed or desired?   To all practical intents, the whole of her arithmetical skill consisted in counting; what she could see and handle she could count; but I accidentally overheard a childish conversation between her and my little son, which will illustrate how deficient she was in some of the most common mental processes.

Charles said, "Enna, how many are sixteen and four?"

"Sixteen and four what?" said Enna.

"Why, sixteen and four any thing; just the figures."

"'Just the figures' don't mean any thing, Charles. I don't know, without you tell me what it is that you are counting."

"Why, yes, Enna! sixteen and four beans will make just as many as sixteen and four apples will."

"Oh! now I can tell, because you said apples and beans, and I know just how they would look on the table; but when you said only the figures, I can't think of them anywhere. It's—(stopping a long minute to count to herself)—it's twenty apples, Charles; and (stopping again to count carefully) its twenty beans too."

"Well, it's twenty anything," persisted Charles; "sixteen and four are twenty, of course."

But Enna looked bewildered, and for the hundredth time repeating her exclamation, "I don't like figures," turned away to some more congenial employment.

The dullness and dislike of the little girl to his own favorite study, were as marvelous to Charles as were his skill and absorption in his intricacies to the mind of Energine, and the mystery of their contrasting capacities and likings might have puzzled older and wiser heads than theirs.

But who shall measure or curb the windings or eccentricities of mind ? Who assign its bounds or decree its compass ? We see one individual gifted in a remarkable degree with some one faculty—is it greater wonder that to another the same faculty is almost wholly denied? Much may be done by cultivation and education, we know, but if there be an entire lack of mental aptitude, it is in vain for man to attempt its creation.

It was not alone in the particulars I have mentioned, that Energine was so different from many children of her age as that she was always spoken of by my neighbors in that phrase of so indefinite significance—"a peculiar child." Though by no means bold and forward, she was yet fearless, and her quick sense of the ludicrous, led her many times to discover great amusement in the very occurrence which to other children would have been the occasion of fright and alarm.

When she was not five years old, I was ill one day, and while by chance alone with the child, I suddenly fainted and fell to the floor. It was probably but a few seconds before consciousness returned, and as I raised my dizzy head and opened my eyes, I saw her, instead of crying with fear and apprehension, as many children would have done, dancing, skipping, and laughing, and with childish glee repeating,

"You fell down, didn't you Ma' ? You fell down !"

She had many little winning, childish ways, but withal

was so capricious in her wayward whims, that one could never tell what she might do next.

One cold November morning, I recollect, we rose early, long before the grey dawn, when nothing would pacify her, but she must follow a sudden caprice, to go to the orchard to get some late sweet apples to eat. So off she went alone, in the dark, frosty morning, and returning with hands and apron full, called loudly at the door,

"Ugh! Ugh! Cold as a frog! Cold as a frog! Ugh! Ugh! Cold as a frog!"

And her aching fingers taught her for the time, better than my words could have done, the folly of yielding to such unseasonable impulses.

She had a faculty of handling everything with the tips of her little taper fingers with a most dainty touch, and of hopping about from place to place like a little bird, and almost as blithely and as free.

Bright, gay colors, too, were her especial admiration; she delighted to deck her hair fantastically with blossoms, marking the different effect of her varied embellishments by watching my countenance as she came to display her rustic adornings, for, in truth, I must say, that vanity was early one of the prominent characteristics of my little Energine, and the love of admiration almost a ruling passion.

She possessed a ready tact at reading the opinions of others, which in later years contributed not a little to gain for her the popularity she craved. Blending with a quick, intuitive sympathy, it led her to be readily interested in whatever occupied the mind of a companion.

I used sometimes to fancy that she was so absorbed in the thoughts and feelings of others that she had none of her own, excepting as thus derived.

A nature gifted with sympathies so spontaneous, could not be selfish, and she was ever ready to yield whatever she possessed or preferred to the importunate request of a schoolmate—sometimes to my great inconvenience.

Such was the child thus entrusted to my care and training. A gentle, fragile plant, seemingly ill calculated to withstand the storms of adversity, yet ever bending gracefully before the blast, and gaily rising again in the returning sunshine.

> " Heaven bless thee, little flower ! I prize thee more
> Than all the pride of female stateliness."

CHAPTER LV.

"A FAYRE GIRL, WITH A CHANGEFULLE SPIRIT."

"She who neither dazzles by her genius, nor much enlightens by her philosophy, does what neither wisdom nor genius always succeed in doing—*wins hearts.*

WHEN Energine was sixteen, I began to consider seriously the necessity of her acquiring, by some means, more practical views of life, and more actual preparations for its coming realities. Up to this time she had been but a gay, light-hearted child, sometimes saddened, indeed, by her own imaginary sorrows, but none the better prepared by these for the weightier cares of womanhood.

She had always wrought at our household labors, as a matter of course, and she had always received the supply of her wants as to food, clothing, and all necessary comforts, equally, as a matter of course.

After much thought upon the matter, I concluded to place her for a time in some good family where she would be expected to labor, and to look only to herself for the care of herself, and thus the qualities she lacked might be developed by necessity. Yet, though I had determined upon this plan, I still deferred the acting upon it, dreading the day which would send her from my own fireside to the less loving home of strangers. I looked around among my friends, to see where I could assure myself she would find the tenderness, the firmness, and the consideration which her young and undeveloped nature demanded ; where, with wholesome restraint, might yet be mingled cheerfulness and moderate indulgence.

After some delay, I was so happy as to secure for her a place, possessing in good degree these requisites, in the household of Samuel Dudley, the husband of Mary Lyman, as mentioned in a former chapter.

I took my children and went with Energine to her new home, that, by the social chat of a friendly visit, the change might be made less painfully to myself. The house was one of some elegance, in the busy street of the flourishing village of Dudleyville. A broad, green slope, with a wide path in its centre, was in front, and a large shaggy dog, lying upon the step, gave notice, by a surly growl, of our approach My old friend Mary met us with a cordial welcome. Our girlish acquaintance had been in a measure kept up by occa- sional visits, as we lived only four miles apart, and she had always taken an affectionate interest in Energine, as well as in my own children, especially since my sad bereavement.

Energine, always animated and elated in new scenes, behaved her prettiest ; and I could easily see that she was likely to find favor with all the family.

The father and mother of Mr. Dudley lived with them, and though Mary was nominally and really the mistress, the more imperious and dictatorial Madam Dudley was sure to exert a felt sway upon the household, and I was gratified to observe the kindness and evident partiality with which she already regarded my foster-child.

My little Anna was delighted with all she saw at the Dudleys'. The large, wide hall, and spacious rooms, quite impressed her with their superiority to the smaller, but comfortable house in which we lived ; and I have often recurred, with no small amusement, to her serious exclamation, as we came again to the brow of the hill overlooking our own home—"There is our humble cottage !"

Here Energine lived two years. Her exuberant spirits, with her good looks, and a ready and pleasant humor ever peeping out in a witty repartee, carried with them a sort of fascination which made her a favorite with all ; and the more particular preference of my friend's only son was beginning to make itself manifest, when it was discovered by the quick eye of his grandmother.

The old lady—the reigning impulse of her life not a whit abated by any subduing influence of growing age—could not willingly think of the possibility of a marriage, even in the third generation, which would bring no wealth to her own side of the house. She found means, soon after becoming aware of the incipient liking of her grandson for my pretty Energine, to persuade Mary to dismiss her.

By ingenious questionings, the ambitious and meddlesome woman assured herself, before she left, that Energine had attached no particular importance in her own mind to the young man's attentions, and wisely forbore to enlighten her upon the point, though the proof was plain to her own wary observation. She probably thought, by sending Energine out of the way, and exerting a counter influence upon the mind of the youth, the danger might be seasonably arrested.

Energine came again to me, and spent the ensuing winter at home, attending the school near by. For a while Mr. Samuel—for he too had inherited from his father and grand-father the same good Scripture name—was a pretty frequent visitor. But he met with no very decided encouragement, and his calls becoming less and less frequent, at length ceased entirely.

Energine laughed and joked as gaily as ever—her heart had not been touched—and she had no lack of admiring attendants, though not always such as I could desire or approve.

21

CHAPTER LVI.

TRUST.

> " And may not I, by Heaven's kind mercy aided,
> Weak as I am, with some good courage bear
> What is appointed for me ?"

I FELT much solicitude at this time about Energine. Her grace and attractions, her dependent situation, added to the native deficiencies of her mind and character, exposed her to many captivating allurements of youthful vanity and folly. During the past two years she had improved much in looks and in a certain assumed steadiness and self-possession which sat becomingly on her.

She had a naturalness peculiarly her own ; she was small, lithe and flexile in figure, full of ease and prettiness in motion, and her laugh, so out-gushing and bird-like, would betray her in a room full of her young companions. She could converse quite fluently upon the surface-ground of almost any subject she heard discussed, though a few pertinent questions might easily have shown her deficient comprehension of it, and her entire ignorance where close study or reflection were required. I had often been surprised to see how she would seize upon a thought she had heard another express, and clothe it in her own words before the astonished speaker could claim his property. In this way she continually gained credit for more knowledge than she possessed, though by no means intentionally aiming at such a result, quite conscious of, and often frankly declaring her own ignorance and superficial attainments. The influence of the companions among whom she was now by necessity thrown, was in many respects bad for a nature like hers.

Esquire Ross had always in his employ a large number of workmen as well as apprentices, who were often young men without firm principle, without intellectual cultivation, frivolous, and sometimes, I feared, even vicious. With no apparent effort, Energine invariably won from the other sex the admiration and attention she so well loved, and I often regretted that her two abundant vanity was thus easily fed. I could hardly forbid her associating with the other young people, for she was a general favorite and the life of their little companies, and such refusal must have had the appearance either of pride or moroseness in me, besides requiring great self-denial on her part.

Besides my anxiety for my adopted daughter, I had at this time many other perplexing cares. My little farm was losing not only in remunerative profit but in actual value, from the necessity of employing only hired laborers. Even these it was often difficult to obtain, and their mercenary efforts were of course confined to securing the most money for the least work, so that many things which would have been advantageous, and even highly desirable, for the proper improvement of the farm, were wholly neglected. From this cause, my means of support and of education for my children, were diminishing at the very period when they should have been increasing.

My boy was at an age now, too, when every boy requires the guidance of a strong mind and a good judgment, and though he yielded, as ever, implicit deference to my authority, yet I was often myself at a loss to know what was the best course to advise for him. The same evil influences, too, to which I have alluded in the case of Energine, were fraught with no less danger to him than to her.

At times I was almost dispirited by the difficulties thus surrounding me, but a retrospect of my own experience in some measure reassured me. I had learned that all human power is utter weakness, and I trusted not in my own. Strength always flows from the Fountain of Strength, in the hour of trial, if it is sought with humility and earnestness, and I was thus enabled still to

> " depend
> On the One hitherto providing."

I remembered how, in the time of my loneliness and sorrow in Maine—a young girl exposed to many and various dangers—a home had been provided for me, and kind friends raised up. How I had been restored to my father's house after that long absence, and had afterwards enjoyed years of untold happiness. How I had been strengthened and sustained in the great trial of my life ; and how the apparent obstacles in the way of an amicable settlement of the estate had been all removed and harmony secured between the conflicting interests.

Calling to mind all these timely benefits from the Divine
Hand, with many instances of kindness shown to me in my
widowhood, I seemed to trace, as a silver thread running
through the whole web of my past history, the working of
Providence in my behalf, and should I now begin to distrust
its continuing care ?

Still I pondered much upon these subjects of my solicitude, though with a growing faith that a way would be
opened for me, a plain path in which I should be led to
walk.

> " These are my cherished dreams to day,
> And who has dreams more fair ?
> *Dreams* will they prove ?—I fear it not—
> I communed with my secret thoughts,
> Nor selfish wish was there—
> One only—and it will endure—
> ' Oh, keep my dear ones good and pure !'
> And Heaven will hear my prayer !"

CHAPTER LVII.

GREENVALE.

"Calm huts, and lawns between, and sylvan slopes,
White mists, suspended on the expiring gale,
Moveless, o'erhang the deep secluded vale ;
The beams of evening, slipping soft between,
Gently illuminate a sober scene;
Winding its dark green wood, and emerald glade,
The still vale lengthens underneath the shade."

In the ensuing spring I received an unexpected visit from a cousin of my husband's, a lady who had some years before married and removed to the Genesee country, as it was then termed. This lady, Mrs. Fisher, had been unfortunate in her marriage connection, and being, after some years, cruelly deserted by her unprincipled husband, now found a home in the family of her son, in a new settlement in the interior of New York. She had made the long journey to Massachusetts alone, with an intrepidity scarcely comprehensible in these days of quick travelling and certain conveyances. But she dreaded to encounter alone the repetition of all the inconveniences and annoyances on her return, and taking a fancy to Energine, she proposed that she should go with her, and find a home for a time in her son's family, at Greenvale.

At first the idea seemed quite preposterous to me, of allowing Energine to go so far from home and friends, but the more I reflected upon the matter, the more inclined I grew to favor the plan, especially as Mrs. Fisher was one with whom I could entrust her with confidence, that she would be carefully guarded from temptations, and led in the paths of rectitude and morality.

Energine herself was delighted with the prospect before her. She listened with avidity to all the descriptions which Mrs. Fisher gave us of their woods, their lakes, and the broad, level fields, so different from our own rugged hill country. She was not less amused with her accounts of the people—their manners and customs, their log-houses, rude vehicles, and their many peculiar forms of expressing their frank cordiality, and universal familiarity. She told us, too, of their rides, their quiltings, and their various " bees" or frolics, when all the men within a circuit of several miles would collect on some appointed day to help a neighbor in clearing a " piece," gathering in a crop, or in any other job of work too large for him to accomplish alone, and for which it would have been difficult, if not impossible, for him to hire the requisite assistance. The neighbors, thus rallied, worked " with a will," well knowing they, in turn, would receive the like favor, whenever occasion required.

These lively descriptions, made still more vivid to the mind of Energine by her own fancy, invested the new home to which she was invited with a charm scarcely to be depicted. She could see no possible evil in the way of her going, except the unavoidable one of leaving my own family, and for this she was in a measure prepared by her absence during the two previous years.

To my own more sober view, many objectious presented themselves, as I thought of her youth, her inexperience, her want of serious reflection, and her love of admiration. I almost shuddered, as I thought of the possible evils to which she might be exposed in that land of strangers.

But, on the other hand, I remembered my own inability to do for her as I could wish, the unhappy influences by which she was surrounded at home, and the necessity which existed that she should be enabled to maintain herself.

With these considerations, and in the full faith that " He who was able to keep her from falling" would hear my many petitions in her behalf, I gave my consent to Mrs. Fisher's urgent request, and, after a few weeks of busy preparation they left.

No doubt the "golden vapors of romance" passed from Euergine's picture as soon as she reached Greenvale ; for the familiar and near seems trivial, and only the distant and unknown are wonderful and grand. Still she was not the less happy in the reality, for hers was a bright and joyous nature, finding its pleasure in whatever was placed within its grasp, without reaching after impossibilities. She did not, like too many, " while gazing at the stars, forget the sweetness of the violets at her feet."

I cannot better give an idea of her western life to the reader, than by inserting here a letter she wrote to me not long after her arrival at Greenvale.

CHAPTER LVIII.

THE LETTER.

MY DEAR MOTHER :—

I have so much to tell you about this place and the people I have seen since I came here, that I hardly know where to begin. Young Mr. and Mrs. Fisher are very kind to me, and I have not been homesick at all, except a little Sunday nights.

Many of the people here are Dutch, and their ways are curious enough. Their houses are almost all of logs, and some of them have wooden chimneys—"stick chimneys," they call them. I should think they would take fire, but Mr. Fisher says they do not very often, they are so large and wide. In these log houses there is generally only one room, besides a narrow bed-room, which is along one whole side of the house. Up the stairs, which are sometimes a ladder, is a dark chamber, without any partitions, except as they are made by hanging up sheets or blankets from the rafters. The people visit a good deal, though there is so much hard work to do—going in whole families in a big wagon or in a cart drawn by oxen.

Mr. Fisher told me that when a young Dutchman begins to think of getting married, he thinks it essential to his success to have a fine horse to drive. The one Mr. Fisher has now, has been bought at four different times by as many dif ferent young men, who employed him on this service, and then sold him again after they were married. He is a beautiful horse, the best one in the town—they call him "Top-notch," or "Top"—he is of a clear white and his nose is bright pink ; his head is always up, and he is a very swift trotter, yet he is so gentle that I can drive him anywhere.

But I must tell you of a quilting I went to last week. I was invited by a young man whom I had seen once, at our nearest neighbor's—a brother of the young lady who gave the quilting party. He came to our house the evening before, and after talking with Mr. Fisher awhile, he turned to me and said,

"Sally Mari 's going to have a quilting to-morrow, and she'd like to have you come over, if you will."

After a few inquiries I accepted his odd invitation, and he left, saying he would come for me next day. At eleven in the forenoon he drove up in a smart red sleigh, or "cutter," as they call it here, and we rode over the smooth snow at a fine rate to Mr. Van Kromp's.

There were at least thirty quilters, with only a few of "the boys," the rest of whom were expected in the evening. Those who were already there had only come to bring the girls—mostly in large sleigh-loads—and tried to make themselves useful by handing spools, threading needles, and helping when the quilt was rolled. When we had worked till almost dark, we were invited to go into the other room (the long, narrow bed-room) while the supper-table was set.

The quilt had been suspended by the four corners of the frame, with strong cords, from the hooks in the beams above, and it was now, by some contrivance I did not fully understand, drawn up to be out of the way.

We were a good deal crowded in the bed-room, for there were three beds in it, besides chests, boxes, and some chairs. How many more things that we did not see were there I don't know, but " Aunt Jane "—as they all called Mrs. Van - Krompt—came to the door once, and called out to one of the young men,

" Here, Joachim ! you sit nigh, you reach under the bed and give me that pan of fried cakes there."

He did as she told him, and handed out a great pan full of cakes, each as big as an apple and as brown as a nut, keeping one of them " for toll," as he said, and eating it while he sat talking with some of the girls. All were full of fun and frolic, and we were soon called out to supper. Oh, I wish you could have seen the tables, for there were two of them, loaded down with food. There were two tur·keys on each, with two chickens at every corner ; then there were ham and roast beef, potatoes, beets, turnips and squash, all put on with various whimsical arrangements— the beets sliced into circles and hearts, the long potatoes and round turnips alternating upon the same dish, and the squash put in little cups or bowls at the side of each plate. Besides, there were mince-pies and apple-pies, custards and pumpkin-pies, cookies, doughnuts, and cake of two or three kinds, and great piles of warm biscuit. I had almost forgotten to mention the pickles and the preserves, of which there were a great many sorts, and the honey and the apple-butter. After all, a great waiter full of apples was carried round. I could not possibly eat all they piled on my plate, but I found they thought I was proud and impolite, so I did as much as I could in that line.

Before supper I had been introduced to almost every one in the room, by a handsome, bouncing Dutch girl, with red checks, and short curls all round her neck. A good many of the names were odd, but when she whispered " this is the schoolmaster," and then said—" Miss Energine Harlow," for they always give the whole name, " I make you acquainted with Mr. Eager Poppletony"—I thought I should laugh out. Mr. Poppletony said he was " glad to see me, as he was from the East, and heard I was too ;" and he talked away to me, while I could hardly listen to what he was saying for the looks of the man. He had a narrow face, light blue eyes, and white hair, a short nose, and a chin that looked as if it was trying to run away. Then he had on a long yellow vest, and a short-waisted blue coat with a velvet collar, and his great white hands, which he continually rubbed together as he talked, came ever so far out of his sleeves. His voice was soft and whining, and he laughed once in a while in a sort of a whimpering way, as if he was ashamed of himself for something or other. After supper, he came and began to talk to me again, and told me the names of a good many of the young people, and who they were, and what he thought of them. Two or three couples, he said, were engaged, and soon to be married ; and then added,

" Some folks are always in fits to get married, but I am not one of that sort."

I don't know why he should have volunteered this information, without he was afraid I might fall in love with his good looks.

At last he asked me "if I came with anybody?" I stared, for I wondered if he thought I had come all that two miles alone, but he explained that "he meant to inquire if I came in a large sleigh 'promiscuous,' (as he termed it) or with some enviable gallant alone ; *because*, if I was not thus appropriated, he should like to take me home in his cutter." I told him that Mr. Van Krompt had brought me, and he rolled up his eyes and said, "Ah, happy man !"

I was really glad when Sally Mari came to ask me to go and help them sing in another part of the room, and I did not see Mr. Eager again that evening.

I have written so much about this quilting that I have no room left to tell you of our singing-school, and a good many other things I want you to know about. If I could only sit down with you at home, it would be a great deal pleasanter to talk over all these things than it is to write them. I wonder how I could have been so willing to come away, for now I would be a great deal more glad to go back again. But I remember what you used to tell me—that we made our lot good or bad by our own feelings—so I try to look at the sunshine more than at the shadow.

Tell Charles the squirrels are all black here

Please write soon to your affectionate daughter,

ENERGINE HARLOW

CHAPTER LIX.

ENERGINE'S RETURN.

> "Be it ever so humble,
> There's no place like home."

ENERGINE's stay at Greenvale was prolonged to four years. She kept me informed, by occasional letters, of the general tenor of the life she passed in that remote and then newly settled region, dwelling much in them upon the unwavering kindness of her friends, the Fishers.

Her duties were not too arduous, while they were softened and made pleasant by the unfeigned generosity of heart which strove to make her feel that her place with them was that of a daughter or sister, rather than of a stranger or a common friend ; yet was she so thrown upon her own resources, in respect to the supply of her ordinary wants, and in the guidance of her own conduct, as to furnish for her a steady course of discipline, most salutary in its effects.

But amidst all the happiness which she certainly enjoyed in their good-will and affection, and in the flow of her own exuberant cheerfulness—not less the effect than the cause of the very favors showered upon her—her heart still yearned for her old home, and pined for the scenes of her childhood. The love she bore to me and my children—her brother and sisters, as she loved to call them—could scarcely have been exceeded, had she been indeed my own. Though she knew that we were no longer in the cottage at the foot of the hill in Valleybrook—that that loved spot could never be home again—my removal to another residence only quickened still more her impatience to return and join me ; as it afterwards proved, however, not to be, as formerly, a member of my family, though ever a welcome guest at our fireside.

She was for some time delayed in the fulfillment of her wishes, by the want of a suitable companion for her long and difficult journey.

Much entreaty and many inducements were offered by her new friends to persuade her to remain and settle among them, at Greenvale ; the Fishers, in the kindness of their hearts, representing to her the foolishness of wishing to return to the hills and rocks of New England, when she could so easily be provided with a comfortable home of her own, in the midst of their rich, fertile valleys. The rich man of the town, who had been successively honored with nearly all the offices the good people could bestow—being at once supervisor, justice of the peace, and member of the Legislature—was now left a widower. He sought long and earnestly to win the young orphan's consent to take the 'place of his lost companion, and be a mother to his four daughters, the eldest of whom was near her own age, the father alleging the desirable companionship of the daughter as an additional inducement for the compliance of Energine with his importunities. His efforts were seconded by the advice, and even entreaties of the Fishers, and the poor girl was for a time almost tempted to yield ; but, happily, the true instincts of the woman's heart prevailed, and she effectually resisted all solicitations to marry him simply because he would make her "a kind husband," and provide for her a home of plenty, while the heart failed to be met in the fullness and wealth of its affections.

Nor were younger suitors wanting, who proffered their sincere and manly love to the stranger maiden, and asked her to share with them a homely lot ; but my child felt in her soul no answering sympathy sufficient to turn her thoughts from her cherished home and the friends of her infancy.

A favorable opportunity at length presenting itself for her return, she left the kind people of Greenvale with affectionate farewells, and followed by their tears and good wishes.

Again restored to me, she was joyfully welcomed to my heart, with gratitude and thanksgivings to Him who had mercifully preserved her from dangers on the way.

I was glad to find that though she had not, apparently, been in a situation where she could command any very great means of improvement, she had yet gained much during her absence. The variety of her experience, with her quickness in seizing upon, and aptitude at appropriating every thing new, had enabled her to turn to some use whatever came within her range. Her mind was enlarged, and rendered more reflective ; her manners had acquired additional ease, and a shade of womanly dignity and polish. But far more than these, there had found entrance the deepest, strongest, highest power to wake up the soul to its energies and to its high destiny. She had experienced the power of religion. In her it had wrought a great and manifest change—steadying, controlling, and directing all the quick and keen sensibilities of her nature, and correcting, in good degree, her too versatile disposition.

The few months she now spent with me were fraught with much sweet and pleasant intercourse, with delight to us both, and on my part with no small gratitude, that I was thus permitted to see the child of my adoption grown to a matured excellence of character I had hardly dared to hope for. I saw in her a humble, self-reliant desire to act well her part, with an all-pervading loveliness of Christian feeling and principles.

To my family, Energine's descriptions and anecdotes of her western home were as entertaining as Mrs. Fisher's had been to her before she left us. She had a good faculty at graphic delineations, and we could almost see the immense wheat-fields, the deep, dark woods, and the clear blue lakes of which she told us.

Some of the incidents relating to her new acquaintances, and especially the Fishers, I still remember with interest. One in particular I will repeat here, as exemplifying the power of self-control evinced by the elder lady—the innate sense of dignity conferred by a consciousness of rectitude under the infliction of undeserved abuse, and the utter callousness to which a course of vice and dissipation will reduce the human heart.

Mrs. Fisher had not heard, for some years, any tidings
22

of her quondam husband, and for several reasons supposed him to be dead, when as she stood one morning washing the breakfast dishes by the little sink under the kitchen window she saw him riding up to the house, accompanied by a woman whom she had never before seen, and two young children.

"I had to hold on to the sink a moment," said she, in speaking of the affair afterwards, "but when he came in I did not turn round."

He asked for breakfast, which was readily given them, for in that new country there were as yet no taverns, and every house was free to travellers.

The woman ate in silence—the man talked to the children, but apparently took little notice of Mrs. Fisher or of her daughter-in-law. After they had eaten, and had smoked their pipes in the chimney corner, they rose to go, and the man for the first time asked for "the man of the house?" Being told that he was at work at some distance from home, he carelessly remarked, "It's no matter, we have had a good breakfast," and with no further thanks than this half-way acknowledgment, went to the door. But as he raised the latch a sudden thought seemed to strike him, and turning abruptly to Mrs. Fisher, to whom he had not before spoken, he said, in a drawling sort of a way,

"Let's see, aren't you the one that used to be Nabby Lewis?" (her maiden name.)

Drawing herself up and looking him full in the eye, she replied—

"You know my name as well as I know yours!"

The contemptible husband cowered a little, but trying to force a coarse laugh, he left, followed by the woman and her children. As soon as they were out of hearing, young Mrs. Fisher exclaimed,

"Mother, who was it?"

"His name is Fisher," said the indignant but sorrowful woman, whose tears were now flowing—"but don't tell your husband, he will be so angered—but, oh! to think that that wretch is really his father!"

"Why, mother! how *did* you feel when you saw that woman?"

"Why, I can't say," she quietly and quaintly replied, "that I felt any *immediate affection* for her!"

From regard to her mother's feelings the daughter forbore any further remarks upon the painful occurrence, and from that time they had no return of the unwelcome visitor.

Energine soon accepted, with my concurrence, a situation in the family of Mrs. Golding, already mentioned, who was now advanced in life. Mrs. Golding was the eldest daughter of old Madam Dudley, whom she closely resembled in character, though with far less native powers of mind.

Her husband was a quiet, inoffensive man, seeming to think he was born for little else but to add field after field to his well-stocked and very profitable farm. They were now wealthy. Of their three sons, the eldest had distinguished himself in boyhood by an aptitude in study, and was now the honored author of a successful series of school-books. The second—incited by the example of his brother, and himself possessed of no mean intellect—conquered the natural indolence of his disposition, and cultivating his mathematical and inventive genius, had won for himself considerable fame as the originator of several important improvements in machinery, and in agricultural implements.

The youngest son was of a less enterprising turn, though all the children displayed a mental organization quite superior to that of their parents. He had now reached the mature age of thirty-five, and was the chief manager at home. He much resembled his uncle, Sam Lyman—the husband of my sister Mary—and this was not only in looks, but in his somewhat pompous manner and language, and in his upright, honorable, and independent character.

Living as he had so long done, with no female companionship but that of his peevish and exacting mother, the coming of Energine into their household was like the gleaming ray of a sweeter life upon the ungracious seeming of his own.

It was not a surprising, though to me a most unexpected result, that he was wholly captivated by her winning, sprightly grace and beauty. Her ready sympathy, the cheerful kindliness of her disposition, won his fervent admiration, and filled his entire being with an emotion to which he had hitherto been wholly a stranger.

He succeeded, in spite of the unkindness and opposition of his money-loving mother, who, it must be recollected, was the daughter of Madam Dudley, in awakening a corresponding sentiment in the heart of my child, and after some delay their marriage took place, with fair promise of happiness, which in their subsequent life has been well fulfilled.

Religion had enlarged and improved, not changed, Energine's disposition. The same genial humor, the same love of the bright and gay, even her old craving for admiration, were all perceptible in the matron and mother, which we have seen in the youthful maiden ; but so modified as to have become excellences rather than defects.

Her mirthfulness, subdued to a serener hue, became cheerful cordiality. The beautiful in nature was ever fresh to her eyes, and many a happy thought and feeling did she gain and impart to others from the delighted contemplation of the ornaments with which God has decked the earth.

Her delight in the approval of others led her to strive for their pleasure, and in the endeavor she forgot self, and learned the higher bliss of doing good.

To her husband she was a joy, a sunbeam, and in their children were mingled the solidity and strength of the sterner nature with the delicacy and elegance of the mother.

<blockquote>
" Thou sweetest thing
That e'er did fix its lightly-fibred sprays
To the rude rock ; ah ! woulds't thou cling to me ?
Rough and storm-worn I am ! but if thou lov'st me—
Thou truly dost—I will love thee again
With true and honest heart, tho' all unmeet
To be the mate of such sweet gentleness."
</blockquote>

CHAPTER LX.

RETROSPECT AND CHANGE.

"Whence that low voice?—a whisper from the heart
That told of days long past."

In relating these later circumstances of Energine's history, I have brought my narrative down to a period in advance of actual events respecting myself which happened soon after her departure to the West with kind Mrs. Fisher.

Nearly nine years of my widowed life had now passed, and although there ever hung around my dwelling, like a dark shadow, that "cruel sense of loss;" yet I was not unhappy, for I had a Heavenly Comforter. He who had led me all my life long was with me still—a Presence of light, and joy, and peace.

I looked back to the time of my gleeful, sunny childhood, in my father's house : I seemed to stand on the brow of the hill, and view the brown cottage peeping out from behind the little clump of cherry trees, and my heart warmed at the thought. My first great journey to Boston, and to Maine, came up fresh and glowing with the vision of my happy girlhood. Then rose to my mind the remembrance of life's golden prime, when the cup of earthly happiness was full—when

"The soberness of undisturbed bliss
Held even empire in the mind,
Like steady sunshine in a cloudless day."

Again, the ever-present consciousness that

"The storm had been with me, and I was left
Torn and uprooted and laid in the dust."

In childhood, in youth, in maturer years, the Merciful One had guided my path and led my steps, and was preparing for me even now, when I knew it not, greater blessings and new happiness.

The lapse of time will bring *change*—change of circumstances, change in the aspects of things, and in the views we take of them—change ever, too, in that successive, inextricable net-work of present scenes, duties, particular pursuits and feelings, in which we are each involved and form a part; and that makes up the machinery of our strange, busy, mysterious, ever-flitting life. But change, so all-powerful, need not, cannot, touch the affections of the heart—our inner selves. The world of cherished, happy associations links the past with the present—and the chain is bright! True, the happiness of yesterday is not that of to-day; the peculiar delights and pleasant things of the past are gone, and they will not be recalled; the fountain may rise as high, the stream flow as deep and as broad now as then; but that THEN still remains a distinct charm of the past, rendered, perchance, still more dear by a conscious feeling of half regret that it has thus drifted back on the resistless current of time.

Let me return again to my story. I have spoken of my perplexities, on several points, before the departure of Energine with our cousin, Mrs. Fisher, and though relieved by that event as respected her, still there were other things

which gave me no little disquietude. My next neighbor, it
will be perhaps recollected, was David Hill, whose wife,
·Eunice Cotting, was a dear friend, the sister of Bessy's
husband. She was a pale, delicate woman, suffering all her
life from frequent illness, and I had seen her fade away
gradually, step by step, until, with the coming of the early
spring flowers, she died, and was laid in her peaceful grave,
leaving behind her two little girls, about the age of my own.
I had been with her much during the long, slow progress
of the disease—that insidious, but fell disease, consumption—which, while it too surely marks its victim, leaves the
mind clear and unclouded to the last ; and much consolation
I had in the serenity and truly Christian joy which smoothed
and lighted her way through the dark valley.

After the lapse of some months, Mr. Hill, always quite
neighborly and social, began to make more frequent calls,
and ere long became a regular visitor every Sunday evening,
after the services of the day were over, chatting awhile on
various trivial subjects, and then taking leave.

These visits troubled me, not only that they drew forth
certain sly hints and intimations, unpleasant to me, from
my neighbors, but more especially because they occupied
that portion of the holy day which I was accustomed to
devote to my children, and which I prized too highly,
willingly to spend in frivolous conversation.

Besides this, I could not avoid the thought that some
particular purpose prompted the unusual attention—a purpose to which I should be utterly averse. Neither was it
difficult to guess at motives on his part not particularly flat-

tering to me, nor indeed very creditable to himself; for my little, though valuable, farm adjoining his, would make a very pretty and commodious addition to his own snug property. Altogether, I was uneasy, almost vexed, at the proceeding; yet could I find no way, without resorting to absolute rudeness, to free myself from the unwelcome intrusion and real annoyance.

A pleasant and friendly neighbor, David Hill, could be to me nothing more, and I was often reminded of our "sisterly conferences," of which he was the unconscious subject in reference to our dear Grace.

In the midst of my embarrassment, an unexpected event brought about a new phase in my affairs. An old friend, a gentleman whom I had not seen for several years, came one day to see me. He prolonged his stay for several hours; he asked and obtained permission to come again: but I will reserve to another chapter the fuller explanation of what was to me of so much importance.

CHAPTER LXI.

THE WIFE.

"How much tranquillity and contentment in human homes ! Calm onflowings of life shaded in domestic privacy, and seen only at times coming out into the open light."

ONE bright day in March, two single horse sleighs might have been seen passing fleetly over the well-trodden snow toward the East ; their destination the pleasant town of Rawley, twelve miles from Wayland. In the foremost sat, comfortably wrapped in furs, hopeful and happy, the one, gentle reader, so often brought before your notice in this narrative, for some time past known familiarly as "the Widow Coke," no longer so—by my side, conversing in an animated manner, was Mr. Isaac Howard.

Behind us were my three children—Charles was the driver—his two sisters with him, going, in all the trust and joy of childhood, to their new home.

About dark we arrived at a neat white house, on an elevated spot, surrounded by fine scenery, and commanding an extensive prospect.

As we entered the spacious family room, a cheerful, blazing fire was brightly reflected in the large, brass andirons, the tea-table was awaiting our arrival, loaded with tempting viands, and an air of comfort and plenty pervaded the whole. Two young maidens, busy in the last touches of preparation, came promptly forward to welcome and assist us in removing cloaks and shawls, and arranging all comfortably.

Soon I was seated at the head of that table—my two smiling little girls on my right—my son, staid and serious, yet with a half-roguish expression, by the side of his new father, whose eyes beamed upon me with a clear, living light, such as only full trust and serene happiness can enkindle. After the tea things were removed, we passed into the adjoining room, and my husband, taking my hand, said,

" Here, my Anna, is the place where I hope we shall enjoy much together."

It was a small room, with pleasant windows, and bookshelves tastefully arranged and well filled—quite a little boudoir was the room. It was finished with some elegance, according to the style of those days ; and the color, being the lightest of all blues, with paper to match, gave it a lively and even gay appearance, lighted up as it was by the cheerful fire.

Here, indeed, were spent many delightful evenings, full of calm enjoyment, in the converse of congenial minds, or in the mutual pleasure derived from the perusal together of improving and entertaining books. My children had found a father ; he sought their good ; he instructed them from the stores of his own knowledge. It had been my delight in my hours of lonely leisure to lead them, step by step, through the toilsome routine of school studies, and they were ready scholars ; now a fresh impulse was given to their endeavors.

My children were, indeed, most happy and favored in this new relation ; they had no remembrance of their own father, and easily transferred to my husband the filial affection due to a parent, to which he on his part heartily responded. He delighted to guide their young minds, taking a deep interest in their rapid development, and seeing, almost with a father's pride, any quickness, attractive qualities, or ability in them.

We were now in a neighborhood, agreeable, orderly, and social, free, in great measure, from the untoward influences to which I have before alluded as the source of anxiety to me. Most pleasant and cheerful, too, were the surroundings of our home in Rawley ; there was not, it is true, the quiet and picturesque beauty of Valley Brook, with its winding streamlet and its hill-sides crowned with verdure, but a beauty no less real, though grander in outline. A gentle slope to the south gave a sunny exposure, on which the light rested pleasantly, while the morning sun threw across the broad, green plat in front the slender shadows of the flourishing young maples bordering the rustic road.

On the north, a bare and rocky mountain loomed up, grey and misty, in the distance ; while just beyond the orchard, were two small, gracefully rounded hills, rising from the plain field, so green, so lovely in their patches of waving grass, half-hidden rocks, and clumps of trees, that they were like a picture before the eye. But, above all, adown the smooth, green slope in front, were the pleasant, open woods, so beautiful in their every variety of hue and shade, with many sunny glades and dim recesses ; the " quivering aspen," the thrifty beech and birch, a sprinkling of the pure verdure and graceful tassels of the larch, with the dark, solemn firs, their tall cones pointing skyward, and the lofty pine, the hoary inhabitants of the forest.

When, as a young man, " Master Howard " sought my love, my girlish, maiden heart beat no response; it had already its secret image within ; but when the matured man of forty, courteous and dignified, proffered me the support of his manly arm—the strength and guidance of his well-cultured and gifted mind, my soul, chastened, yet quickened to larger, nobler aim and purpose, found sweet repose and solace in the true friendship and faithful affection of such an earthly guide and protector. Again I experienced the pure and ennobling exercise of those affections on which the seal of Death had been placed ! That wonderful, mysterious, precious sympathy—wedded love !

Years succeeded, not indeed exempt from trial, dimmed, too, by frequent ill health and many weighty cares, yet cheered by new joys and hopes, and solaced by the kindness and devoted love of my noble husband.

He was a tower of strength unto me. In him, all my purer, better feelings, my nobler aspirations, met a ready response, and I was thus led, in delighted companionship, to a higher range of thought and mental attainment, fitting me the better, I trust, for the important responsibilities of mother.

Four more were added to the number of my treasures—three gleeful, sprightly boys, and one fair, gentle girl. With us were never known the differences so unwisely made in my father's family, but we were all one loving, united household.

A few more years glided on, and my husband, at the earnest solicitation of friends, established himself in Boston, as furnishing more ample scope for his profession, and also greater advantages for our children.

In this favored city—the Queen of New England—we found a quiet, pleasant home, encircled with its elegances, refinements, and numerous facilities for the liberal culture of the mind and heart. Our children—the elder ones just entering upon busy life—availing themselves of their increased means of advancement, were rapidly improving, and we looked forward with high hopes of future prosperity and happiness.

Here let me stop—let me be spared the record that follows, lest I darken the picture by the recital of fresh scenes of sorrow—for sorrow, deep and bitter, was again my portion.

I was again a widow! Yet let me gratefully remember, that in this second hour of grief there was comfort mingled even with the bitter cup; for my husband, so beloved, so lamented, died in the assured hope and peace of the Christian.

Many years have now gone! Their even course has not indeed reflected a cloudless sky, though comparatively unruffled and serene. In casting my eye along the winding, "backward track" of life, thankfulness to my God and Saviour is the feeling that, more than all others, pervades my heart.

My later years have been passed in tranquillity and content, blessed in the dutiful affection of my sons and daughters, now all-happily married and settled in life.

Time has silvered my hair, and dimmed my eyes, but in my children's children I live over again the scenes of my youth.

How beautiful the dewy freshness of the dawn of day! when, with the bright morning sun, all things rejoice in fragrance and in beauty.

So, in early youth, the spirit looks forth, joyous and free; each fair, smiling path strewn with roses, and an ever-widening vista opens of loveliness and bliss.

But, as surely as the sultriness of the deepening noon, the dust and strife, the tumult of the crowded street and busy mart, follow, not with lingering steps, the quiet coolness of the summer morning, so surely must the green and flowery paths of the spring-time of life lead to the rough slope and steep ascent. All must thread the tangled maze of life—each with his burden of perturbed and anxious thoughts, alternate hopes and fears, and longing aspirations ever unfulfilled! And is this all of life? Is there then no light, no hope to cheer, amid thick-coming cares and blighting disappointments? There is a Hope, never fading;

there is a Light, shining clear and steady. Its beams are shed on a path shady and sequestered, but not lonely—where the pure breezes softly echo back the pleasant voices of a happy company, singing as they journey on—where verdant boughs, overhanging with thickly clustering branches, drop fruits of love and kindness. It is the path from Earth to Heaven.

LIST

OF

NEW AND POPULAR BOOKS,

PUBLISHED AND FOR SALE BY

D. W. EVANS & CO.,

677 BROADWAY, NEW-YORK.

WORKS OF TRAVEL.

BY REV. WALTER COLTON.

THE works of Mr. Colton have outlived most American books of this character, simply on account of their raciness and beauty of style. The Superintendents of Ohio, Indiana, and Michigan, have recommended most of those volumes for the libraries of their States.

SHIP AND SHORE,

In Madeira, Lisbon, and the Mediterranean. By Rev. Walter Colton, U. S. N., late Alcalde of Monterey. It was in this work that Mr. Colton made his first essay as an author without a name. The favor with which it was received was a prophecy of the success of his after works, for it procured him an honorable fame, both as a poet of promise and a spirited author of lively prose. Illustrated. 12mo, cloth. Price $1.

"This is one of the most charming books of travel that ever was placed before the American public. Probably more beautiful passages and pages have been transcribed from this book than any other American work."—*Boston Cour.*

LAND AND LEE,

In the Bosphorus and Egean; or, Views of Constantinople and Athens. By Rev. Walter Colton, U. S. N. Athens and Constantinople, with all the traditions, peculiarities, manners; and customs of their people; their political, religious, and social life, occupations, &c., are placed before the reader of this volume in a clear and attractive style. Illustrated. 12mo, cloth. Price $1.

"This work will be remembered as a bright, sketchy, sparkling picture of the classical shores of the Egean and Bosphorus. It abounds in shrewd remarks and buoyant enthusiasm, reflecting the joyousness of the climes it portrays."—*New-York Evangelist.*

DECK AND PORT;

Or, Incidents of a Cruise to California, with Sketches of Rio Janeiro, Valparaiso, Lima, Honolulu, and San Francisco. By Rev. Walter Colton. This work is full of highly interesting scenes and incidents, detailed by a master hand. Everything related is clothed in the rich garniture which is afforded by a well-stored and well-cultivated mind, governed by high moral principle.

"His pen has the wand-like power of making the scenes which it describes live and move before the mind of the reader. We can cheerfully recommend this as a charming book."—*Hartford Christian Secretary.*

THE LAND OF GOLD;

Or, Three Years in California. By Rev. Walter Colton. This volume gives an interesting description of the country and its inhabitants at the time of the breaking out of the gold fever, and the excitement and tumult which ensued. Nothing of interest to the public in this new world—its towns, villages, and settlements, its gold digging, gold explorations, etc.—escapes the author's notice. Illustrated. 12mo, cloth. Price $1.

"While the reader is instructed on every page, he will laugh about a hundred, if not a thousand times, before he gets through this captivating volume."—*Washington Republic.*

LIVES AND EXPLOITS OF HIGHWAYMEN AND ROBBERS,

Embracing the career of Claude Duval, Jack Shepherd, Dick Turpin, Eugene Aram, the Golden Farmer, Tom Jones and the German Princess, and more than thirty other celebrated highwaymen and robbers. Fully illustrated. 12mo, cloth. Price $1.

THE SEA AND THE SAILOR.

Notes on France and Italy, and other literary remains of Rev. Walter Colton. With a Memoir, by the Rev. H. T. Cheever. This volume is composed of Mr. Colton's most valuable miscellaneous writings, and will be read by many who knew and esteemed him with thrilling interest. His aphorisms, maxims, and remarks demonstrate the mind of a keen observer of men and manner. 12mo, cloth. Price $1.

"The Sea and the Sailor is a real addition to our religious literature, and we doubt not it will be widely useful."—*New-York Observer.*

THIRTY YEARS IN THE ARCTIC REGIONS;

Or, The Adventures of Sir John Franklin, The fate of Sir John Franklin has not ceased to be a theme of deep interest throughout the world. The narrative of the expedition, the first in 1816, the fourth and last undertaken in 1845, we have the final solution; his fate being the great problem which has awakened more interest than that of the discovery of the Northwest passage itself. All the information that has been acquired, respecting his last expedition, is here given, together with a sketch of McClintock's expedition sent out in search of him, and the final success attending it.

The chief merit of this volume of nearly 500 pages, is that it gives for the first time, in a cheap and readable form, Sir John Franklin's own account of his early voyages, condensed, of course, but containing all the pith of his relations. No inconsiderable amount of labor must have been expended in making this compilation, the material for which could not have been very easy of access. The investment of labor, however, was a safe one, for the Arctic regions have long held an inscrutable hold on the public mind—a hold rendered a thousand times firmer by the sad fate of Franklin. In the sad loss of the brave navigator has nearly been swallowed up the memory of his successful voyages; and only a small body of general readers remember the important aids to geographical science which he rendered during his thirty years of occasional effort in Arctic exploration. The popular publication of this book will do a good office in imparting a more general knowledge of these facts; and for the mere pleasure reader it has the strange interest of all Arctic narratives. Large 12mo, cloth. Price $1 25.

INDIAN BATTLES.

With incidents in the early history of New England. Large 12mo. 425 pages. Price $1.

A book of wonderful and intense interest, containing thrilling and stirring narratives of Battles, Captivities, Escapes, Ambuscades, Assaults, Massacres, and Depredations of the Indians. The Habits, Customs, and Traits of Character peculiar to the Indian race. The Life and Exploits of Capt. Miles Standish—The history of King Philip's War—an interesting account of the coalition of Indian Tribes in New England to exterminate the English Settlers—the gallant deeds of Capt. Church, Major Waldron, Capts. Stone, Lovewell and Wainwright. The youthful adventures of General Putnam, and historical incidents in the Revolutionary War, containing many interesting items of local and historical interest, never before published.

The talented compiler, in his preface, says : " It is exceedingly desirable that these incidents should be extensively read—hitherto they have been confined to a few rare works, so that to most persons they have been inaccessible, and to a great degree unknown. The design of this volume is, to embody these incidents, and present them to the reader in one view, and if it assists to influence the patriotism, strengthen the faith, interest and instruct the mind, and promote the morality and religion of the community, the object of the author is attained."

THE TRAIL OF BLOOD.

A record of crime from the earliest to the present day, containing the trials and confessions of the most celebrated criminals of this and foreign countries, with biographical sketches of the most cold-blooded murderers, who have been tried and executed in this country. Fully illustrated with numerous engravings and portraits from life, with many other narratives—with an engraved vignette in colors. Large 12mo, cloth. Price $1 25.

MOST NOTED PIRATES.

The History of the Lives and bloody Exploits of the most noted pirates, their trial and execution, including a correct account of the large piracies in the West Indies, with the remarkable adventures of Capt. Kidd. Fully illustrated. 12mo, cloth. Price $1.

VIOLA ; OR, THE TRIUMPH OF LOVE AND FAITH.

By Wm. Earle Binder, author of "Madelon Hawley, &c., &c. 12mo. Beautifully illustrated from designs by Orr, executed in the highest style of the art. Price $1.

Viola is not merely a work of fiction for which we claim the attention of the public, nor do its highest merits rest in creating a sensation. The high moral tone infused throughout its pages, sustained by irresistible logic, without detracting from the interest, claims for it a place by every fireside.

The sensation seeker, and intellectual epicure will read it—the one for its startling plot, and inexpressible interest ; the other for its constant warnings to the right path, and beautiful delineation of every-day life. Nothing has been spared to render this book attractive in every form. The illustrations presenting some of the most thrilling scenes to the eye of the reader, and executed in effective style, from designs by Orr, the well-known artist.

LIGHT AND SHADE ;

Or, THE YOUNG ARTIST.

A Tale by Anna Harriet Drury, author of " Friends and Fortune," " Eastbury," &c. 12mo, cloth. Price $1.

" It is a beautiful and ably written story."—*Churchman.*

" The scenes of this work are portrayed with a delicacy and a natural pathos that give to them an irresistible attraction."—*Courier and Enquirer.*

" It deserves, and will doubtless receive, an extended circulation, and will do good wherever it may go."—*Newark Advertiser.*

" It is a romance that the most fastidious objector to novel reading might peruse with advantage as well as with pleasure."—*Worcester Palladium.*

" We are disposed to rank this work, in point of talent, more highly than any of Miss Drury's previous volumes."

" It is pleasant to recommend a volume like this, which every mother can place in her daughter's hand with the certainty that the lesson it teaches must strengthen within her every virtuous thought, and better prepare her to pass worthily through the conflict of life. We cannot do the reading public a better service than to recommend the circulation of this work."—*Albany State Register.*

" A book of high order and rare interest, and worthy to rank among the foremost works of that class of fiction, which invigorate but do not intoxicate."—*Com. Advertiser.*

HOME IS HOME.

A book for the fireside. 12mo, cloth. Price $1.

"The higher walks of life, the blessedness of doing good, and the paths of usefulness and enjoyment, are drawn out with beautiful simplicity, and made attractive and easy in the attractive pages of this author. To do good, to teach others how to do good, to render the home circle and the neighborhood glad with the voice and hand of Christian charity, is the aim of the author, who has great power of description, a genuine love for evangelical religion, and blends instruction with the story, so as to give a charm to all her books."—*N. Y. Observer.*

"Whoever misses reading this book, will miss reading what is, in various respects, to the best of our judgment and experience, the most remarkable book of the day—one, indeed, that no thoughtful, inquiring mind would miss reading for a great deal."—*New Monthly (London) Magazine.*

"The language is chaste and appropriate, the characters finely drawn, and the whole makes a fine family picture, which some great artist, like Powers or Durand, might chisel into palpable form, or cause to glow upon the almost breathing canvas with admirable effect."—MRS. JANE MARIA MEAD.

"The excellency and beauty of the Christian Virtues, as here presented, cannot fail to commend them to the readers' approval, and to make a salutary and lasting impression upon their minds; while the intrinsic interest of the work will delight, instruct, and improve."—*Syracuse Journal.*

DARING DEEDS OF AMERICAN HEROES.

A record of the Lives of American Patriots and Heroes, including full and accurate biographies of the most celebrated American Generals. The Life and Services of Gen. Jacob Brown, including a History of the Invasion of Canada during the War of 1812, with a spirited account of the battles of Fort Erie, Chippewa and Niagara. Life of Gen. Gaines, including a History of the Seminole and Black Hawk Wars. Life of William Henry Harrison, Defeat of the Northwestern Indians, Attack on the Chesapeake, Battle of Tippecanoe, Defence of Fort Harrison, Massacre at Frenchtown, Siege of Fort Meigs, Perry's Victory Battle of the Thames. Life of Andrew Jackson, Attack on the Wax Haw, Battle of Hobkirk's Hill, the Creek War, Battle of Talluschatchee, Battle of Talladega, Battle of Emuckfaw, Battle of Enotochopco, Battle of Tohopeko, Capture of Pensacola, Battle of New-Orleans. Life of Gen. Macomb, Capture of Fort George, MacDonough's Victory, Battle of Plattsburgh. Life of Gen. Pike, Expedition against York. Life of Major-General Winfield Scott, Attack on Queenstown, War with the Sacs and Foxes, Expedition against Vera Cruz, Battle of Cerro Gordo, Battle of Contreras, Battle of Cherubusco, Battle of El Molino Del Rey, Capture of Mexico, &c., &c. Bound in one volume. Large 12mo., cloth. Price, $1.

GOOD NEWS OF GOD.

Sermons by Rev. Charles Kingsley, author of Yeast, Alton Locke, &c., &c. 12mo, cloth.   Price $1.

The following review by Evert M. Duyckinck, author of the Cyclopedia of American Literature, will give an idea of its merits : " When we open the book, and enter upon its thirty-nine discourses, following the heart-stirring deductions of the spiritual life, the fine-thoughted improvements of scriptural narratives and apologues, the cheerful words throwing light upon the darker paths of daily life, we recognize the words of one, who, by sympathy and the best knowledge of mankind, is eminently fitted to be a teacher of men. These sermons are animated, yet not rhetorical; full of subtle perceptions of truth, yet not obscure ; indeed, the subtlety fulfils its proper work in unriddling what is dark before us. We may take, as an instance of this apt subtlety, one which we have alighted upon at the opening of the book, an elucidation of the text, " *Take no thought for the morrow*," which might be very easily misconceived as a plea for neglect of labor. Mr. Kingsley takes the difficulty in hand at the out-set. It is not prudence or effort, he tells us, that we are taught to avoid or be indifferent about, but anxiety and troublesome fears which are to be shunned— for the very reason that they are foes to prudence. " Let me say a few words to you on the text," in his language. " Be not anxious, it tells you. And why ? Because you have to be prudent. In practice, fretting, and anxiety, help no man toward prudence. On the contrary, I know nothing which cripples a man more, and hinders him working manfully, than anxiety. The wholesome truth is enforced by many familiar illustrations."

THE LIFE OF MARTIN LUTHER,

Gathered from his own writings, by M. Michelet, author of " Love," " Woman," "A History of France," &c., &c. 12mo., cloth. Price, $1.

This valuable work is the best Biography of the Great Reformer ever written ; best, because the frequent reference to the diary and correspondence of Luther renders it almost an autobiography, so that every page glows with the truth, piety, and fearless virtue of this Representative Man of Modern Times. It is not only a biography of the man, but a history of his work, the Reformation, and as such is doubly valuable to the general reader.

THE UNIVERSAL GENIUS;
OR, THE COMING MAN.

By M. W. Savage, Esq., author of the "Bachelor of Albany," "My Uncle the Curate," &c.   One vol., 12mo. pp. 443, cloth.   Price, $1.

A most entertaining story, by the author of the "Bachelor of Albany." It is full of life and character, and is written sensibly, humorously, and often satirically.—*N. Y. Courier.*

The story is well told, and the moral a most instructive one.—*Daily Standard.*

The narrative is remarkably lively and amusing, and the varied characters are depicted in a graphic and sparkling manner.—*Christian Messenger.*

The story is very skilfully and yet naturally wrought out, and he will be a fortunate reader who does not find parts of it bearing closely on passages in his own life.—*Albany Reg.*

A satirical novel, written in a style of high art and careless carefulness rarely excelled We have seen nothing more lively, polished, and piquant for many a day.—*N. Y. Post.*

It is written in a dazzling and joyous style, which certainly recommends it.—*Troy Whig.*

HEARTS UNVEILED;
OR, I KNEW YOU WOULD LIKE HIM.

"There is a glare about worldly success which is very apt to dazzle men's eyes. When we see a man rising in the world, thriving in business, successful in his speculations—if he be a man out of our own line, who does not come in competition with us, so as to make us jealous of him—we are apt to form a foolishly high opinion of his merits. We are apt to say within ourselves, 'what a wonderful man this must be to rise so rapidly,' forgetting that straw, and dust, and feathers, things with neither weight nor value in them, rise the soonest and easiest; and yet, though he push his fortunes, he may not have a grain of real greatness about him. He may be utterly without sympathy and fellow-feeling for others; he may be utterly devoid of all true wisdom; he may be without piety and charity—without love, that is, either for God or man." A book of sterling value and interest. 12mo. Price, $1.

LIFE AND ADVENTURES OF LEWIS WETZEL.

Together with Biographical Sketches of Simon Kenton, Benjamin Logan, Samuel Brady, Isaac Shelby, and other distinguished Warriors and Hunters of the West. By Cecil B. Hartley. With splendid illustrations, from original drawings by George G. White. 12mo., cloth. Price $1.

THE YOUNG LADY'S CABINET OF GEMS.

A CHOICE COLLECTION OF PIECES IN PROSE AND POETRY.

Poetry is one of the most powerful aids to human refinement and spiritua progress. With the aid of flowing numbers, it impresses great truths indelibly on the mind, and in making this collection, the object has been to present the reader with pieces that are really gems, not only in expression, but in thought and sentiment. It has been a constant endeavor to present the real spirit of the present age, so eminently an age of progress.

It will consequently be found that not only are the pieces here given the productions of living or very recent writers, for the most part, but that the poetry, breathes that high spirit of philanthropy and Christian benevolence which marks the present era, and which serves to keep alive the high tone of moral feeling. which the real philanthropist is happy to recognise as one of the features of our best current literature. Bound in one handsome volume. 12mo., cloth. Price, $1.

LIFE OF THE EMPRESS JOSEPHINE,

First Wife of Napoleon. Illustrated with steel portraits. By J. T. Laurens author of "Heroes and Patriots of the South." 12mo., cloth. Price $1.

LIFE AND ADVENTURES OF DAVID CROCKETT.

Written by himself, with notes and additions. Splendidly illustrated with engravings, from original designs. By George G. White. 12mo., cloth. Price $1.

LIFE AND TIMES OF DANIEL BOONE.

Including an account of the Early Settlement of Kentucky. By Cecil B. Hartley. With splendid illustrations, from original drawings by George G. White. 12mo., cloth. Price $1.

LIFE AND TIMES OF GENERAL FRANCIS MARION,

The Hero of the American Revolution; giving full accounts of his many perilous adventures and hair-breadth escapes among the British and Tories in Southern States, during the struggle for liberty. By W. Gilmore Simms. 12mo. cloth. Price $1.

THE PRINCE OF THE HOUSE OF DAVID,

Or Three Years in the Holy City.   A series of letters of Adina, a Jewess of Alexandria, supposed to be sojourning in Jerusalem in the days of Herod, addressed to her father, a wealthy Jew, in Egypt, and relating, as if by an eye witness, all the scenes and wonderful Incidents in the Life of Jesus of Nazareth, from his baptism in Jordan to his crucifixion on Calvary.   New edition' carefully revised and corrected by the author, Rev. J. H. Ingraham, LL. D. Rector of Christ Church, and of St. Thomas' Hall, Holly Springs, Miss., with five splendid illustrations.   One large 12mo. volume, cloth.   Price $1 25.

THE PILLAR OF FIRE;

Or, Israel in Bondage.   Being an account of the wonderful Scenes in the Life of the Son of Pharaoh's Daughter, (Moses,) together with Picturesque Sketches of the Hebrews under their task-masters.   By Rev. J. H. Ingraham, LL. D., author of the " Prince of the House of David."   Price $1 25.

"The Pillar of Fire" is a large 12mo. volume of 600 pages, illustrated, and contains an account of the wonderful scenes in the life of the Son of Pharaoh's Daughter (Moses), from his youth to the ascent of Sinai; comprising, as by an eye-witness, his miracles before Pharaoh, Passage of the Red Sea, and the reception of the Law on Mount Sinai, &c.

THE THRONE OF DAVID;

Or, the Rebellion of Prince Absalom.   Being an illustration of the splendor, power and dominion of the Reign of the Shepherd, Poet, Warrior, King and Prophet, Ancestor and Type of Jesus; in a series of letters addressed by an Assyrian Ambassador, resident at the Court of Jerusalem, to his Lord and King on the throne of Nineveh ; wherein the glory of Assyria, as well as the magnificence of Judea, is presented to the reader as by an eye-witness.   By the Rev. J. H. Ingraham, LL. D., Rector of Christ Church, Holly Springs, Miss., author of the " Prince of the House of David," and the " Pillar of Fire."   12mo, cloth. Price $1 25.

LIVES OF FEMALE MORMONS.

A Narrative of Facts Stranger than Fiction.   By Metta Victoria Fuller 12mo , cloth.   Price $1.

JOYS AND SORROWS OF HOME.

An Autobiography. By Anna Leland. One volume, 12mo., cloth. Price $1

" This is one of the most beautiful domestic stories we have ever read, intensely interesting, with a natural flow and easiness which lead the reader imperceptibly on to the close, and then leave a regret that the tale is done."

BOOK OF ANECDOTES AND BUDGET OF FUN.

Containing a collection of over One Thousand Laughable Sayings, Rich Jokes, &c. 12mo., cloth, extra gilt back. Price $1.

" Nothing is so well calculated to preserve the healthful action of the human system as a good hearty laugh."

BEAUTY OF WOMAN'S FAITH;

A Tale of Southern Life. One volume, 12mo., cloth. Price $1.

" This volume contains the story of a French Emigrant, who first escaped to England, and afterward settled on a plantation in Louisiana. It is charmingly told, and the strength and endurance of woman's faith well illustrated."

THREE PER CENT. A MONTH;

Or, The Perils of Fast Living. A Warning to Young Men. By Chas. Burdett. One volume, 12mo., cloth. Price $1.

" The style of this book is direct and effective, particularly fitting the impression which such a story should make. It is a very spirited and instructive tale, leaving a good impression both upon the reader's sensibilities and morals."

LIGHTS AND SHADOWS OF A. PASTOR'S LIFE.

By S. H. Elliott. One volume, 12mo., cloth. Price $1.

" This is a well-written, highly instructive book. It is a story of the life-teachings and life-trials of a good man, whose great aim was to elevate, morally and intellectually, his fellow-men. Like many of his nature and temperament, some of his views were Utopian. But his successes and failures, with the causes of these, are painted with a masterly hand. There is unusual strength and vitality in this volume."

THE ENCHANTED BEAUTY,

And other Tales and Essays. By Dr. Wm. Elder. 12mo., cloth. Price $1.

"This is a volume of beautiful and cogent essays, virtuous in motive, simple in expression, pertinent and admirable in logic, and glorious in conclusion and climax."

THE DESERTED FAMILY;

Or, the Wanderings of an Outcast. By Paul Creyton. 12mo., cloth. Price $1.

"An interesting story, which might exert a good influence in softening the heart, warming the affections, and elevating the soul."

RECORDS OF THE REVOLUTIONARY WAR.

Containing the Military and Financial Correspondence of distinguished officers; Names of the officers and privates of regiments, companies and corps, with the dates of their commissions and enlistments. General orders of Washington, Lee, and Green; with a list of distinguished prisoners of war; the time of their capture, exchange, &c.; to which is added the half-pay acts of the Continental Congress; the Revolutionary pension laws; and a list of the officers of the Continental army who acquired the right to half-pay, commutation, and lands, &c. By T. W. Saffell. Large 12mo. Price $1 25.

THE ROMANCE OF THE REVOLUTION.

Being a history of the personal adventures, romantic incidents and exploits incidental to the War of Independence—with tinted illustrations. Large 12mo. Price $1 25.

THE MASTER SPIRIT OF THE AGE.

THE PUBLIC AND PRIVATE HISTORY OF NAPOLEON THE THIRD.

With biographical notices of his most distinguished Ministers, Generals, and Favorites. By S. M. Smucker, LL. D. This interesting and valuable work is embellished with splendid steel plates, done by Sartain, in his best style, including the Emperor, the Empress, Queen Hortense, and the Countess Castiglione. 400 pages, 12mo. Price $1 25.

The following books are by T. S. Arthur, the well-known author, of whom it has been said, "He has not written a word that, dying, he would wish to erase." They are worthy of a place in every household.

ARTHUR'S SKETCHES OF LIFE AND CHARACTER.

An octavo volume of over 400 pages, beautifully illustrated, and bound in the best English muslin, gilt.   Price $2.

LIGHTS AND SHADOWS OF REAL LIFE.

With an Autobiography and Portrait of the Author.   Over 500 pages, octavo, with fine tinted engravings.   Price $2.

TEN NIGHTS IN A BAR-ROOM, AND WHAT I SAW THERE.

This powerfully-written work, one of the best by its popular author, has met with an immense sale.   It is a large 12mo., illustrated with a beautiful mezzotint engraving, by Sartain; printed on fine white paper, and bound in the best English muslin, gilt back.   Price $1.

A HISTORY OF ITALY,
AND THE WAR OF 1859.

Giving the causes of the War, with Biographical Sketches of Sovereigns, Statesmen and Military Commanders; Descriptions and Statistics of the Country; with finely engraved Portraits of Louis Napoleon, Emperor of France, Francis Joseph, Emperor of Austria, Victor Emanuel, King of Sardinia, and Garibaldi, the Champion of Italian Freedom.   Together with the official accounts of the Battles of Montebello, Palestro, Magenta, Malegnano, Solferino, &c., &c., and Maps of Italy, Austria, and all the adjacent Countries, by Madame Julie de Margucrittes; with an introduction by Dr. R. Shelton Mackenzie.   One volume, 12mo., cloth.   Price $1 25.

This is an able, interesting, and lively account of the War and the circumstances connected with it.   The author's residence in Europe has given her facilities for preparing the volume which add much to its value.

Not only does she give a description of Italy in general, but of each Sovereignty and State, showing the extent, resources, power, and political situation of each.   Throughout the volume, are found anecdotes, recollections, and even *ondits*, which contribute to its interest.—*New-York Courier and Enquirer.*

THE SPIRIT LAND.

12mo., cloth, with mezzotint engraving. Price $1.

" These pages are submitted to the public with the counsel of the wisest and best of all ages, that amid the wily arts of the Adversary, we should cling to the Word of God, the Bible, as the only safe and infallible guide of Faith and Practice.

THE MORNING STAR;

Or, Symbols of Christ. By Rev. Wm. M. Thayer, author of "Hints for the Household," "Pastor's Holiday Gift," &c., &c. 12mo., cloth. Price $1.

" The symbolical parts of Scriptures are invested with peculiar attractions. A familiar acquaintance with them can scarcely fail to increase respect and love for the Bible."

THE WORLD IN A POCKET-BOOK.

By William H. Crump. New and revised edition, brought down to 1860. This work is a Compendium of Useful Knowledge and General Reference, dedicated to the Manufacturers, Farmers, Merchants, and Mechanics of the United States; to all, in short, with whom time is money, and whose business avocations render the acquisition of extensive and diversified information desirable, by the shortest possible road. This volume, it is hoped, will be found worthy of a place in every household—in every family. It may indeed be termed a library in itself. Large 12mo. Price $1 25.

ANNA CLAYTON, OR THE MOTHER'S TRIAL.

A Tale of Real Life. 12mo., cloth. Price $1.

" The principal characters in this tale are drawn from real life—imagination cannot picture deeper shades of sadness, higher or more exquisite joys, than Truth has woven for us in the Mother's Trial."

LIFE OF CHRIST AND HIS APOSTLES.

By the Rev. John Fleetwood. With a History of the Jews, from the earliest period to the present time. Large 12mo., bound in cloth. Illustrated. Price $1.
Octavo edition, with steel engravings. Turkey Antique, $3 50.

The Ladies' Hand Book of Fancy and Ornamental Needle-Work:

Comprising full directions, with patterns, for working in Embroidery, Applique Braiding, Crochet, Knitting, Netting, Tatting, Quilting, Tambour and Gobelin Tapestry, Broderie Anglaise, Guipure Work, Canvass Work, Worsted Work, Lace Work, Bead Work, Stitching, Patch Work, Frivolite, &c., &c., &c. Illustrated with 262 engraved patterns, taken from original designs. By Miss Florence Hartley. One volume, quarto, cloth. Price $1 25.

BUNYAN'S PILGRIM'S PROGRESS.

Including "Grace abounding to the Chief of Sinners." Large 12mo., 500 pages Cloth. Beautifully illustrated. Price $1.

Octavo edition, with steel engravings. Turkey Antique, $3 50.

SWEET HOME, OR FRIENDSHIP'S GOLDEN ALTAR.

By Frances C. Percival. Mezzotint frontispiece, 12mo., cloth, gilt back and centre. Price $1.

"The object of this book is to awaken the Memories of Home—to remind us of the old Scenes and old Times."

THE LIFE AND TIMES OF ALEXANDER HAMILTON.

By S. M. Smucker, LL. D. Large 12mo., with portrait. Over 400 pages. Price $1 25.

THE LIFE AND TIMES OF THOMAS JEFFERSON.

By S. M. Smucker, LL. D., author of "Life and Reign of Nicholas I., Emperor of Russia," &c., &c. Large 12mo. of 400 pages, cloth, with fine steel portrait. Price $1 25.

THE LIFE AND REIGN OF NICHOLAS I.,

Emperor of Russia. With descriptions of Russian Society and Government, and a full and complete History of the War in the East. Also, Sketches of Schamyl, the Circassian, and other distinguished characters. By S. M. Smucker, LL. D. Beautifully illustrated. Over 400 pages, large 12mo. Price $1 25.

THE BATTLE FIELDS OF THE REVOLUTION.

Comprising descriptions of the different battles, sieges, and other events of the War of Independence, interspersed with characteristic anecdotes. Illustrated with numerous engravings, and a fine mezzotint frontispiece. By Thomas Y. Rhoads. Large 12mo., cloth. Price $1 25.

PERILS AND PLEASURES OF A HUNTER'S LIFE.

With fine colored plates. Large 12mo., cloth. Price $1 25.

From the table of contents we take the following as samples of the style and interest of the work:—Baiting for an Alligator—Morning among the Rocky Mountains—Encounter with Shoshonees—A Grizzly Bear—Fight and terrible result—Fire on the Mountains—Narrow Escape—The Beaver Region—Trapping Beaver—A Journey and Hunt through New-Mexico—Start for South America—Hunting in the Forests of Brazil—Hunting on the Pampas—A Hunting Expedition into the interior of Africa—Chase of the Rhinoceros—Chase of an Elephant—The Roar of the Lion—Herds of Wild Elephants—Lions attacked by Bechuanas—Arrival in the Region of the Tiger and the Elephant—Our first Elephant Hunt in India—A Boa Constrictor—A Tiger—A Lion—Terrible Conflict—Elephant Catching—Hunting the Tiger with Elephants—Crossing the Pyrenees—Encounter with a Bear—A Pigeon Hunt on the Ohio—A Wild Hog Hunt in Texas—Hunting the Black-tailed Deer.

Dr. Livingstone's Travels and Researches of Sixteen Years in the Wilds of South Africa.

One volume, 12mo., cloth, fine edition, printed upon superior paper, with numerous illustrations. Price $1 25. Cheap edition, price $1.

This is a work of thrilling adventures and hair-breadth escapes among savage beasts, and more savage men. Dr. Livingstone was alone, and unaided by any white man, travelling only with African attendants, among different tribes and nations, all strange to him, and many of them hostile, and altogether forming the most astonishing book of travels the world has ever seen. All acknowledge it is the most readable book published.

"FASHIONABLE DISSIPATION."

By Metta V. Fuller. Mezzotint Frontispiece, 12mo., bound in cloth. Price $1